BLOOD SACRIFICE

BLOOD SACRIFICE

This is a work of fiction. All characters, organizations and events in this novel are products of the author's imagination and are not to be construed as real. Any resemblance to persons, living or dead, is entirely coincidental.

ISBN: 978-1-938745-64-5

Published by Angry Sheep Publishing LLC
Findlay, Ohio

Cover Design by For the Muse Design
Interior Design by JW Manus

BLOODLINES #5

Blood Sacrifice

SUZAN HARDEN

More Books by Suzan Harden

(Each series is in suggested reading order)

Bloodlines

Blood Magick

Zombie Love

Zombie Confidential

Zombie Wedding

Amish, Vamps & Thieves

Blood Sacrifice

Love, War & a Bulldog

Zombie Goddess

Ravaged

Sacrificed

Reality Bites

Ghouls in the Grocery Store

Resurrected

Bloodlines Shorts Anthology

Bloodlines: The First Boxed Set

Justice

Sword and Sorceress 28

("Justice")

Sword and Sorceress 30

("Diplomacy in the Dark")

Justice: The Beginning

A Question of Balance

A Modicum of Truth

A Matter of Death

A Touch of Mother

A Twist of Love

A Virtue of Child

A Hand of Father

A Measure of Knowledge

A Hint of Thief

A Cup of Conflict

Seasons of Magick

Spring

Summer

Autumn

Winter

The Seasons of Magick Anthology

The Justice Thalia Stories

Snowfall

Murder Most Fowl

The Sweetest Poison

A Granddaughter of Mine

Too Many Fish in the Sea

Tales of the Twelve

The Trickster Priestess and the Demon

Crossover Worlds

Invasion!

888-555-HERO

Hero De Facto

Hero Ad Hoc

Hero De Novo

A Very Hero Christmas

Hero De Jure

Hero In Camera

Hero Amicus Curiae

A Very Hero Wedding

A Very Hero New Year

Hero Ad Litem

Queer Eye for the Super Guy

Solar System Services, Inc.

Alone Is Not Lonely

Halloween Harvest

("A Place at the Table")

A Place at the Table

Millersburg Magick Mysteries

Spells and Sleuths

Fae and Felonies

Magick and Murder

Feline Navidad

Soccer Moms of the Apocalypse

Pestilence in Pumpkin Spice

Famine in French Vanilla

War in White Chocolate

Death in Double Mocha

Demons Run at Halloween

Miscellaneous

Sword and Sorceress 31

("Pig-Headed")

Sword and Sorceress 32

("Unexpected")

Practical Witches

Revenge Served Hot

The Yule Switch

Chocolate for Dinner

Silver Shoes and Pigs' Ears

Snipe Hunt

For updates, news, and giveaways, join Suzan's mailing list at suzanharden.blogspot.com/p/contact-me.html, or visit her website at www.suzanharden. com. You can also check her out on Facebook @SuzanHardenWriter.

To Jody and John, whose love has endured as much as Phil and Alex's, and to Kevin Smith and Kevin Smith, who showed me how much fun messing with religion and myths could be.

AUTHOR'S NOTE: The events in this novel take place concurrently with the events in *Amish, Vamps & Thieves*.

Prologue

Four months ago . . .

Marcus Giovanni grimaced. His eardrums ached at the sheer decibel level of the prisoner's howls of rage. Spell-threaded metal groaned at his efforts to break his chains. Even if he tore through those, there was still the matter of the box in which he was locked. Or the safe room itself. Both of which were made from the same material as the prisoner's fetters.

The elderly *strega* standing next to Marcus grinned in delight. He motioned for her to follow him upstairs. The Boulder safehouse and a couple of offshore accounts were the last of the family assets that hadn't been seized by Augustine Coven after the disaster in Los Angeles. Or hadn't been wasted on the ridiculous attempt to turn the Vampire Nation and a host of other supernaturals against Uncle Caesar.

Marcus hadn't realized how much he missed solid food until Grandmother Selene dangled the possibility in front of his nose. But her efforts to create a cure for the V-virus had failed.

Spectacularly.

He closed the insulated titanium door and leaned his head against the cool metal. Finally, he could think, but those thoughts were not comforting. Grandmother's desire hadn't been for just a cure, but a way to keep the advantages of being a vampire and losing all the detriments. To live forever and still walk in the sun.

And now? Everything had been lost.

He straightened and glared at the *strega*. "The plan has failed. My grandmother is dead. We should just let him go."

The old witch smirked. "And what do you think the god will do if you release him? Pat you on the head and tell you he won't hold a grudge?"

"I'm not the one who imprisoned him," Marcus growled. "That was you and my grandmother."

Ginger and the faint hint of reptile filled the air. She smiled even wider, showing rotted teeth between chapped lips. "Do you think he'll care?" She laid a claw-like hand on his arm. "It won't be much longer, my dear boy. I'm waiting on a delivery. Once I have it, you will help me. Or don't you have the stomach—or the balls—anymore?"

Marcus's eyes narrowed as he examined the strange witch. She had shown up on Grandmother's doorstep after their banishment from the coven, claiming she was Lucien's teacher. Grandmother had welcomed the *strega* with open arms, which never made sense considering her disdain for any witchbreed, including her eclectic servant Lucien.

Maybe two thousand years and her obsession with destroying her twin brother had warped Grandmother's mind. She had ignored Marcus when he'd questioned the *strega*'s claims.

And he sure as Hades didn't trust the old bat, but he no longer had a choice in the matter. She was his only hope for staying alive.

Marcus jerked away from the witch's touch. "Once he's sacrificed, then we'll be done."

She cackled. "Oh, we will be quite done, my boy. We will be quite done."

Chapter 1

When Alex Stanton appeared in the frame of her new store's smashed front doors, Phillippa Mann gritted her teeth. Out of the hundreds of languages she'd learned in her 5,000-plus years of existence, only one word sprang to mind.

"Shit."

Her assistant manager Jane glanced up from her half of the antique store's inventory. "What's wrong?" She whirled toward the front. "Hubba, hubba."

"Don't even think about it." Phillippa shot the twenty-eight-year-old a stern look. "He's an enforcer."

Jane responded with a pouty lip. The woman was hornier than all the nymphs in Los Angeles County. Maybe promoting her hadn't been such a good idea. How was she going to control the rest of the staff if she couldn't control her own libido?

The pencil in Phillippa's fingers snapped. Maybe she shouldn't be casting aspersions. She clamped down on her emotions.

What the hell was Stanton doing here? The break-in at the new facility for her antiques business was nothing more than a standard smash-and-grab. She returned her attention to her own portion of the inventory, trying to ignore the blue eyes looking her way. Eyes that still haunted her dreams despite their current neon glow.

She tossed the broken pencil back into its box and grabbed one of its sharpened siblings. A series of quick checks on the sheet covered the nineteenth century letter openers. Nagging unease filled her as she audited the merchandise. Nothing was missing. Not even a single diamond from the heirloom brooches. Why would someone break in, shatter the display cases and not take anything?

Glass crunched behind her. Electricity sparked the instant before a large hand touched her shoulder. His cool skin permeated the thin t-shirt she threw on when the alarm company had called.

"Are you all right?" The Texas drawl remained even though he'd lived in Los Angeles for nearly a century now.

Not that she kept track of those things.

She jerked away from his touch and faced him. "Everyone's fine. No one was here when it happened."

Alex surveyed the mess. "What's missing?"

"This isn't your jurisdiction." Phillippa set her expression to what Jane referred to as her "bitch scowl."

He glanced at the uniformed sheriff's deputy standing three yards away and scribbling furiously in her notebook. Phillippa's muscles clenched when he took a half step closer to her and lowered his voice. "This is a Family business, which is why Jorge called me."

"It's a Normal crime," she shot back.

Light flashed in his shaggy blond hair when he nodded toward the detective standing near the ruined front doors. "He says this doesn't smell right."

She snorted. "This isn't Sifuentes' jurisdiction either. He's a homicide detective."

Alex shrugged. "He was the only Family with rank on duty when the call came in."

Phillippa closed her eyes. This night couldn't possibly get more aggravating. Deep down, she knew the detective meant well. She was too entwined with Augustine Vampire Coven. One more item in the stack of reasons for her to leave Los Angeles.

She opened her eyes to find Alex staring at her with concern. The last thing she needed was any man's concern, least of all Alex Stanton's. "He's also full of wolf shit. Just because he's married to one—"

Jane shoved her way between them. Part of Phillippa was relieved by the interruption. The other wanted to snap the girl's neck like the pencil she had a moment ago. *It's in the past.* So why couldn't Phillippa get Alex out of her head?

"Hi." Jane thrust her hand into Alex's. "Jane Chevrette."

The grin Alex gave her was a few watts short of the one he'd first given Phillippa over a century ago. But he'd also had a tan back then. "Pleased to meet you, Jane."

The second his hand touched hers, Jane's smile faltered. A smidgeon of glee fluttered in Phillippa's heart at the girl's expression. She'd warned Jane he was a supernatural.

To the assistant manager's credit, she recovered quickly, for a Normal, and shook Alex's hand. She turned to Phillippa, all business. "Nothing's been touched in the safe. The only thing missing from the showroom is the fake tumi from the Madison estate."

Phillippa grabbed Jane's inventory sheaf. "You're sure?"

Jane nodded.

"Tumi?" Confusion marred Alex's face.

Detective Sifuentes sauntered across the room to join them. "What the hell's a tumi?"

"An Incan ceremonial knife." The answer came as an afterthought while Phillippa flipped through both sets of pages. "That makes no sense."

Jane shrugged. "It's the only piece I can't find." She surveyed the showroom. "Doesn't mean it's not buried somewhere under this mess."

Alex's attention flipped between Jane and Phillippa. "You're sure it's a fake?"

The lights in the showroom flickered. Phillippa forced down her irritation. How dare he question her?

Sifuentes' eyes widened, but Alex regarded her with amusement. Her jaw muscles quivered as Phillippa reined in the threads of her control. Electrocuting five members of the Los Angeles County Sheriff's Office along with the vampire wasn't conducive to keeping a low profile.

Jane's offended expression helped. "The metal on the piece wasn't gold or any of the alloys used by the pre-Columbian cultures indigenous to Peru, so we had it tested. The tumi was made of titanium, a ceramic composite and another substance our assayer couldn't identify."

"Which means . . . ?" Sifuentes prompted.

"Someone used leftover space shuttle parts," Phillippa said. "It couldn't possibly be authentic."

The detective rolled his eyes. "And you had a fake for sale?"

"The piece was clearly marked as a replica. It was unusual enough we thought we could sell it for Mrs. Madison." Anger punctuated Jane's sharp words, but the girl's pique helped Phillippa gain control of her own mood.

Sifuentes rubbed a palm over his face. "I was pulled down here for this?" He flipped his notebook shut and thrust it in his jacket pocket. "Look, Mann, I'll write this up as vandalism so you can file with your insurance company." He shot a suspicious look at her. "You do have insurance, don't you?"

She may have her powers under control, but that didn't squelch the urge to deck the detective for questioning her. Alex must have read her expression because he tensed and edged in front of Sifuentes.

Not wanting to give Stanton an excuse to touch her, she muttered, "Yes."

Sifuentes nodded and smacked Alex on the arm. "If you need anything, let me know. I'll have the report on your desk in twenty-four hours." He pivoted to leave.

Alex's desk, not hers. The lights flickered once, and Sifuentes looked back and smiled. The evil smirk honed his blade-like nose and pointed chin. "I can turn the investigation over to Ziva or John if you want."

"No, thank you," she bit out. It was just her bad luck the vampires were up on the supernatural law enforcement rotation. On the other hand, the witch high priestess was worthless, and the alpha werewolf was a little too enthusiastic in meting out punishment rather than seeking justice. No, it wasn't the rotation schedule. She could have dealt with any other vampire enforcer. Just not Stanton.

Sifuentes stepped closer to her, and like Alex had earlier, lowered his voice so the other deputies wouldn't hear. "This would be a lot easier for everyone if you demigods would band together and get a seat on the Council."

Of course, he knew. Nearly every supernatural in Los Angeles had seen her throw lightning bolts when zombies had attacked her ward's wedding. And they had spread the gossip as fast as telepathy and the internet could carry the titillating tidbits.

So much for keeping a low profile the last four millennia.

"Not in your lifetime. And you will send a copy of your report directly to me." She gave the detective a smile, one that had sent Mycenaen soldiers fleeing in terror on the battlefield of Ilium. To his credit, Sifuentes didn't flinch. But then, he was a Normal married to a werewolf.

"Sure." He motioned to the rest of his people, and they filed out the hole where the front doors used to be.

Phillippa shifted her attention to Alex. "You can leave, too."

"No, I can't." He smiled a real smile this time, one that displayed his extra pointy canines. "Don't particularly wanna get staked by my boss for not taking care of you."

Of all the audacious—

"I do not need to be 'taken care of.'"

"Don't worry, Phil." He cocked a dark blond eyebrow as his expression grew haughty. "It wasn't an offer. I don't do one-night stands with women older than my great-great-granny anymore."

Chapter 2

Alex resisted the urge to laugh when Phillippa's mouth gaped open. But he was through with her insults and frigid attitude. She'd made her point that she preferred him only when his blood had been Normal temperature. And she was so full of herself, she assumed his practical joke at the San Francisco mansion had been retaliation for her rejection, instead of being aimed at someone else. Dammit, he'd apologized enough over the last one hundred years.

"Um, maybe the coven could send someone else to assist you, Mr. Stanton?" Jane asked. The poor girl had paled noticeably during his and Phillippa's verbal sparring.

Pink flared in Phillippa's cheeks and her heart rate jumped. Interesting. He couldn't read her mind, but she couldn't hide the little things, like her pulse.

He crossed his arms and gave Jane his full attention. "Sorry, darlin'. I'm the senior enforcer in Los Angeles until my boss returns. My coven master values his business relationship with Miss Mann here, so I'm stuck babysitting her."

Sure enough, the overhead fluorescents flickered on cue.

He ignored the Olympian temper-tantrum. "Could you get me this Mrs. Madison's number and address?"

"No." Phillippa's voice resembled the low rumble of thunder.

"And, I'll need an inventory of the other items y'all are handling for her." He gave Jane a gentle smile.

Phillippa stepped between him and her assistant. "I said no."

He shifted around the irate demigoddess to face Jane. "You mentioned this was an estate sale. Does the widow have documentation for the items?"

Phillippa whirled to face her assistant. "Don't you dare answer him."

Jane flicked a glance at her boss before her attention returned to Alex. "I'll get it for you."

Once again, the lights in the shop brightened and dimmed. Alex had to give Jane credit. Most Normals would be quivering with terror when caught in the middle of an argument between a vampire and a demi-goddess. Unless she didn't know what her boss was. But she damn well knew what he was. He'd caught that much in her surface thoughts when he shook her hand.

Instead, the girl raised her chin a notch as she faced her employer. "Somebody went to a lot of trouble to steal that replica. Don't you want to know why?" She pivoted and marched toward the store's office.

Phillippa whirled to face him again, her fists clenched at her sides. "How dare you glamour my employee." One of the halogen spotlights popped. The acrid smoke overrode the saltpeter scent of her anger.

He watched her, trying to keep his amusement in check. "You keep throwing a hissy fit, and you'll fry the building's wiring. Do you want to explain an electrical fire to your claims adjustor or the arson investigator?"

She took a deep breath. It was all he could do to keep his attention on her face and away from her perfectly proportioned breasts. Only one time with her, and the feel of her skin had burned into his cells. Not even the V-virus wiped that away.

Alex shook his head. "I didn't have to do anything to your assistant. She's as upset and confused about this break-in as you are."

"I am not—" she began. Then she took another lungful of air and crossed her arms, matching his body language, as her gaze swept the wreckage. "I really don't want to explain to my insurance company why my store was trashed twice in less than a year."

His eyes widened in disbelief. "Augustine Coven didn't compensate you for that rogue attack in January?"

One of Phil's perfect shoulders lifted and dropped. "Caesar paid for the furniture and equipment that was destroyed and the building damage. What he can't pay for is the time it takes to acquire such a collection in the first place or my reputation. The landlord refused to renew my lease because of the incident. While the insurance company was thrilled not to pay on the first claim, they *will* question this one a lot more thoroughly."

Jane walked back with a piece of paper. "Here's Mrs. Madison's info. I can have everything else to you in the morning."

Phil reached for it, but Alex snatched it first.

"Getting slow in your old age, Mann?" He ignored Phil's look of outrage and scanned the address before checking his watch. It was a little late for a social visit, so he may have to glamour the widow. God, he hated messing with anyone's mind.

He did another slow sweep of the mess. This may have been sheer vandalism, but something about the break-in just didn't sit right. There was too much damage for a simple robbery. Someone took precious time to shatter every single display. And why take a fake when there were pieces more valuable and easier to fence?

He folded the paper and shoved it into the back pocket of his jeans. "Thank you for your help." He handed her a business card. "If you wouldn't mind e-mailing me the information?"

The girl beamed. "No problem, Mr. Stanton."

"It's been a pleasure, Jane." He faced Phil. "Since you insist you don't need my help, have a good evening."

Phil stepped in front of him. "Wait. Where are you going?"

For a second, the jiggle of her breasts almost made Alex forget her question. He forced his eyes to meet hers. "Out to do my job. We've been a little short-handed lately. It's not like I can foist it off on someone else." He tried to walk around Phil, but she inserted herself again between him and the gaping hole where the front doors used to be.

"You're going over to Mrs. Madison's tonight, aren't you?" Accusation ran thick in her voice.

"Didn't you just tell me this wasn't my jurisdiction?" He gestured at the broken display cases.

"You are not harassing one of my clients." She planted her fists on her hips. Unfortunately, the motion gave her perfect breasts another little jiggle. Did she still taste like the sweetest white grapes?

Once again, it took all his willpower to meet her gaze. A gaze that literally flashed lightning. "Why do you care?" His was a simple question, delivered in a flat voice because he would be damned if he acted like a lovesick puppy around her anymore.

He wasn't sure if it was his question or his tone that rocked her back on her heels. Her mouth opened and closed. She stared at the ruined jewelry case beside them for a moment before she said, "If something about this piece is the reason for the break-in, Beatrice may be in trouble."

"Then someone needs to check on her. You coming with me, or you driving your own vehicle?"

For a split second, it seemed like she'd give him more shit. Then she grimaced and turned to Jane. "Will you be all right alone until the contractor gets here with the plywood?"

Jane nodded. "I've got my Taser if they come back before Roberto arrives."

Alex tried to hide his wince. The mention of a Taser brought back too many memories he'd rather forget. He motioned for Phil to follow him out to his truck.

Fifteen minutes later, Alex stole another glance at the woman next to him. Passing headlights illuminated the worried look on her face. If it were any other female, he'd take their hand and tell them everything would be all right. If he tried that with Phil, she would cut off the offending appendage before she beheaded him.

Instead, he focused on the case. "Did Mrs. Madison say where she acquired this tumi?"

She shook her head. The motion sent her high ponytail swinging. "Not in detail. Her husband got it on a business trip to Peru a few years ago."

"If a tumi is a cultural artifact, how'd he get it through customs?"

She snorted. "Because customs isn't going to stop you from carrying a fake. That's what it said on the declaration she showed us."

"What if it's not a fake?"

He could feel her eyes boring into him as he kept his attention on the road. "You don't believe me," she finally said.

"I didn't say that." They passed the Beverly Hills sign, and Alex repressed a shudder. Nothing good came out of Beverly Hills. The last time had been a horde of zombies. "But someone went to an awful lot of trouble to steal one fake when everything else would have been more profitable."

Phil chewed on a thumbnail. He wasn't going to get anything more out of her now. She was touchier about her honor than most of the older vampires he knew.

He guided his pick-up into the Madison driveway. The second he stepped out of the truck, a sickly-sweet smell assaulted his olfactory nerve. He reached for his semi-automatic tucked at the small of his back. While teeth and claws were great for hand-to-hand, the specially designed bullets in the magazine gave him a decided advantage.

Phil's worried expression melted into anger. "Where's the spare?"

"Under your seat," he said softly. He reached out with his mind, but the only thing he found was muddled thoughts that screamed canine. With his luck, it could be a were instead of someone's pet.

She had the second gun in a tight grip as she circled around the bed of the truck to meet him. He held up one finger. With hand signals, she asked, *Normal or supernatural?*

He shrugged. If neither of them could tell, this could turn nasty fast. It would be so much easier to communicate mentally, but he sincerely doubted she'd let him create a tight telepathic bond so they could talk silently. He'd have better luck getting into her bed again.

She motioned she would take the back entrance. With a blur even his vampire vision had difficulty tracking, she was across the front yard and over the stone privacy wall.

Alex eased up to the main door, senses extended. Faint sounds came from the house along with the snarl of animal thoughts.

He pulled his shirttail from the waistband of his jeans. The material covered his hand as he tried the door handle.

Unlocked.

With his boot, he toed open the huge mahogany door. The smell of decay gagged him.

He followed the sound of whimpering to his right. For once, he cursed his ability to see at night. Dark cinnamon spots covered nearly every surface of the living room. Including the tiny dog huddled next to the head of the dead woman lying spread-eagle in the middle of the carpet.

A middle-aged woman with a gaping hole in her chest. From the arcing splatter pattern, whoever killed her had started cutting while she was alive.

The dog had white fur where she wasn't coated with her mistress's dried blood. A small scrap of black fabric lay nearby. Something that hadn't been in the room when the killer had cut the aorta. From the smell and the dried puddle under the woman's chest, she'd been dead for nearly forty-eight hours.

He scanned the room. Trashed. Furniture overturned. Cushions slashed. Odds and ends scattered across the carpet. Whoever did this tossed the room before they started cutting into Beatrice.

While the smell of old blood didn't trigger the extension of his fangs, anger did.

Phil appeared in the doorway to the back of the house. He caught a hint of what may have been grief before she steeled her thoughts and her expression. She couldn't hide her scent though. The brimstone of rage poured from her. She pointed at the rest of the house.

Without a word, they checked the rest of the first floor before they swept the second floor. Like the living room, every other nook and corner had been upended.

When they returned to the entrance of the living room, Alex pulled out his phone and hit the speed dial icon for Sifuentes. The only positive in this whole mess was the fact that Madison's house sat just outside the Beverly Hills city limits. The last thing he needed was LASO and BHPD butting heads during the investigation.

"Hey, Jorge, I've got something for you that's more up your alley."

Sifuentes swore in a streak of Spanish before he said, "Madison."

"Yeah." Alex gave him the address before he clicked off the call.

"Alex."

He looked at Phil with a start. It was the first time she said his name without the word dripping with contempt since he'd been Turned.

"Do you have any rags or an old shirt in your truck?"

He followed her gaze to the poor dog shivering next to her mistress. Well, former mistress. "Yeah. I'll be right back."

Phil ignored Sifuentes's rant as she sat in the front yard of Beatrice Madison's house. Instead, she concentrated on shaving the blood-matted fur from Beatrice's Maltese. Unfortunately, all she had to work with was one of Stanton's throwing knives, but it kept her focused enough that she wasn't affecting any nearby electrical equipment.

When Sifuentes paused for a breath, she looked up at him. "Kiki hasn't eaten or had any water for at least two days, Jorge. Was I supposed to let her starve? Die of dehydration? I didn't think even you were that much of a shit."

"You contaminated a crime scene," he repeated for the thirty-eighth time.

"Tracking a teaspoon of dog urine through the kitchen is hardly contaminating a crime scene."

"I'm talking about shaving the dog!"

She fed the Maltese a piece of kibble. "The real evidence is the scrap of fabric by the . . . body." Kiki pawed at Phillippa's hand holding the knife, and she resumed trimming the dog's fur.

Sifuentes threw up his hands in exasperation. "Stanton . . ."

"In this case, I've got to agree with Phil." The familiar twinkle in Alex's eyes sent unwanted tingles through her body. "You're acting like a shit, Jorge."

Sifuentes repeated his rant in Spanish, throwing in the occasional colorful metaphor.

She returned her attention to Kiki and gave the dog a few more pieces of kibble. She'd doled out the food while they waited for the sheriff's department to arrive. The last thing she wanted was to make the traumatized Maltese sick.

"Detective?" One of the deputies approached them. The scent of ginger surrounded the man, not the tart apple of a Normal. *Witch.* "It looks like Madison may have been getting ready to leave town. Suitcases are in the trunk of the car in the garage. Her purse was in the car as well. The killer or killers may have caught her in the garage, then dragged her into the house."

Sifuentes shoved his hands in his trouser pockets. "Were the suitcases ransacked, too?"

"Yeah. But the odd thing is they didn't take any money. Cash and credit cards are still in her wallet. We also found her passport in her purse along with a boarding pass."

Sifuentes glared at the deputy. "Where was she headed?"

"Lima, Peru." The deputy lowered his voice. "Her ghost isn't around for me to question, sir. Sorry."

The detective shrugged. "Don't worry, Wolowitz. It was a long shot. Nothing appears to be missing except the vic's heart."

Phil looked up at the deputy. Honestly, men could be such dumbasses when something was right under their noses. "What about the demon?"

All three men turned to stare at her.

Alex crouched next to her. "What demon are you talking about?"

"The one that was in the house two days ago." She eyed Alex for a moment before she shaved the last couple of swatches of ruined fur off Kiki.

"Are you saying a demon killed Mrs. Madison?" Alex's voice broadcast his disbelief.

"No." She set down Kiki, who gave herself a good shake before she turned and nudged Phil's hand for more food.

"Then would you mind spelling it out for the rest of us," Sifuentes growled.

"All I can tell you is a demon was in the house around the time of Beatrice's death." Phil held out a nugget that Kiki enthusiastically took. "I'm not saying the demon killed her. The back door was wide open when we got here. It may have stumbled on the scene after the fact, attracted by the scent. If it was here before she died, she invited it in."

Which only added to the questions of this whole weird situation. Why would Beatrice be dealing with a demon?

Phil grimaced as Wolowitz bagged the shaved fur for Sifuentes. There hadn't been anything in her dealings that indicated Beatrice Madison was nothing more or less than a grieving Normal widow. She had wanted to sell her late husband's "collection of junk" before she put the house on the market.

Alex held out his palm to Kiki. "Phil, have you been to Madison's house before tonight?"

Kiki trotted over and licked Alex's hand. Weird. Most dogs avoided vampires.

Phil nodded. "Yes. Twice. Once for the initial appraisal. The second when she signed the consignment contract. I didn't smell or detect anyone other than humans and Kiki both times."

"Why don't you think the demon murdered her?" Alex said as he petted the Maltese.

It reminded her of how gentle he'd been with her . . .

Phil quashed the memory. "The opening is too neat. If a demon, no matter the pantheon, goes after the heart, it likes getting messy."

"Detective Sifuentes!"

Phil and Alex climbed to their feet at the shout. Before she could say anything, Alex scooped the tiny dog in his arms. A little green monster rose behind Phil's eyes. *Don't be stupid. Kiki's not even your dog.*

They followed Jorge through the gate to the courtyard. Another deputy knelt near a flowerbed with a flashlight.

Sifuentes snorted. "Dog tracks? You called me over to look at dog tracks?"

"Not the dog tracks, sir. The gold pin."

Alex crouched next to the deputy to examine the shiny object. Kiki growled low in her throat.

Phil leaned over him to see for herself. It was an odd little pin, still attached to a scrap of black cloth. Just like the black cloth they found next to Beatrice's corpse. The gold pin was about an inch long. A coiled snake-like creature superimposed over a star. Except the reptilian figure had eight tiny legs.

"What the hell is that?" Sifuentes whispered.

"A cult symbol," Alex said. "The Sunshine Believers."

Chapter 3

Alex's stomach lurched. Most of the Sunshine Believers were supposed to be locked up in the state psychiatric facility. The handful declared sane enough to stand trial had been sentenced last month and had been transported to the state pen.

Phil looked at him "The Sunshine Believers? Aren't they—"

Phil! Shut up!

Wolowitz, the witch deputy, winced in pain at his psychic shout. Obviously, it got through Phil's shields from the ugly look she shot Alex.

He could see in her eyes when she realized what she almost said in front of the Normal member of the sheriff's department.

"—disbanded?" she finished.

Even Jorge had a pissed look on his sharp face. "You two are done here. Why don't I walk you to your truck?"

Alex shoved the dog into Phil's arms and latched onto her elbow. For a second, the look on her face said she'd deck him. Instead, she jerked free from his grasp and marched for the gate.

The sway of her hips sent a jolt straight to his groin. Dammit, what the hell was wrong with him? A woman had been brutally murdered, and his dick wanted to do all the thinking.

He stalked after her, Sifuentes puffing behind him as he tried to keep up with the supernaturals.

Phil was already standing by the passenger door, staring straight ahead when Alex reached his truck. He thumbed the key on his fob. The second Phil was inside, she slammed the door hard enough to emphasize her anger, but not rip it off its hinges.

"Stanton, wait!"

He paused, his hand on the door handle.

Jorge wheezed for a couple of seconds before he said, "We need to work together on this."

"And why is that?" Alex snapped. He closed his eyes. His own bad mood wasn't Jorge's fault. "Sorry, *amigo.*"

"*De nada.*" Sifuentes glanced at the house, then back at Alex. "It's gonna take both sides to figure out what happened to the vic. There's a good chance that whoever murdered Madison was the same person or persons who trashed Mann's place."

Alex could see his own suspicions mirrored in Sifuentes's eyes. Phil or Jane or any of the other employees could be lying on the debris of the antiques store, her chest sliced open and her heart missing. "What are you proposing?"

"My people can deal with the Sunshine Believers. But I need your help with the demon equation. Supes could have been the ones who summoned Mann's unknown player."

Alex couldn't help smiling. He'd never known Sifuentes to ask for any kind of supernatural assistance before now. And if the detective needed it, he would have gone to his father-in-law first. The demon angle must bother Sifuentes more than he was willing to admit. "Then we share all information. No holding back. Otherwise, someone else may die."

Sifuentes dipped his head. "Agreed."

Alex yanked the driver side door open. "Did you recognize the scent of the demon?" For a long moment, he didn't think Phil would answer him. She sure as hell wouldn't look at him.

Finally, she sighed. "No. All I can tell you is what it wasn't. It's not European, North African, Middle Eastern or North American."

"That only leaves the rest of the world." He couldn't stop the sarcasm that leached into his voice.

Her eyes met his. "And all the other dimensions."

"Other . . . dimensions?" Sifuentes's voice rose an octave.

Alex bit his tongue to keep from laughing out loud. Leave it to Phil to play her god card. Good to know she didn't consider him her only verbal punching bag if she was messing with Sifuentes. Alex returned his attention to the detective. "I'll eliminate the local demon species before

I start checking outside of Earth." He inclined his head toward the house. "The deputy who's a witch . . ."

Sifuentes gave a rueful chuckle. "Wolowitz's got potential. He's excellent at pulling answers out of ghosts at crime scenes, which is why I recruited him for homicide, but he's a baby by witch standards."

"I'll call Ziva and see if she has a demonology expert." Alex eyed Sifuentes. "I don't suppose you could put in a word with the in-laws . . ."

"Do you have a problem with my wife?"

This time Alex let his laughter loose. "Not one damn bit. She's got the best nose in the pack."

Sifuentes rubbed his jaw. "I'll have her meet you here once the crime scene unit's done."

"See you in a few hours." Alex climbed into the truck and started it. Once he was out of the driveway, Sifuentes waved the arriving CSU van into the spot.

Phil still wasn't talking, which Alex had to admit to himself was just fine. Concentrating on his job kept him from thinking about how her body had felt under his. How much he wanted to feel her again after all these decades.

While a cold shower would do wonders, what he really needed was a computer whiz since he wasn't anywhere near a secure line. He punched Tiffany Stephen's number into the truck's built-in phone.

"What the fuck do you want, Alex?" So much for pregnancy mellowing *her* attitude.

"I need some research."

"I can't. I'm on goddamn maternity leave until December 31st. Remember?"

Figured that she'd still be pouting about Duncan's orders. The girl was damn lucky she hadn't lost her baby after zombies pummeled her during her aborted wedding two and a half months ago.

He sucked in a deep breath and dropped his tone. "And I'm acting chief enforcer while Duncan and Caesar are out of town. Do you want to work on a murder investigation or not?"

Silence crackled through the speaker for a moment before she said, "Go."

"The victim is Beatrice Madison. A Normal whose heart was cut out of her chest. We can place a demon and possibly the Sunshine Believers at the scene around the time of death."

Tiffany's sharp intake of breath whistled through the phone. "Those bastards are all locked away after Jessie's kidnapping last winter."

Alex couldn't help smiling. Only Tiffany would be more concerned about a Normal cult than a demon. "Not all of them, so double-check for me. And I need everything you can find on Madison. Focus on phone calls, incoming and outgoing, over the past four days. Also, she had a boarding pass for a flight to Peru. Find out what flight and when she bought the ticket."

"Anything else?"

He glanced at Phil. "What's her husband's name?"

"Dennis Madison." She focused on stroking the dog, which had gone to sleep in her lap.

"Hey, Phil!"

"Hello, sweetie." Phil's voice noticeably softened toward her former ward.

Alex prayed Tiffany wouldn't say anything about Phil being in his truck. Some angel must have heard his silent plea because Tiffany said, "Is he a suspect?"

"No." Phil cleared her throat. "He died in an automobile accident two months ago."

"Did you get that, Tiffany?" Alex said.

"Yeah. You'll want his background info and the accident report. Anything else?"

"One more thing. He brought items into the U.S. from Peru for several years before his death. See if you can get a listing from the Customs database."

"How soon do you need this?"

The waste over such a senseless, obscene death hit him in the gut. "We needed it two days ago, kid."

Phillippa winced. Alex's words felt like a slap across her face. If he hadn't insisted on visiting Beatrice, Gaea only knew when her body would have been discovered. And devoted little Kiki would have starved to death before she would've left her former mistress.

The tiny body in her lap shook and whined. Phillippa stroked the dog's fine fur, and she calmed, still asleep.

Phillippa wished she could find comfort in a simple touch. What she really craved was a target and a weapon. Electricity rippled along her skin, making the hairs on her arms stand straight up.

If she didn't get her agitation under control, she'd fry the truck's electrical system. And she'd be damn to Tartarus before she'd give Alex the satisfaction of watching her lose it again tonight. "What should we do while we wait for the CSU to finish and Tiffany to pull the Madisons' information?"

"'We?'" Alex glanced at her before returning his attention to the road. "There's no 'we,' Phil. I'm taking you back to your shop so you can get your car."

Like Hades. "No. I'm your shadow until we find Beatrice's killers."

He glanced at her. "And as you've repeatedly said, you won't get mixed up in other supernaturals' internal matters."

"And as you've repeatedly said, Augustine Coven is short-handed these days between Selene's betrayal and the zombie attack at Tiffany's wedding."

Wood smoke overlaid Alex's normal sandalwood scent. Phillippa suppressed a twinge of satisfaction. Good to know she was getting under his skin too. Not that she would have thrown Selene's bullshit in Caesar or Duncan's face.

"Besides, these bastards hit my place," she added. "And Beatrice is, was, my client, not the coven's or the pack's."

A wry smile spread across Alex's face. "You really cannot handle the fact that I was right about checking out the Madison house tonight, can you?"

"Men are never *right*." She stared out the window.

Of course, Alex couldn't drop the subject. "Really? I've noticed you don't get this snippy with Caesar or Duncan."

"They are . . . reasonable."

"In other words, you haven't screwed either of them."

There it was. The thing that always lay between them. All because she made the mistake of falling for a Texas Ranger in San Antonio over 125 years ago. A Normal she thought was dead.

Ugly truths danced too close to the surface of her emotions. Except this time, it wasn't anger that consumed her, but immense sorrow. "Beatrice died because of something none of us understand yet. Can you please leave yours and everyone else's penises out of the equation? Even I understand how short-staffed you are when it comes to daytime personnel if a zombie is your only choice to accompany another vampire to Ohio."

Alex's attention flicked to her, then back to the road. "How did you know Sam went with Anne to visit her brother?" Understanding washed over his features. "Tiffany bitched."

"Don't worry. She only spoke with me." Phillip smiled. "She's not happy about the forced maternity leave."

He sighed. "I can't blame her. But you know how Duncan gets any time one of his nieces becomes pregnant."

She laughed. "Yes, I do. And I've seen a few more centuries of his macho act than you have."

Alex grinned for a moment, then abruptly sobered. "If I accept your offer of help on this case, that means you'll have to follow my . . . instructions."

He'd been about to say, "Orders." She'd lay a month's income on it. His acknowledgement of her feelings without his usual pathetic ass-kissing thawed a tiny bit of her reserve.

"Fine."

He shot her an odd look. "I mean it, Phil. I can't have you going off half-cocked until we know for sure who tossed your store and killed Mrs. Madison."

"I swear I won't do anything stupid."

"On the River Styx, Phil." Alex made a point of saying it in Ancient Greek, not English.

Okay, now she was pissed. The world righted since they were back to their usual acrimonious relationship.

She sighed, a perturbed sound. "I swear by the River Styx I will obey your directions during the course of the investigation of the break-in of Seven Wonders Antiquities and Beatrice Madison's murder," she answered in Greek. She switched to English. "Happy?"

"Deliriously."

She leaned her head against the passenger door window. There was only one little problem with assisting Alex during the next few days.

How was she going to keep her hands off him?

Chapter 4

<hr>

When Alex pulled into the parking lot at Phil's store, the front windows and doors were boarded up, and Jane's little Paseo was gone. He popped open the driver's door as Phil climbed out. "Why don't I follow you back to your condo? We can take my truck back to Madison's house—"

Crash!

He whirled toward the store and drew his gun at the same time. His mind extended, identifying everything in the surrounding area. Phil, Kiki, drivers in the street, a Normal next-door working late in his office.

There was something inside Phil's store he didn't recognize. Something that didn't feel remotely human-related or even fae.

Alex glanced at Phil. She set Kiki on the seat with a whispered, "Stay." For the second time that night, she reached beneath the passenger seat for his spare gun. With the front of the store boarded and no sign of tampering, there was only one way in or out of the building.

Another *bang* came from inside. Alex motioned for her to follow him. He eased around the corner of the stucco exterior.

He tried to quell his surprise that she obeyed. The idea of her swearing on the Styx had been grabbing at straws on his part. Of course, she could simply consider him cannon fodder.

The back door stood open, the steel frame gouged in order to pry the two deadbolts free. No lights were on inside. More clattering confirmed that whatever was inside the store was near the smashed front doors.

Alex leaned toward Phil. Communication would be so much easier with telepathy, but if she was honoring her promise, the least he could do was respect her space. "Where's the switch for the showroom?"

"On the inside wall to the right at the entrance."

He crept through the storage and office area. Whoever was in the shop muttered to himself. An odd sing-song language like nothing Alex had heard before.

Clang!

He motioned to Phil, and with the palm of her hand, she flipped the row of switches. Light flooded the room.

Jane and Roberto had obviously cleaned up as best as they could. Merchandise had been neatly stacked on one side of the room. Debris had been swept to the other side.

A creature the size of a large chimpanzee or a small gorilla, Alex couldn't decide, sat near the piled merchandise. It resembled someone's taxidermy project—a capuchin monkey that had been partially devoured by a swarm of moths, except the taxidermist used orange LED lights instead of glass eyeballs. The creature's scent made the zombies that had attacked during Tiffany's wedding smell like the finest French perfume.

What was equally obvious was that it had been rummaging through the antique pieces and tossing them aside.

"Demon!" At Phil's shout, she fired. One of the LED eyes disintegrated into a mass of orange goo.

The thing shrieked. It jumped straight into the air, claws scrabbling for purchase on the acoustic tile ceiling.

The same talons that had cut through the steel back door shredded the tiles as well as the aluminum framework. Foam and fiber floated through the air. Metal ricocheted off the walls before hitting the floor in rapid-fire *pings*. For a split second, the demon imitated a hellish version of Wile E. Coyote running in mid-air. Gravity had other ideas, and the creature crashed to the floor.

For something that looked like a giant dead monkey, it was fast. It leapt, and Alex ducked and rolled to avoid its claws. No doubt it could take off his head with one swipe from what it had done to the rear door.

It headed straight for Phil and knocked the semi-automatic from her grip. Alex raised his own gun and fired.

The thing shrieked again when part of its head disintegrated. It shoved Phil into the wall before it turned and glared at Alex with its one good eye. Before he could squeeze the trigger again, it dove through the doorway to the storeroom.

Alex jumped to his feet and ran after it, Phil hot on his heels.

A series of sharp high-pitched yips preceded another shriek from the creature. Alex raced out the back door to find the thing perched on top of the dumpster. It cringed while Kiki danced around the base, barking for all she was worth.

What the hell? The creature tore through a vampire and a demigoddess like they were nothing, and it was terrified of a shaved Maltese?

From the ashy scent penetrating the thing's body odor, there was no doubt. It was scared shitless of Kiki. More strange, chittering language issued from its mouth.

It looked at Alex and Phil approaching and back down at the tiny white dog. Resignation appeared on its mottled face. It reached for Kiki.

"*No!*" Phil's scream was telepathic as well as auditory.

Horror seized Alex's heart. He brought his gun up and squeezed the trigger the same moment the demon touched the hyper canine.

The monkey demon exploded into a cloud of ash before the silver bullet hit it.

Chapter 5

Phillippa tucked Alex's spare gun in the waistband of her jeans before she snatched up Kiki. Thick gray ash covered her shorn coat. The dog sneezed twice and squirmed as Phillippa checked every inch of the Maltese. Not so much as a scratch.

"Is she okay?" Alex brushed ash off his shoulders and jeans.

Phillippa nodded. She set down Kiki, who shook her little body with fervor. Another cloud rose into the air and set both Phillippa and Alex coughing and sneezing.

"What the hell was that thing?" Alex asked once he wiped the pink-tinged tears from his eyes.

"A demon," she answered. "The same demon that was in Beatrice's house." A shudder rippled through Phillippa. "The one that killed her."

"Wait a minute." Alex laid a hand on her shoulder. "Think about this. Earlier you said the demon probably didn't kill Mrs. Madison. What if you were right and it searched her place after she'd been murdered. It was in your store, looking for something. Probably your missing tumi."

Red-hot anger settled in her bones, and she shrugged off his touch. "Maybe I was wrong, and it tortured and murdered Beatrice to find out where the tumi was."

"Then why didn't Kiki destroy it while it was at Madison's house? The dog's been running loose inside for the last few days, remember?" Alex's fingers ruffled through his thick, blond hair to shake out the ash.

She raked her fingers through his long hair as he slowly entered . . .

Phillippa crossed her arms and pinched the tender underskin to interrupt the memory. What the Hades was wrong with her? Her client was dead, and she kept thinking about Alex. It irked her that she still dwelled on their night together a century after the fact.

It irked her even more to admit he may be right about the demon. She looked down at Kiki, who sat primly next to her. "Maybe you're right. Kiki refused to leave Beatrice's body during our initial search. She might have ignored the demon, too."

Alex cocked his head. "Speaking of which, exactly how does a Maltese blow up a demon?"

"They're divine," Phillippa said.

"Come again?" Alex shot her a look that clearly said she was crazy.

She smirked. "That's the problem with men. Short-term memories."

Alex sighed. "Phillippa, tell me what you know about Maltese dogs."

The compulsion tugged along her nerves. What in Hades' name had possessed her to swear an oath of obedience to Alexander Stanton? Much less on the River Styx?

Because you wanted revenge for Beatrice's murder.

"When the Phoenician goddess Astarte married the Egyptian god Set, the sky god Haddad created the original pair of Maltese from two small white clouds. They were her companions while she was away from the Phoenician pantheon."

Alex looked at the tiny canine. "Might be worth getting one myself. She came in handy in a fight."

The image of Stanton with a fluff-mop of a dog was too much. Phillippa roared hysterically. Alex glared at her while she leaned against the dumpster to catch her breath.

"If you're done laughing at my expense—" His pocket beeped.

With a final dirty look, he pulled out his phone and thumbed the "Answer" icon. "What have you got for me, Tiffany?"

He was silent for a second, then he said, "She's right here. Let me put you on speaker."

"Like I told Alex, I pulled Beatrice Madison's home records first." Tiffany's voice had a tinny quality coming through the phone. "The two-day thing stuck in my head. There's a call from her house to Seven Wonders at one-twenty-seven p.m. on Saturday. It lasted for five minutes and thirty-three seconds."

Phillippa frowned. "I wasn't here."

"Yeah, I kno-o-ow. You were at lunch with me and Bebe." Tiffany's "duh" wasn't implied. It was forcefully clubbed over Phillippa's head. "What did the staff say when you got back?"

Concern wiggled up her spine. Beatrice's call could have been something simple. Checking if any sales of her consignment had been made. Or finding something else she wanted to sell.

Except with everything between the break-in and the demon, Phillippa wasn't about to assume anything anymore. "No one mentioned her call to me. Let me check into it."

"In the meantime, can we use your shower?" Alex asked.

"Sure," Tiffany said. "I should have more for you by the time you get here."

When he ended the call, Phillippa asked, "Why Tiffany's?"

"Tarzana is closer to the Madison house than either of our places." He scratched his scalp. "And frankly, that demon dust is making me itch."

Despite the size of Tiffany and Max's sprawling three-bedroom ranch, Alex was very aware when Phillippa stepped out of the bathroom on the opposite side of the house. The scent of sea and grass and wind filled the air.

Tiffany looked up from her notebook computer and rolled her eyes. "You really need to get laid."

"Seriously?" Irritation made him itch almost as much as the demon ash had. He leaned back in his chair. "This coming from the knocked-up nineteen-year-old?"

She bounced a yellow number two pencil off his head. "I'm twenty."

"You weren't when you got pregnant."

She snorted. "It's not my fault the condom broke. Besides, you don't have to worry about getting someone pregnant."

No, just infecting them with an incurable disease. The one woman he couldn't infect, the one woman he wanted, would prefer it if Kiki could blow him into ashes.

He shoved thoughts of Phil away, tried to ignore Tiffany's smirk, and typed another search criteria into her old laptop. He would have preferred his state-of-the-art desktop, but beggars, blah, blah, blah . . .

"What about Rhoda, the Karnak casino manager?"

Nope, the kid definitely wasn't going to drop the subject. And it wasn't like Rhoda hadn't made her interest known over the last fifty years. The problem quite simply was the lady vamp wasn't Phil.

He blew out an exasperated breath. "Just because you got hitched, does *not* mean everyone else around you has to get married or otherwise coupled."

"That's not what I mean. I'm just tired of you mooning over Phil. And I've only had to deal with it for the last twenty years. I can only imagine what the rest of the coven thinks."

"I am *not* mooning," he ground out between clenched teeth.

"Ri-i-ight." She stood and stretched. On her petite frame, her belly already bulged even though she was barely half-way through her term.

An image of Phil, heavy with his child, rose in his mind. He brutally shoved it away. As a demigoddess, she may be immune to the V-virus, but the disease still left him sterile.

"Alex?"

He shook his head to clear his mind. "What?"

A smirk twisted Tiffany's lips, one that said she knew exactly where his thoughts were without any telepathy. "Do you want some more blood or coffee?"

"Coffee, please." He pushed the super-size mug, with the word "Bazinga!" stenciled in bright primary colors, across the table.

A whine came from the floor, and a dainty paw brushed his bare big toe.

Alex reached down and picked up Kiki. The dog was slightly damp from her own bath. She licked his nose and whined again.

"Tiffany, you got any meat?"

She waddled to the table and set down his coffee. "I've got some leftover roast beef."

"Can we have a few small chunks?" he asked. Kiki panted and gave Tiffany a doggie smile for good measure.

She laughed. "I don't need both of you making puppy eyes at me. She can have some."

Kiki jumped from his lap and raced for the refrigerator.

Tiffany crossed the kitchen at a more sedate pace and pulled out a large baking dish. She brought it back to the table along with a knife. Once she settled back in her chair, she sliced off teeny bits of roast. Somehow she managed to feed the Maltese with one hand and type with the other.

A few minutes later, she said, "Bingo."

Alex looked up from his own search through the Customs database. "Whatcha got?"

Tiffany's eyes darted back and forth as she read her screen. "Dennis Madison's SUV blew a tire on the freeway. He lost control of the vehicle, slammed into the concrete barrier and flipped. He died at the scene. Witnesses reported that he and another vehicle, a black Suburban, seemed to be racing, but CHP never found the other driver. Apparently, the license plate was obscured by dirt."

"What time?"

"The accident was reported to 9-1-1 at three-oh-two a.m."

It could have been an accident. Or maybe was someone chasing Dennis Madison? If so, why?

Tiffany shook her head. "Reconstruction found a puncture that possibly blew the tire. No definitive cause though."

Alex's index finger tapped a restless rhythm on the tabletop. "Could have been an accident. Picked up a nail."

"Or someone in the other vehicle could have tossed a spike."

"Or shot out the tire," he added.

Alex and Tiffany stared at each other over the screens of their respective computers.

"I don't believe in coincidences," he said.

"Highly overrated," she added.

Phil sauntered into the kitchen. While most of the Augustine enforcers kept extra clothing at each other's residences for emergencies, she had to borrow a t-shirt and a pair of knit athletic shorts from Tiffany's husband Max.

Her perfectly shaped breasts stretched the cotton shirt and made it definitely clear that she wasn't wearing a bra. The curves of her hips pulled the seams of the shorts taut.

Alex quickly sat straight. His cock showed its enthusiasm for Phil's display a little too much. Would she take off her clothes if he ordered her to? Did her oath stretch that far?

Stanton, you are one sick bastard. Maybe he needed another shower. A very cold one. He took a gulp of coffee instead.

Phil sat on the chair between Tiffany and him before she reached for the knife. "I spoke with everyone that worked in the store on Saturday. No one talked to Beatrice on the phone, and she didn't come into the store while I was at lunch."

Alex watched her hand a pebble-sized morsel of beef to Kiki. "How can you be sure they were telling you the truth?"

Phil ignored his gaze while she sliced off a larger hunk of meat. "Because everyone who works there is a nymph except Jane. And even a Normal isn't stupid enough to lie to me when she knows what I am." She popped the beef into her mouth.

"Why *did* you tell her?"

She chewed on the roast for a full minute before she swallowed. "Because I'm looking for someone to take over the business."

"Why?" he pressed.

Another long pause as she fed Kiki and sliced herself more meat. "Because this is the longest I've ever stayed in one place. I'm getting restless."

Tiffany stared at Phil, her dark eyes wide with pain. "You stayed because of me, didn't you?"

Wetness shimmered in Phil's blue-green eyes, and she lowered them. "I'm sorry, sweetie. This isn't how I meant to tell you. I'm staying until the baby is born." She laid a hand over Tiffany's. "And I'll keep in touch."

A rock settled in the pit of Alex's stomach. Phil was leaving. Anything he said right now would only drive her faster and further away from Los Angeles.

He stared at the computer screen. It took a minute for him to realize he was looking at the information he'd been searching for over the last hour.

"Phil, when did Mrs. Madison say her husband brought the fake tumi into the country?"

She handed another bite to Kiki. "The sale paperwork she gave me was dated three years ago. Why?"

"Because according to this customs declaration, Dennis Madison brought a ceramic and titanium replica into the United States three days before he died."

Chapter 6

Phillippa rose from her chair and stepped over Kiki to look at the scanned form on Alex's computer screen. Impossible. The paper Beatrice had given her couldn't possibly be . . .

The computer screen flickered. One of the bulbs in the lamp hanging over the table popped.

"Phil, if you blow up my computers and the wiring in this house, I swear I will shoot you through the heart with my crossbow." Tiffany glared at her.

"Sorry, sweetie," she murmured. She yanked the threads of her anger back under control before she read the form again. "Why would Beatrice counterfeit the customs paperwork for a fake? That makes absolutely no sense."

Footsteps shuffled in the hallway. Phillippa looked up from the computer to find Tiffany's husband, his hair ruffled and glasses askew.

"Honey, it's one-thirty in the morning. Why is my alarm clock going off?" Max blinked rapidly under the bright kitchen lighting.

Tiffany winced. "Sorry about that." She shot an evil look at Phillippa. "It won't happen again. Why don't you go back to bed?"

Max's groggy brain finally seemed to register Phillippa and Alex's presence. "What's going on?" Alarm flashed across his face. "Sam hasn't done something stupid again, has she?"

Phillippa crossed over to Max and laid a hand on his shoulder. "This has nothing to do with your sister. Tiffany's helping us with some research."

"Why?" Suspicion glinted behind his wire-rim glasses. He turned to Tiffany. "You're supposed to be on maternity leave." He spun to face Alex. "She's supposed to be on maternity leave." Max twisted to face Phillippa. "Tiffany is *supposed* to be on maternity leave."

"She is." Phillippa squeezed his shoulder. "We won't let anything happen to her and the baby."

Max's blue eyes narrowed. "You mean like at our wedding?"

"Which one?" Alex muttered. "Ouch!" He glared at Tiffany. "My feet are bare."

Tiffany shook another pencil in his direction. "Don't make me use this on you."

Phillippa closed her eyes. Gaea help her, those two were worse than her sisters. She opened her eyes and met Max's concerned look. "I swear all she's doing is helping us with background research on a murder case."

"Murder?" Max was decidedly awake now. "A supernatural?" Slippers slapped the linoleum as he crossed the kitchen and pulled the fourth chair closer to his wife's.

"No," Alex said. "A Normal, but it's related to a break-in tonight at Phil's shop."

In the minute it took Tiffany to fill Max in on the situation, Phil returned to her former position at Alex's shoulder.

Alex folded his arms over his chest. Sandalwood and his own distinctive evergreen scent teased her. He looked up at her, blue eyes glowing slightly. Apparently, she wasn't the only one irritated by tonight's puzzles.

"I'm beginning to think this tumi is not a fake. Did you pick up *anything* from it while it was in your store?"

She shook her head, damp hair heavy against her neck. "No."

"No unusual energy? No magick?"

"No," she repeated. "I . . ." She rifled her memory of the day she and Jane went to Beatrice's house to review the items the widow wanted to sell. "Actually, I never touched it. I looked at it, but Jane handled it. In fact, Jane handled everything. Packing the merchandise. Logging it in. Unpacking."

Phillippa leaned on Alex's chair to read the customs declaration one more time. Her motion only drove his scent further into her brain, prompting scenarios of everything she'd planned to do to him when he came back to San Antonio all those decades ago.

Except he never returned.

"And you didn't supervise?" he prompted.

She straightened abruptly. "This was Jane's first estate sale. I wanted her to have the experience if she's going to take over for me. The only thing I did was tell her to send the tumi to the assayer when she said she thought the metal was titanium."

"But you never touched it?" Alex prompted.

Phillippa shook her head again.

Alex wiped a palm over his face. "If we didn't have to meet Jorge and Siobhan soon, I'd say let's question Jane a little more."

Phillippa glared at him. "Are you accusing one of my employees of theft?"

"No, Phil, I'm not." His voice sounded weary. "But she might have noticed something at the Madisons' house or the assayer's that was out of the normal. Maybe a customer at your store who acted or said something about the tumi that might give us a clue of what the hell is going on. We've got someone willing to kill for what's supposed to be a fake Incan artifact."

"You're right."

He raised an eyebrow, but otherwise let her acknowledgment pass. No pleased look. No teasing. No emotion whatsoever. Something tugged at her that had nothing to do with her oath. Was he really over her?

She should be gratified that his infatuation was gone. So why did it feel like someone had hit her in the gut?

Alex hit a few keystrokes, and a printer whirred to life in another room. "Get some sleep, Tiffany."

"What about the rest of the research?" she countered.

"Work on it during the day, and e-mail it to me."

Max looked from Tiffany to Alex and back. "You're supposed to be on maternity leave."

She fixed her husband with a nasty look. "Shut up, or this will be the only child you ever conceive."

Kiki started barking from the tension in the kitchen.

Phillippa bit her tongue to keep from smiling. "Tiffany's not going to be on street duty, Max."

Tiffany glared at Phillippa. "That's not your decision."

"No, but if your uncle Duncan asks me, I will enforce his will. Understand me, little girl?"

A pout appeared on Tiffany's elfin features, and she crossed her arms over her belly. "I thought Amazons didn't do what men told them."

For the first time in Tiffany's short life, anger rose from deep in Phillippa. "You're being a selfish brat. Duncan's order has nothing to do with your competence. That baby is dependent on you. Honor the life you created."

Tiffany's jaw dropped. Crimson spread across her pale face. "Yes, ma'am."

The men exchanged surprised looks, but thankfully, they kept their mouths shut.

"Jorge's about to call. I'll go get my shoes." Phillippa pivoted and headed for the front porch.

Alex's phone beeped behind her. She smiled to herself as Max marveled over her psychic abilities, and Alex confirmed to Jorge they were on their way back to the Madisons' house.

Alex tried to keep his eyes on the road. Honestly, he did, but Phil's breasts subtly swayed with the motion of the truck. Irritation jangled his nerves.

Irritation that Kiki was curled up on Phil's lap instead of him. Irritation that the two of them were tagging along on this investigation. Irritation with his inability to control himself.

"You enjoy messing with people, don't you?"

From the corner of his eye, he could see her turn toward him. Her rich chestnut hair had dried into a glorious mass of curls that framed her oval face. Over one hundred and twenty years later, he remembered how it looked spread out over her pillow.

"What's that supposed to mean?" A frown tugged at the corners of her mouth.

"That thing with pretending to predict when a phone's going to ring." He shouldn't be taking his pissy mood out on her. It wasn't fair.

Like she hasn't been taking hers out on you for the last century? a little voice said in the back of his mind.

"Is that what crawled up your ass tonight? That I know when a phone's going to ring?"

"Answer my question." He glanced at her. An odd look crossed her face. The oath. She was actually trying to fight the oath.

Finally, she muttered, "Yes." She crossed her arms over those heavenly breasts. "But I didn't make it to my fifty-third-hundredth birthday by not using every talent I have to my advantage."

The cab remained silent for another mile before she said softly, "Aren't you even going to ask how I know?"

Alex spared another glance at Phil. Her lips were parted, anticipation on her beautiful face. Her expression only spiked his irritation. "I already know how." He needed to keep his attention on the street and not think about kissing her.

"Y-you—"

The moist sound of her tongue on her lips sent signals to his groin he should damn well be ignoring.

"How?" she whispered.

"Since you've got your granddaddy Zeus's talent for throwing lightning bolts, I figured you can pick up other electrical signals as well. Like between a cell tower and a phone. I've just been trying to figure out the why-I-pretend-I'm-precognitive part. What does it have to do with survival?"

"Seriously? You didn't read any of the Greek classics?" Sarcasm dripped from her voice.

"Yes, I have. What's that got to do—"

"Everything!"

The truck's running lights brightened, then dimmed.

Phil stared out the window. Her chest heaved, which certainly did not help his libido. "Everything," she whispered. "All of my sisters, every single one, died because some dickwad had to prove himself."

With no siblings, Alex could hardly put himself in Phil's position and claim he understood. But something else made sense with her confession. "How'd you manage to erase yourself from history?"

Her head whipped back to face him. "What?"

"Look, I'm not disputing your view that guys like Heracles, Theseus and Achilles were assholes. Let's face it. Homer and the other poets and historians don't exactly paint these guys as Boy Scouts, and they were on the heroes' side. But you're never mentioned in any legends or stories like your sisters. How'd you manage to disappear?" A quick look at Phil revealed her shocked expression.

"How-how did you know?" she choked out.

"Like I said, I read the classics." He couldn't help a smile. "Otrera, the daughter of Eurus the East Wind and the first queen of the Amazons, had a long-term relationship with Ares, the god of war. They had several children, all girls. Your sisters. But there's no mention of a Phillippa as one of the daughters. So how'd you manage to disappear from all the stories?"

"You wouldn't understand." She stared out the passenger window again.

"Why wouldn't I?" His grip tightened on the steering wheel. "Because I'm just a tiny name on a wall in Austin. Because there aren't statues and coins and shit thousands of years after I supposedly died, like there are for Caesar's family and your sisters."

Kiki crawled from Phil's lap to rest her head on his thigh. He reached down with one hand and scratched behind her ears.

Phil turned to face him. "Name on a wall?"

He should've dropped the subject when she gave him the chance. Old bitterness welled. Not over his Turning. God knew that Duncan had saved his life in more ways than one.

It didn't make the survivor's guilt any less difficult to handle at times.

He kept his eyes on the traffic. "There's a wall at the Texas Rangers Museum in Austin. It lists all the men who died in the line of duty."

"Why would you even go?"

He could feel her watching him, and he shrugged. "Part of it was morbid curiosity."

"And the other part?" Her voice was gentle as they turned down the Madisons' street.

He didn't want to answer, but if anyone would understand, it would be Phil. "I couldn't remember the names of everyone in my old battalion anymore."

Phillippa cracked the window for Kiki before she climbed from the truck cab. This time she made sure the door was securely shut.

With all the bickering between her and Alex, she'd forgotten how young he really was. What would he do when he woke up one night centuries from now and had trouble remembering his own name, much less his family and companions.

The changing of identities, creating false histories, had become so ingrained she barely remembered her mother and sisters. Images of Hippolyta in the comic books seemed far more real than the eldest sister she'd loved and admired.

And then there was the matter of Father . . .

Shoving the thought aside, Phil stalked after Alex.

Jorge Sifuentes waited for them on the front step, female clothing in his hands. The front door stood open, and the scent of wolf permeated the yard.

The detective nodded. "Siobhan decided to get started."

Phil smirked. "Just like her father."

Alex looked at her. "Behave."

She opened her mouth for a snide remark, but the compulsion yanked on her jaw. Instead, she said, "Is it okay if we do another search through the house?"

Sifuentes shot her an odd look before he said, "Go ahead."

Old blood and death filled her head when the three of them stepped inside the foyer.

"By the way," Alex said. "We caught our mystery demon inside Phil's store a few hours ago."

"And?" Sifuentes propped his hands on his hips, curiosity on his face.

A bitter laugh erupted from her throat. "It committed suicide rather than talk to us."

The detective's expression turned incredulous. "How the hell does a demon commit suicide?"

Alex grinned. "Apparently by touching a Maltese dog. Another interesting tidbit is that Dennis Madison brought the tumi into the U.S. two months ago. Three days before he died."

Sifuentes stared at Phil. "You told me it was a fake brought back years ago."

Phil folded her arms over her chest. Alex quickly found interest in a painting that decorated the stairwell. Maybe he wasn't as over her as he pretended.

"Beatrice gave me a fake customs declaration, so I'm guessing the bill of sale is also a forgery. The demon was rummaging through the merchandise, probably looking for the tumi. I want to go through her paperwork."

Jorge gestured toward the stairs. "Have at it."

She jogged up the steps, Alex on her heels. It took them minutes to sort through the chaos of what had been Dennis and Beatrice Madison's office.

"Notice anything strange?" she asked as they surveyed the neat piles.

"Yeah." Alex wiped a hand over his face. "Anything regarding artifacts from Peru is missing."

Phillippa propped her fists on her hips. "Well, a demon sure as Hades wouldn't have bothered taking paperwork."

A whisper of movement came from the hallway. Siobhan Lannigan Sifuentes appeared in the doorway. "My guess is it was the Normals."

The Los Angeles pack's beta was naked. A tiny thrill spiked in Phillippa that Alex didn't seem remotely interested in the attractive redhead. Of course, his refusal to peruse her nude body might have more to do with the fact that Siobhan would gut him in an instant if he showed the were any disrespect.

Phillippa tapped her finger on her cheek. "Did you have a chance to examine the body? Could you tell who killed Beatrice?"

"Yeah, the kid picking up the corpse was Augustine Family so he let me have a sniff. My money's on the Normals. Steel was used. Also, no ozone. The whole purpose of a sacrifice is to raise power." Siobhan shrugged. "I'd double-check with someone from Silver Bear though if I were you. Demons aren't my forté."

Wonderful. Phillippa's stomach grumbled around the roast beef she snacked on at Tiffany's. The last thing she wanted was to involve the Los Angeles witch coven, but Alex may not have a choice. Not when even her experience couldn't identify the demon that had been searching her store.

Sifuentes appeared behind his wife. "Thanks for dumping the problem back in my lap, honey."

Siobhan grunted.

Phillippa looked at Alex. "If Normals killed Beatrice, then why cut out the heart? And why trash my shop since they obviously beat the demon to it?"

Alex stared back. His eyes brightened. Not a full-blown vamp-out, but enough to show he was disturbed. "The bigger question is why a demon wants a supposed replica of an Incan artifact."

"You don't think it's a fake?"

"Not anymore, darlin."

Chapter 7

Too many questions tumbled through Alex's mind as he drove back to Phil's store. The top of the list—what the hell was the item Beatrice Madison tried to sell, and why was it worth killing for?

"We need to check your files."

"My files?" Oncoming headlights flashed across her face. "Jane said she'd get them for you. You can't wait until the morning?"

Alex grimaced. "Under normal circumstances, I'd respect your time and hers. But the sooner I can get this resolved, the sooner I'll be out of your hair."

Phillippa sighed. "Fine."

Was that reluctance he heard in her voice?

Stop the wishful thinking. You're over her, remember?

Out cold, Kiki didn't budge when he pulled into the parking lot and braked to a stop behind the shop. Phil reached for the dog, and Alex laid a hand over hers. Electricity sparked, not her powers but the old-fashioned attraction between a man and a woman. She licked her upper lip.

As much as he wanted to accept the invitation, he didn't dare. "Let her sleep. I doubt if she has for the last couple of days." Reluctantly, he slid his hand from hers at her acknowledgement.

They climbed out of the truck and gently shut their respective doors. He followed Phil to the back door and helped her push the steel frame they'd bent to secure the building out of the way.

She flipped on the backroom lights and headed for her office. He walked behind, doing his best not to watch the sway of her hips. It didn't matter what she wore. Phil made anything look good.

He leaned against the doorway while she slid into her leather desk chair and started rifling through her files. "Since you'll be busy with the insurance company this morning, why don't I take Kiki back to my place for the day?"

Phil glanced up with a wry smile on her face. "And how are you going to walk her?"

He shrugged. "She can use newspapers on my patio."

She laughed, a low melodious sound he remembered far too well. "Newspapers? Really, Mr. Computers-Are-The-Wave-Of-The-Future?"

He grinned back. "They come in handy. Like when I need to babysit a Phoenician divine dog."

Instead of laughing some more or shooting a quip, she frowned. Her fingers flew over the folders in the drawer a second time. Then she rose and shuffled through an entire five-drawer cabinet.

Alex straightened. "What's wrong?"

"It's not here." Phil turned and started going through the plastic paperwork trays on her desk.

"Mrs. Madison's file?"

"No! Your brains, cowboy!" She slammed down the files she held. Loose sheets flew into the air and fluttered to the carpet. "Beatrice's file is gone."

The overhead lights flickered.

"You need to calm down right now."

If Phillippa were her cousin Medusa, he'd be stone from the look she gave him. But the lights steadied and brightened.

Tell her to take off her t-shirt, his second brain whispered.

Instead, Alex said, "But you have the main inventory that lists the items, right?"

"Yeah." She swiveled her chair around and hit the power switch on her computer. "I scanned in the paperwork as well. And Duncan set up the backup program that dumps everything into an Augustine server."

"You're welcome," he drawled.

She looked up at him. "What?"

"He made me set up your system because I let Tiffany drink too much soda pop one night when she was eight."

Phil covered her mouth, but he could see the light dancing in her eyes. "That was twelve years ago."

"Yeah, and my boss, being a stereotypical Scorpio, carries grudges for a lifetime. And since he's a vampire . . ."

She gave up trying to hide her humor and laughed outright. "Considering I had to take a grumpy, sleep-deprived third grader to school the next day, you're not getting any sympathy from me."

As much as he wanted to stay with Phil, a familiar tightening of his skin told him it was time to go home. Dawn came too damn early in June. "You going to be okay here?"

That question earned him a reproving look. "I think I can manage."

"Then I'll go home and see what Tiffany's come up with." Except his feet didn't want to take that first step out of Phil's office.

She deliberately stared at her computer screen while she clicked on the necessary documents. "Alex, you've got forty-five minutes to beat the sun home. I really don't want to explain to Caesar why he lost another enforcer."

"Give me a call if something else happens."

This time she turned to face him. "I will. Now, go."

Alex pivoted on his boot heels and headed out the back door. For only the second time in one hundred-twenty-five years, he regretted his Turn.

Phil made a couple of calls. The nymphs spread the message, and within an hour, all ten of them were at the store, shoveling debris and evaluating the damage to the merchandise. The only person not answering her phone was Jane. Both her home landline and her cell kept rolling over to voicemail.

Surprisingly, Sifuentes sent a deputy out with the official report and copies of the photos his team had taken.

Both the insurance adjustor and her contractor arrived by nine a.m. Phil tried to stay out of the way as the two of them did their jobs. She gratefully accepted the large cup of coffee Melissa handed her.

"Should I try Jane again?" Worry lay in the nymph's amber eyes.

Phil shook her head. "No, she was here late last night dealing with the police and this mess. She probably turned off her phones and forgot to set her alarm clock." Except she couldn't shake her own concern. One person had already died over a fake artifact.

Was the tumi a fake? Alex seemed sure there was more to the object than what the assayer reported.

"Humans," Melissa murmured, disapproval in her tone. "They would be so much healthier if they simply followed Apollo's chariot."

Another possibility occurred to Phillippa. "You helped Jane with the Madison estate. Did you ever touch the tumi replica?"

Melissa stared at the ceiling while she replayed her experiences of the last few months in her mind. Sometimes, the nymph's eidetic memory came in handy. "I only handled it directly once. Two weeks ago, a couple came in looking for something unusual and one-of-a-kind for her parent's fiftieth anniversary." She took a sip of her tea and frowned. "Something felt . . . off about it."

"How?"

Melissa's fine brows crinkled, then smoothed as she shrugged. "I can't say. Our perceptions aren't as clear as they used to be, m'lady. Not in the two centuries with the power grid and pollution."

The adjustor walked over to them, and the nymph darted away to distribute tea and juice to her compatriots.

He rubbed the bald spot at the back of his head. "I've got good news and bad news, Ms. Mann."

She gave him a rueful smile. "You'll pay the claim, but you're dropping my policy."

He laid his clipboard on the solid mahogany counter, one of the few pieces in the store that was intact. "Your agent already spoke with you."

She nodded.

"You've got to admit that two incidences of vandalism in less than six months is an issue. Especially when we're dealing with some high dollar items."

A sad laugh trilled in her throat. Maybe this was the Moirai's hint for her to leave Los Angeles sooner rather than later. "I'm all too aware of the issue. I thought moving outside of the city proper would alleviate your company's concerns." She scanned the room. In a corner, Melissa flirted with Roberto as she handed him a steaming cup. "And provide less of a target."

The adjustor leaned against the counter. "These girls will be out of a job if you shut down your business, won't they?"

"Yes." The problem was more than the employment. It was giving the nymphs a sense of purpose in the twenty-first century, in a world that no longer believed in them, much less honored them. Like Duncan asking Phil to help raise Tiffany had given her a sense of purpose.

"Damn," the adjustor muttered. "It'll be next to impossible for them to find something in this economy. My son lost his job two years ago, and still can't find anything above minimum wage. The bank foreclosed on their house just after my daughter-in-law had my grandson."

Determination filled the man's face. "Let me talk to my regional director." He held up a hand. "I can't guarantee anything, Ms. Mann. If I get her to agree and there's another claim . . ."

"I understand." Phillippa stuck out her hand. "I'd appreciate whatever you can do." She glanced over at the nymphs. "For their sakes."

Once Roberto delivered his estimate and paperwork was signed, copied and traded between him, the adjustor and Phillippa, both men left.

But not before Roberto promised to return at seven a.m. tomorrow with a team to install the new doors and windows. All ten of the nymphs volunteered to come to the store at dawn to meet the contractor, though Melissa looked more peeved at the extra volunteers than excited. Phillippa distracted the potential nymph fight over the attention of mortal men by promising the girls they could decide on the new colors for the interior once they removed the last of the debris.

She handed the swatch book to Melissa. "Can you keep everyone on track? I'm going to run over to Jane's to check on her."

"Yes, m'lady." Melissa saluted her. If it were anyone else, Phillippa would have smacked them for mocking her. From the nymph, the gesture was sincere.

"And keep your hands off Roberto."

Melissa pouted, but said nothing.

"I mean it. I need him to finish this job." Phillippa glared at the nymph.

Melissa's sullen "Yes, ma'am," was the best she was going to get. She turned and stalked out the back door to her car.

The drive to Jane's apartment complex drew Phil's nerves taut. She couldn't shake the feeling something was terribly wrong. This wasn't like Jane. The girl was so damn efficient and punctual, even if she chased everything with a penis.

Maybe Jane was part-nymph herself.

Phillippa parked her Mustang and jogged up the exterior flight of stairs. She hammered on her assistant's door. No one answered.

She scanned the area. Jane's blue Paseo wasn't in the parking lot. The girl didn't live in the best of neighborhoods, but the people here seemed to be good folks the couple of times Phillippa had visited. A few children played in the pool under the watchful eye of two older women.

"Yo, gringa, whachoo want?" A middle-aged man approached along the open walkway. His mustache was thick and full, but it carried the same salt-and-pepper as his hair. His light blue workshirt was embroidered with "P. Rodriguez, Manager."

Phillippa switched to Spanish. "I'm Phillippa Mann, Jane Chevrette's employer. She didn't come to work today and isn't answering her phone. I came to check on her."

"Miss Jane?" Rodriguez shook his head. "Miss Jane hasn't been around in two weeks."

"What are you talking about?" It would be understandable if Jane had met somebody, but she hadn't mentioned dating anyone lately.

The fine hairs rose on the back of Phillippa's neck. *Two weeks.* The same time that Melissa said she felt something strange from the tumi. It couldn't be a coincidence.

"No one's seen Miss Jane in a couple of weeks. In fact, the postman asked me yesterday if I had a forwarding address for her because her box was full." He shrugged. "But she hasn't turned in her notice and her rent's paid through the month."

The little worm of worry became a full-blown leviathan. Jane had been at the shop last night. She would have been the first one at the store this morning. "Would you please unlock her door for me?"

The manager gave her a measured look. "Maybe we should call the police."

Phillippa smiled. "If she's in there and okay, then you can blame everything on me. But if she's sick . . ."

Rodriguez pulled the key ring from his belt. "You're right. Miss Jane doesn't cause any trouble." He slid what looked like a master key into the lock and twisted.

The stench of rotten meat hit Phillippa as soon as Rodriguez popped open the door. She entered, the manager right behind her. "Jane?"

"Mother in heaven, what is that smell?" Rodriguez muttered.

Silence. Nothing was out of place in the tiny living room, but the odor . . .

Phillippa arrowed for the kitchenette, the source of the Gaea-awful smell, and yanked open the refrigerator door. Rodriguez whirled away at the sight that greeted them and heaved the contents of his stomach across the living room carpet.

"Oh, Jane," Phillippa whispered. She closed the door, pulled her cell phone out of her pocket and punched a number she really shouldn't have memorized.

Alex answered on the first ring. "What's up, Phil?"

She swallowed the bile at the back of her throat. "I need an enforcer at Jane's apartment." She could hear the scratch of a pencil on paper as she gave him the address. "And I need you to contact Sifuentes."

"Sweet, Jesus," he muttered. "Is Jane . . . ?"

Phillippa's fingers squeezed the case of her smart phone until the plastic squealed. "Somebody cut her up and shoved the parts into her refrigerator at least a week ago. Whoever was at my store last night was not Jane Chevrette."

Chapter 8

Phillippa wasn't the least bit surprised when Tiffany pulled into the parking lot twenty minutes later. Alex must have woken her because she wasn't wearing her usual black and white goth make-up. The tiny girl climbed down from her huge black SUV.

Woman, Phillippa had to remind herself. It was hard to remember Tiffany was an adult when her mind still wanted to paint a picture of the toddler she took to the park.

"You shouldn't be here," Phillippa said when the kid reached the curb.

Tiffany smirked "Sounds to me like all the danger is over." She carefully lowered herself to the concrete where Phillippa sat. Tiffany had finally accepted reality and bought some maternity clothes. Phillippa didn't want to know where she'd found the black t-shirt with the words, "Parasite on Board," and an arrow pointing down.

"Duncan's going to have a fit that Alex dragged you into this."

"Uncle Duncan can sink his fangs into my lily-white ass." Tiffany watched as yet another deputy came out of the apartment and leaned over the railing to puke into the bushes below. "Pretty bad up there, huh?"

"You have no idea."

"Any demon scent in the place?"

"Couldn't tell over the smell of . . ." Rage flooded her once more. The siren on one of the sheriff's cars someone had left running blared once before it squealed like a dying rabbit.

Shit. She thought she was far enough away from LASO's equipment.

Why couldn't she feel grief like everyone else? But no, the rage was one more nasty little legacy from Daddy Dearest.

Tiffany scowled at her. "Phil, if you can't get a grip, then you're no help to me or Alex."

She clenched her fists on top of her thighs. "I'll keep it together."

Tiffany's doubtful expression said everything. "I've never seen you this pissed off before."

"Jane was a good kid. She just needed some guidance. This—" Phillippa waved a hand toward the apartment. "Her death was totally unnecessary."

"Why *did* you hire her? Why not turn the business over to the nymphs?"

Phillippa chuckled. "You really think a bunch of nymphs could handle a modern business?" She faced Tiffany. "I need someone with a strong enough personality to keep a leash on the staff. As for 'Why Jane?' I guess you wouldn't remember. You were three. She broke into the old store one night when you were sleeping over."

Tiffany tilted her head. "She broke into your place?"

"She was a starving runaway looking for something to pawn."

"And you hired her?"

"After I beat the shit out of her stepfather for trying to rape her, and after she promised to complete her education and not run away from her mother again." Phil smiled.

Tiffany laughed, a sound laced with black humor. "And here, I thought she was secretly a more socially adept nymph."

Sifuentes strode through the waves of heat shimmering across the concrete parking lot. Phillippa climbed to her feet. Tiffany held up her hand for some assistance, and was upright by the time the detective reached them.

"You know my first question, Mann," he said, his voice a low-pitched growl.

She raised her chin. "I don't know who was at my store last night. She fooled both Alex and me."

"If you two weren't so busy sniping at each other, maybe you would have noticed something."

"Whoever it was, she's fooled me and the entire staff for at least a week. Possibly two, if Mr. Rodriguez and the other tenants are correct."

"Crap." Sifuentes kicked at a loose piece of concrete. "The rest of the staff are supes?"

"Yes. Jane was the only Normal."

Her white-hot rage and Sifuentes frigid anger canceled each other out. They both sagged as the significance of the imposter sank in.

Sifuentes wiped a hand over his face. Dark circles smudged his eyes like bruises. He hadn't slept since the break-in at Seven Wonders either. "They're getting ready to remove the body. Once the movers are done, come upstairs. See if you can pick up anything. This may be your demon's work."

"Really? Because . . ."

"You didn't see it since the head was sitting in front of the torso. This time, the heart's missing and it *is* messy."

Phillippa stepped into Jane's apartment once again. The deputies had opened every single window, but the ninety-degree temps mitigated their efforts to eliminate the smell of decay as they worked.

She took a deep breath. The stench of death was one odor among many, and she had smelled far worse on battlefields over the millennia.

Crisp Macintosh permeated the room. Jane. Alive.

Beneath the apple of a Normal, honey, acorn and morning glory. Three of the nymphs visited. Melissa probably instigated the social call in order to take the measure of the woman who would replace Phillippa. She made a mental note to question Melissa about the time and confirm the reason for the visit.

Something else was here. The scent spoke of cool, dark caves, scales sliding over soapstone and obsidian, reptilian musk but with a hint of something ancient. So subtle, she would have missed it if she hadn't been concentrating.

Underneath everything, a vibration hummed. Alien energy crawled along her every cell. A song that maggots would sing while they searched for death.

"Jorge?"

The detective stepped closer, his voice soft. "Siobhan's on her way. Her dad owns the apartment complex." His gaze begged Phillippa not to say more in front of the Normals.

Alex had pulled the drapes across the huge plate glass windows of his condo as soon as Kiki did her business on the papers covering a corner of the terrace. The last thing he needed was the distraction of the skyline as the city woke.

But after Phil's phone call, what had been a typical puzzle of his job had become personal.

Kiki curled on his lap while his fingers flew across the specially designed keyboard, one that could handle a lot more abuse than a Normal keyboard. The systematic check of each airline gave tedious a whole new definition, but the imposter wasn't going to slip past him again.

Anger smoldered over someone managing to pull the proverbial wool over his eyes. She acted, smelled and felt Normal, dammit!

Chevrette, Jane popped on the screen. Whoever pretended to be Jane was using the girl's passport. They'd missed her by four hours.

If two women weren't dead, he'd laugh at the irony that Fake Jane took the same flight from LAX to Lima that Beatrice had booked. And he'd bet his entire stock portfolio the imposter had the tumi in her one carry-on.

It was an hour before sunset when the knock on Alex's door came. He set Kiki on the floor before he stood and crossed the living room to answer it. Tiffany brushed past him, a small cooler in her hand. Phil followed with several bags from a local fast food place. The delicious odor of fried chicken and mashed potatoes nearly cancelled her scent. What surprised him though was Jorge and Siobhan Sifuentes on the women's heels.

Kiki parked herself between Alex and the werewolf, barking her fool head off until he picked her up and soothed her.

Siobhan smirked at the Maltese and shook her head.

Jorge smiled, a wan imitation of his wolfish grin, and held up the two bags he carried. "Dos Equus and José Cuervo. It's been one of those days, and it's not getting better when you hear everything."

"Then, I hope you brought limes—" Alex started.

Siobhan socked him in the bicep. "Of course, we brought the limes."

Kiki growled.

"Forty-five seconds, right, Alex?" Phil yelled from the kitchen.

Okay, things were worse than he thought if Phil was heating his blood. And mentioning the double entendré would come under the heading of the stupidest thing he'd done since his practical joke that backfired nearly a century ago. He'd never convinced Phil that Caesar's twin sister had been his real target.

Add in his and Phil's surprise to learn the other was alive, and the chance for any reunion he might have wished for was gone.

Once everyone had filled their plates, or in his case had a warm mug, they gathered around the hunk of petrified wood that served as his coffee table. Kiki circled around, sniffing at everyone and occasionally growling at Siobhan. Or she did until the were bribed the Maltese with a few bites of chicken.

Alex laid out his suspicions. "I've already booked Phil and me on tomorrow's flight to Lima and contacted the Huamán Vampire Coven. We've got some local support when we need it."

Phil groaned. "Caesar really needs to buy another plane."

"You got a problem flying with the masses?"

Her eyes shifted from blue-green to gray. "I'm not sure what's worse, some TSA agent copping a feel or claiming you at baggage."

"If it makes you feel better, flying in a transport coffin is not my first choice." He shrugged. "But with Caesar in Africa dealing with the IC over the Seelie involvement in last spring's zombie attacks, this is the fastest way to chase our imposter."

Alex turned to Siobhan.

She held up a hand before he opened his mouth. "You don't even have to ask. I've already had a long talk with my father. If Tiffany can coordinate between me and the senior Augustine enforcer for the rest of the month . . ." She frowned. "Who's in charge if you and St. James are both out of town?"

"Right now, it would be Miko Osaka."

Siobhan's green-gold eyes widened. "A Normal? You've got to be kidding me. Where's Anne?"

"Helping her brother with a domestic problem."

Siobhan ripped at a chicken breast. "In other words, you have no one."

"Hey!" Tiffany protested. "What am I? Chopped liver?"

Siobhan didn't have to say a word. Her expression said everything. At least, she represented the Los Angeles wolf pack in this little war council, instead of her father. John Lannigan and Tiffany would have traded insults until claws and weapons came out.

Alex leaned back against the couch. "It's been a real shitty couple of years."

Jorge set his bottle on the table with a harsh *clink*. "Has it occurred to you this is a wild goose chase? A way for an enemy to fragment Augustine resources even further."

"Yep." Alex finished the last of his blood and reached for the tequila. "But my gut says something else is going on here."

"Alex is right," Phillippa said.

Someone could have shot him through the heart with a crossbow bolt, and he wouldn't have been more surprised.

Phillippa picked at the label on her bottle of beer. "Someone's killed two people to make sure that creature in my store last night didn't get the tumi. He was in Beatrice Madison's house, but something else killed Jane." She looked across the table at him. "Anything from Ziva about our suicidal monkey demon?"

He shook his head as he poured a shot. "None of her people recognized the description. She suspects it may be from a Central or South American pantheon and offered to contact some of the witch covens down there. I told her no."

"What? Why?" Tiffany exclaimed around a hunk of drumstick meat.

"Don't speak with your mouth full," Phil admonished. The girl shot a nasty look at her former guardian.

"We don't want to tip off the imposter or whoever she's working for," Phillippa continued. "Letting another vampire coven know about the situation is pushing our luck. What will the Huamán Coven's stand be when we find her?"

"If she's done something to piss off Master Huamán, he'd just as soon kill her himself. Otherwise, it's our problem." Alex dumped the tequila down his throat. With his Turn, the liquid burned more than he remembered it, but it wouldn't affect him, which was a good thing with Phil in the room.

She gestured for the bottle, and he slid it across the table. Phil poured two fingers into a shot glass before she passed it back to him.

Tiffany's attention swiveled between Alex and Phil. "What about the Sunshine Believers?"

Jorge reached for the last bucket of chicken. "The pin might have been nothing more than a red herring." He waved his thumb between his wife and him. "We're still going to visit the prison tomorrow and the psych ward the day after so I can question them and Siobhan can double-check scents."

Tiffany laboriously climbed up from the couch. "Why all the fuss if this tumi is a fake though? Alex, I have to agree with Jorge. It sounds like someone's seriously fucking with us."

Alex pointed toward the kitchen. "Grab that folder on the counter and I'll show you."

She sauntered back to the couch with the paperwork and a bottle of water. Alex took the manila folder and spread the printouts of the tests Phil had e-mailed him. The sheets glared white against the dark polished stone.

He pointed to the first two sheets. "Phil's assayer was right when he said the tumi was constructed of titanium and RCC."

Siobhan snorted. "Translate that for those of us without a PhD in chemistry."

Alex grinned. "RCC is reinforced carbon-carbon, basically a special type of heat-resistant ceramic consisting of carbon fibers in a matrix of graphite. NASA used it for the nosecone and leading wing edges on the space shuttles. What's more interesting are the other two results. The first one shows the third material composing the tumi. It's nothing known to us."

Tiffany pulled the sheet closer to her. "This isn't a proper chromatograph. This is someone flashing a lightbulb inside the machine."

"That's pretty much Ray Xavier's conclusion." Alex turned to Siobhan. "And yes, he is a vampire with a PhD in chemistry." He tapped the last sheet. "This one is the most interesting."

Jorge turned the page so he could read it. "This is a carbon dating report." He looked at Alex, then Phil, and back. "Twenty thousand? Years?"

Phil rose on her knees so she could see the report better. "The assayer said the carbon dating was inconclusive."

Alex didn't want to embarrass her, but he had to ask the question. "The assayer said that? Or did Jane?"

Surprisingly, her gaze was steady though her eyes were still the disconcerting gray. "I spoke to the assayer directly. Jane was concerned about the conflicting reports." She held up a hand. "Before you say it, this happened a month ago, so it could've been the real Jane. Even assuming it was our fake Jane, she probably wanted to make sure she had the correct object before she stole it. At that time though, given the odd readings on the inlay material and construction of the rest of the tumi, I agreed with assayer that it had to be an oddball reading."

Warmth spread through Alex as he deduced her real reasoning. "And you didn't want to charge Beatrice for a second set of tests."

"No."

Siobhan snickered. "Awww. Big, bad Amazon has a soft spot for orphans and widows."

Phil shot her a murderous look. "I have absolutely no problem kicking dogs."

Jorge deliberately reached between the two women for the tequila bottle. "Before you two start your supernatural smackdown, think about something. Last night, the imposter made a point of telling us the tumi was the only object missing."

Phil snorted. "Because she wanted me sitting here like I am right now, knowing she made a total fool of me."

"Maybe you two shouldn't go." Tiffany played with the condensation on her bottle. She met each person's eyes in turn. "What if Jorge's right and this is just a ploy? Some of Selene's followers haven't been located. And despite a concussion, I know damn well I saw Marcus Giovanni slip out of the chaos at Mallory Labs last February."

"We're not chasing ghosts here." Alex stared into Tiffany's eyes until she lowered them. The girl had to bring up that fucking traitor. He poured more tequila into his glass. "If the tumi is a genuine artifact and was brought illegally into the U.S., then it needs to be turned over to the Peruvian government."

"What if this tumi is something else?" Jorge served himself another shot. "Like an object of power. Jane Chevrette's heart was literally ripped from her chest, and most of her blood was missing."

Alex lowered his glass. "Are you saying this could have been blood magick?"

Siobhan wore a somber expression. ""Something had been done in that apartment. There was the faintest hint of ozone."

Phil nodded. "And there was residual energy." She shuddered. He'd never seen her react this way. Not even when a horde of zombies invaded Tiffany's first wedding ceremony. "I've never felt anything like it before."

She reached for the tequila bottle and poured another shot. "There's something else. Melissa said she felt something odd from the tumi when she showed it to some customers two weeks ago."

Sifuentes froze. "That's the same time the apartment manager said Jane went missing."

Phil slung back the drink. "Yeah. And I checked with the rest of the staff. Melissa was the only supernatural who touched it directly."

Alex set his glass on the table. Puzzle pieces started sliding together. "The tumi could have left some kind of mark on Jane. It would explain why she was targeted. Beatrice Madison, too." He reached for his phone. "I'll ask Ziva to send someone over to the apartment complex."

"No." Phil's hand closed over his. "If her people couldn't identify the monkey demon, I doubt if they'll know what this is. Our best bet is to track down the imposter." He could smell her underlying concern over someone else dying, so he released the phone.

"What about Melissa?" Tiffany blurted. "She could be in danger."

"Probably not, now that the imposter has the tumi." Alex eyed Phil and braced himself. She wasn't going to like his next suggestion. "But a little precaution wouldn't hurt. Why don't you have her stay at the mansion? She can use Anne's room until we sort this out."

To his amazement, Phil nodded. "I'll try, but I doubt she'll agree to it."

"You could order her."

Phil laughed. "The last thing Bebe and Miko need is a pouty nymph causing trouble." She shrugged. "Besides, if Fake Jane's left town and the other demon's dead, I doubt if Melissa will be in any danger."

Siobhan turned to her husband. "I'd like to get a couple of the pack to check out the scents at the two murder scenes. It'll give us a handle on the situation and keep my father in check while Alex and Phil are in Peru."

Jorge climbed to his feet. "Then let's get started before I fall asleep on Stanton's floor." He held out a hand for Siobhan, who clasped it and rose, before he turned drooping eyes to Alex. "We'll funnel any new info to Tiffany while you're out of town."

"Because I live for playing secretary," she muttered.

"You're supposed to be on maternity leave," Alex and Phil said at the same time.

Tiffany responded by using both hands to flash them the bird.

Phil stood as well. "I need to run an errand and pack as well."

The offer for her to spend the night at his condo lay on the tip of Alex's tongue. Just because fake Jane left Los Angeles, it didn't mean other folks, like their monkey demon, weren't after the tumi. Some of them might be powerful enough to question Phil in the most painful way possible. But he knew exactly how she'd take his suggestion.

Instead, he grinned. "Meet you at the morgue at four a.m."

She rolled her eyes. "I can't wait."

Once they left, he turned to find Tiffany still sprawled on his couch and feeding Kiki more chicken. "Can I impose on you to dogsit for a few days?"

"Sure." Tiffany raised an eyebrow as she contemplated him.

"What?"

"A toy breed?" She shook her head. "Man, you really need to get laid."

Phillippa pushed the doorbell of the tiny house in the rundown neighborhood and surveyed the area. Most of the homes had steel bars over the windows. Those buildings that didn't were covered with colorful graffiti and had blankly staring holes where glass and curtains should be. Three men across the street took a little too much interest in her. But it was typical male stupidity, not anything she considered a real threat.

"Yes?" The hesitant voice filtered through the heavy door.

"Kate? It's Phillippa Mann."

Two deadbolts clicked. Kate Chevrette left the chain in place while she peered between the frame and the door. A red, swollen eye stared at Phil. "What the fuck do you want?"

She forced herself to stand still against the waves of grief and hostility flowing from the woman. "I wanted to talk to you about Jane."

Kate sneered. "Well, congratulations. Not only did you chase away my husband, you killed my daughter." Fumes wafted from her breath. The grieving mother hadn't shared her bottle of tequila with anyone.

Phillippa held out her business card. "I'd like to help with Jane's funeral. Please call or stop by my store, and Melissa will assist you with the arrangements."

"What? You too fuckin' good to dirty your precious hands?"

Gaea, if you only knew how many graves I've dug . . .

Phillippa shoved the painful thought away. She debated telling Kate Chevrette the truth during the drive from Alex's place. The agony in the mother's eyes made her decision. "The person who murdered Jane left the country using your daughter's identity. I'm going after the bitch. My flight leaves in a few hours."

Kate's gaze dropped, but she didn't take the business card.

Phillippa couldn't blame the woman. The gods knew she hadn't been able to stay at the hospital after the zombie attack during Tiffany's wedding. Facing the idea of Tiffany and her baby dying still twisted her gut.

Kate's silence stretched into the warm June night. Phillippa slid the thick paper into the mail slot and turned to leave.

"Wait." The door closed. The chain jingled before the door opened again. Kate stepped across the threshold. Strands of gray permeated her dark hair and lines crisscrossed her features. She looked decades older than her actual age. "The sheriff . . ." She swallowed hard. "When they came t-to tell me, they didn't want me to come down and identify the body."

This time, Phil looked at the broken concrete beneath the rubber soles of the athletic shoes she'd pulled on twenty-three hours ago.

When she'd gotten the call from the alarm company.

"Because I already had, Kate. I'm the one who found her when she didn't show up for work."

"Why-why didn't you call me?"

Phillippa met the heart-broken woman's gaze. "Because I didn't want your last memory of her to be the one that's going to haunt me for the rest of my life."

"Y-You're going to beat her, aren't you? The woman who killed my Jane? Like you did my ex when he tried to hurt my baby?"

"No, Kate, I'm not going to beat her." She didn't need the River Styx to make this oath. "I'm going to kill her."

Chapter 9

At three-fifty-five, Phillippa knocked on the service door to the Los Angeles County Morgue.

A young man opened the door with a flourish. "Hey, Ms. Mann! Come on in!"

He carried the prominent nose of the Ptolemaic line. One of Caesar's nephews, but damn if she could remember which one. After two thousand years, she wasn't sure how the vampire master kept track of all his sister's descendants, but somehow he did.

She smiled. "Good morning."

"This way." He waved for her to follow him and took off at a brisk pace.

There was only one hallway so it wasn't like there was any place else to go. Not to mention, all she had to do was follow the vampires' signature sandalwood.

"I'll drop you off at the international terminal before I take Mr. Stanton's casket over to the shipping area." Her guide seemed oblivious to any possible eavesdroppers. At least, he was smart enough not to offer to carry her backpack. She strode after him until he paused at a doorway and waved her ahead.

A bright red fiberglass casket on a trolley dominated the gray room. Just looking at the thing made her chest tighten. She wasn't claustrophobic, but she couldn't imagine being locked in that thing for the fifteen-hour flight, much less the layover in San Salvador plus loading and unloading times.

Alex stood next to his little prison, wearing only a dark blue t-shirt and tan cargo shorts. His feet were bare. He gave her a short nod of greeting, but he focused on power sucking from a blood bag. From the almost Normal color of his skin, it wasn't the first one of the morning.

Doctor Ramon Xavier knelt next to the casket. He glanced up at her through black frames. "Morning, Phil."

"Good morning, Ray." She always found the medical examiner's affectation for glasses amusing. Even though he no longer needed spectacles since his Turn, he claimed his nose was lonely without them.

Ray stood. "Okay, oxygen tanks are full and the system checks out. You're good for twenty-four hours."

Alex tossed the empty bag and straw in a receptacle marked with the biohazard symbol. "Okay, let's do this."

Phillippa couldn't resist teasing him. "Do you have to pee before we leave? You're not going to get a chance before we reach Lima."

He shot her a nasty look. "Do I look like Tiffany at age three?"

Hormones rippled through Phillippa's body. Alex Stanton was many things to her, but never a child. And he'd felt all male when her legs had been wrapped around his waist—

She brutally squished the thought as if it were a scorpion she'd shaken from her boot. The danger of this trip to him hit her in the gut. "Yell if you need help."

Alex grimaced. "No one's going to hear me in the baggage compartment."

She laid a hand on his arm. *You know what I mean.*

His eyes widened at the telepathic contact. But instead of answering her, he merely gave a curt nod before he climbed in the travel casket. Once he had his earbuds in place and his smart phone clipped where he could reach it, he lay down in the tight space.

Ray leaned over Alex. "Got your passport and money?"

Alex slapped the lower pockets of his shorts. "Yep."

"The emergency release—"

"I've done this before, *amigo.*"

The medical examiner pursed his lips. Apparently, Phillippa wasn't the only one worried about this flight. Ray helped Alex adjust the oxygen mask before he lowered the lid. The finality of it snapping shut reminded her of another time. Another place.

She climbed down from her mare and surveyed the disaster. The posse from San Antonio had stopped questioning her abilities two days ago. It didn't matter whether it was the west Texas desert or the steppes of Asia Minor. Horses and tracking were the same.

Three of the men swore in the name of their god. The other two turned away, and one of them heaved the biscuits and hard tack he ate for breakfast.

A few arrows stuck out of the abandoned wagons. Most of the holes had been caused by the new Winchesters. The fake bottom from Duncan's hiding place in the secret compartment of one of the wagons rested on the dirt. She crossed to the abandoned conveyance and ducked to check the padding. No greasy spot or ash.

The vampire had survived the initial attack. Since he hadn't come back to San Antonio, he must have continued on foot to San Francisco.

She smiled to herself. No, that wasn't his style. He would go after his assailants first. Gaea help those stupid bastards. Except . . .

Her gaze swept the area, and her smile faded. Duncan would have buried the bodies before pursuing the bandits, his idea of proper respect. What in Hades' name had happened here? Was the vampire injured? Hiding somewhere?

Predators had scattered body parts across the shallow depression. Pain clutched her by the throat when she spotted the hank of golden hair caught in the brush. She strode past the wagons, knelt and examined the tracks. Panther.

Phillippa followed the trail of old blood to a trampled area. The cat had long since gone. Only gnawed bones were left. She walked back to her mare, a little slower this time, to retrieve her shovel. Somewhere in those few steps, her heart cracked in two.

She blinked the extra wetness from her eyes. If Ray noticed, he ignored it. Caesar's nephew was totally oblivious.

The vampire retrieved a backpack from another bench and handed it to her. She hefted it over her shoulder alongside her own. From the weight, Stanton had his boots, a jacket and a change of clothes. They'd deal with acquiring weapons once they were in Peru.

Ray held out his hand. "*Vaya con Dios, mi amiga.*"

Phillippa snorted. "Jehovah would be the first one to tell you I'm not his responsibility." She grasped his palm in hers. "But thank you."

The drive to LAX was mercifully short. The security line at the airport wasn't.

Intuition crawled under her skin as she shuffled forward. The TSA agent at ten o'clock. Tall, beefy guy. The kind that loved abusing his power.

Great. How in Gaea's name had she managed to get in the pervert line?

Normally, she pounded guys like this into their place.

Here? She didn't dare. Not because she'd spend time in jail.

She couldn't abandon Alex when she swore to be his shadow until this case was solved.

The agent licked his lips. He ignored the easy pickings of the cute college student two passengers ahead of Phillippa. No, he definitely targeted her. Five bucks said he hoped she raised a fuss so he had the excuse to strip search her.

She set the backpacks on the x-ray's conveyor. The metal detector screeched. With a huff, the businessman in front of her stalked back through and cleaned the change out his pockets for his second pass.

Rarely did Phillippa pray, but this time, she sent a tiny plea to Aunt Athena for a strategic intervention.

Musk filled her nose as she crossed through the metal detector. A stout middle-aged woman in a TSA uniform stepped between Phillippa and the salivating pervert.

Werewolf.

The gray hair only made her more threatening. Few weres survived long enough to show that much age. The female agent gestured toward the private screening areas. "Ms. Mann, if you could grab your carry-ons and step this way, please?"

"Teri, I haven't wanded her yet," Pervert complained.

The were stepped closer to him. "I catch you harassing another female passenger, and I'll break your fucking wand." She smiled, a toothy threat.

Phillippa bit her lower lip to keep from laughing aloud at Pervert's sullen expression. She snatched up the backpacks and followed the were into the room.

An aluminum case lay on the table. The were unsnapped the latches and lifted the lid, making sure the contents pointed away from the tiny observation window. Inside, two Glocks shimmered under the fluorescent lights. Matching white boxes nestled next to the arms.

The were smiled. "Compliments of our beta, Ms. Mann."

Phillippa performed a quick check of both pieces. She popped open the boxes of ammunition and took a whiff. Silver-and-garlic-laced rounds. She slid a gun and a box into each backpack. The entire process took less than ten seconds.

She grinned. "Give Siobhan my thanks."

The were nodded. "Good hunting."

Phillippa hoisted the backpacks and sauntered from the tiny room. The hair on the back of her neck prickled. She looked over her shoulder. Pervert's eyes tracked her across the concourse. Her mocking salute turned his face beet red.

Thank you, Aunt Athena.

In the back of her mind, a tiny voice whispered, *You're welcome, child.*

A teeth-rattling jolt shook Alex awake. The edge of excitement from the other passengers filtered through his mind. *Lima.*

Thank the Lord, the trip had been uneventful. Well, except for the two teenage baggage handlers at the layover in San Salvador.

The boys had dared each other to open the casket. They wouldn't have been the first airport employees Alex had to glamour when curiosity about a dead body superseded their common sense. But three other workers had been nearby when the two challenged each other's manhood, which would have been a major problem if they found Alex alive and well inside. Luckily, their supervisor approached and snapped at the boys before they worked up their courage.

Alex tried closing his eyes, but now that the plane had arrived, adrenaline made any additional sleep impossible. He exhaled. It would take Phil an hour or two to clear customs and claim him.

Bumps and thumps accompanied the unloading process. He thumbed the phone's controls and tried to focus on the audio book of Mark Twain essays. Another bang slammed his head against the padded fiberglass.

Damn, don't these guys have any respect for the dead?

Then the slide of being loaded onto a vehicle. Once inside the terminal, he could relax a little. The time on his phone blinked one minute, then two.

When it hit five minutes, worry squirmed in his brain. Whatever the casket was in picked up speed. *Phil?*

Yes?

Where are you?

Two of the Lima Coven escorted me through customs. We'll be downstairs to pick you up in fifteen minutes.

I'm not in receiving.

The soda-fizz of Phil's alarm filtered through his brain. *Where are you?*

He reached out with the odd little directional sense all vampires had. It was better than a GPS. *Someone's placed the casket in a motor vehicle. From the speed, we're on a highway headed south.*

Her focus left him for a minute as she relayed the information to the vampires with her. *We're on our way. Hit the emergency release and get out of there.*

Hesitation grabbed him. Not because Phil's advice was wrong. *Someone knew I was coming. This may be our chance to nab whoever's behind the theft.*

Another presence intruded in Alex's thoughts. Francisco Chavez, the Lima Coven's chief enforcer. *Mr. Stanton, you are in our territory. I will not be held responsible for any harm to you because of your own stub-bornness.*

Alex chuckled. *Don't worry, man. Master Augustine will fry my ass, not yours.*

Phil's sea grass presence was back. *Who has you?*

Normals, from the feel of them.

You certain? Because Jane sure as Hades felt *Normal.*

Dang. The admission Phil was right gnawed on his ego. They had no idea what Fake Jane was. Common sense overrode his concerns.

Chavez, can you catch up with me? I don't want to lose the first lead we've got.

You are seriously loco, *you know that?* The honey and nut taste of Chavez's humor rippled through his mind.

On the other hand, brimstone emanated from Phil. *This is crazy, Alex! We don't have time. The sun rises in a few hours.*

Alex spared a glance at the smartphone's clock. *We've got four. Plenty of time.*

The Greek curses filtering through his head definitely came from the pissed Amazon. Occasionally, she threw in a few from languages he didn't recognize.

As much as Alex wanted to probe the minds of the two people in the vehicle more thoroughly, he didn't dare. If they were the same type of being as the one that had impersonated Jane, tipping them off would demolish his plan.

Then there was the whole getting kidnapped twice in the last year. That *really* burned his britches. Why didn't the bad guys ever kidnap one of the ladies from the coven?

Technically, Selene's rogues kidnapped Anne in December.

You're not helping, Phil.

I'm not transmitting pictures of myself wearing an original Star Trek security shirt while I'm tied to train tracks.

Out of spite, he built a vision of Phil in his mind, dressed in the T.V. series' red mini-skirt uniform.

Asshole.

Was it his imagination, or was there a little humor behind her insult?

Unfortunately Chavez's presence intruded in their banter. *Stanton, one of my people is following a delivery van seen leaving the airport.*

Another vampire tailed Chavez's mind. *I am Isabella, Mr. Stanton.*

Yep, she was definitely closer than Phil or Chavez from the strength of her touch.

At that moment, the vehicle swerved. Alex braced himself as the casket slid across the vehicle's bed. The resulting collision with the wall of the van rang his head. *I think my hosts recognized you, Isabella.*

Light laughter filled his head. *I believe you're right. The van has turned away from the coastal road. The altitude will slow them enough for Francisco to catch up with us.*

Alex hit the emergency release. Free and ready was preferable to his growing collection of bruises. While the V-virus repaired most damage damn near instantaneously, the more injuries he acquired, the sooner he'd need blood. He shoved the lid up and swung his legs over the side.

Fire scorched his soles, and he jerked his feet back into the casket. *What the fuck?*

Mr. Stanton? Isabella asked.

Alex? Phil shouted at the same time.

He raised his phone, using the tiny screen to illuminate the cargo area. Silver flashed back at him. The floor, the walls, the ceiling. Everything was coated in silver.

He yanked the lid back in place. Just in time. The van swerved again, so hard the casket slammed into the wall and flipped. A distinctive crunch beneath his hip said he'd need to buy a new phone.

I'm fine. Like I said, they were expecting me. He relayed his predicament.

Don't do anything else stupid. Phil's anger hurt almost as bad as his feet.

Moi? *Do something stupid?*

The only warning he received was Isabella's curse. The screech of tires. A brief sensation of flight. Then he and the casket tumbled through space.

Chapter 10

Agony ripped through Alex. Out of reflex, he curled into a fetal position. No broken bones or impact trauma from the collision. Just burns from rolling across the blasted silver when the casket popped open and cracked in two.

He sucked in a harsh breath and climbed into the nearest section of fiberglass. A few more seconds to allow the pain to subside before he forced his torso upright. The rivets along the top of the loading doors had popped. Silver-coated steel twisted apart, allowing a gleam of starlight into the interior.

At least, the truck was no longer moving.

His eyes swept the inside. He sat on what had been the lid. The bottom half laid nearby, split in two from the weight of the oxygen tanks. He snagged the closest bottle and pushed it against the floor. Red fiberglass slid along the silvered truck bed slicker than a greased pig before it gently bumped the damaged door.

He stood and lifted the tank. Basic physics as Mr. Newton would say. For every action, there was an equal and opposite reaction. He prayed the opposite reaction involved breaking the lock, not the tank exploding in his face.

One hard swing snapped the latch. It also sent the lid careening across the back of the truck. He dropped to a crouch and rode the fiberglass. Who'd have thought all the times Tiffany dragged him to the beach for night surfing would come in handy?

Using the tank as propulsion once again, Alex launched the casket lid straight for the exit. The van doors sprang open at the impact, and the casket was flying through the air again. He started rolling before the remains of the casket crashed into the packed earth and splintered.

The rich scent of loam, greenery and sandalwood filled the air as the last tumble brought him to his feet. Good. Isabella had brought rein-forcements.

Except it wasn't a member of the Huamán Coven who pointed the modified AK-47 in his face as he straightened. Fury turned his vision blood-red, and his fangs automatically elongated.

Marcus Giovanni grinned above the barrel. Traitor. Rogue. Facts made even worse because he was Caesar's biological nephew.

Fake Jane stepped next to Marcus and smiled. "Told you it'd be the cutie who followed me." The fake tumi swung from a loop on her belt. Behind her, two Normals stood near the van, both armed similarly to Marcus. A quick scan said they were the ones who'd picked up Alex at the airport.

Alex took a deep breath. Nope, the imposter still had the apple-sweet scent of a Normal. "Really, darlin'. Hanging out with slime like this. I got the impression you had better—"

Marcus swung the butt of the gun before Alex could blink. Even the Normals behind Marcus winced at the audible crack when Alex's jaw broke. *That's the problem with taunting an older vampire. Speed increases with age.*

"—taste," he finished when the bone knitted. Between the burns and the broken jaw, he started to feel thirsty. Very thirsty.

Fake Jane ignored him. "Stanton is yours, but I get the Olympian."

Marcus snorted. "Assuming you can control her."

The imposter's eyes narrowed. "I suggest you don't question me again, vampire." The surrounding wildlife grew silent at her threat.

Even more telling, Marcus inclined his head, something the asshole had only done with the oldest vampires in the Augustine Coven. "Merely a legitimate concern. You've never fought an Amazon."

An odd smile appeared on Fake Jane's face. Her cheeks rippled as if a thousand tiny worms crawled underneath the skin. "Then I'll have a new experience to enjoy."

Two more vampires climbed up from the other side of the road. Recognition clicked in Alex's brain. Former members of Augustine who had defected when Caesar banished Selene. They hauled a struggling form between them.

"It's not Mann, sir," one of them called.

Fake Jane stalked over and lifted the woman's head. Blood stained her chin though the cut on her lip had healed. "A vampire." Disgust filled her voice.

Isabella cut loose with a stream of Spanish curses plus a few in what must have been a native Peruvian language. Fake Jane slapped Isabella hard enough blood spouted from the vampire's re-torn lip.

Alex shifted his weight to the balls of his feet. Only six opponents. If Isabella could keep her wits and Marcus would drop his attention for an instant . . .

The semi-automatic rose level with Alex's eyes. Anger burned in Marcus's dark orbs. "Where's Phillippa? We know she was on the same flight."

"Jesus Christ." Alex wiped both palms down his face. His skin still tingled and itched from the silver burns. He settled for staring at Marcus. "What is it about me? Seriously, man. Why do you feel the need to constantly kidnap me? Do you have some sort of crush on me? 'Cause if you do, I've got to tell you you're not my type."

This time the butt caught Alex in the gut. Air exploded out of his lungs. The sternum and two of the lower ribs snapped at the impact. He tried not to think about the internal injuries.

"You're going about this the wrong way, Giovanni." Fake Jane grabbed Isabella's neck and dragged her across the road.

Tension prickled along Alex's spine. Two of Marcus's men had trouble holding the lady vamp, but Fake Jane acted like a child with a rag doll.

"You have one chance, my dear Alex. Where's Phillippa?" The imposter pulled the tumi from her belt.

Alex laughed. "She's still stuck in customs. If Asswipe here hadn't been so impatient to collect his revenge, you would have had both of us."

And the rogue vampire was as proud and as predictable as ever. Alex ducked as Marcus drove the butt of his rifle where Alex's face had been. He swept Marcus's legs out from under him. The follow-thru kick drove

Marcus face-first into the ditch by the time the gun's report became a sound.

Alex twisted and dove for Fake Jane.

She grinned, and inside that grin, her teeth elongated. Not just the eyeteeth, but all of them. A mouthful of wickedly sharp points that would have scared the shit out of a piranha.

Under the sweet apple smell of her, another scent rose. Reptile musk and hatred and damned souls. If souls had a smell, that was.

He latched onto the arm with the weapon. Even if Phil swore up and down it was fake, some instinct told him otherwise. Even if she were correct, the tumi's wicked-looking titanium edge could probably take someone's head off. He damn well wasn't giving Fake Jane a chance to prove him right.

Except nasty-looking claws now held the Incan weapon.

Isabella began struggling in earnest against the talons digging into her neck.

The distraction gave Alex his opportunity. An elbow to the toothy face. A kick that should have crushed the knee if the imposter were human. He snapped her forearm across his thigh. She screamed, a high-pitched, unearthly sound that didn't come from the vocal cords of anything he recognized. He snatched the handle of the tumi as her nerveless fingers released it. Good to know she had some vulnerabilities.

He whirled and slashed at the thing in Jane's skin. She ducked backward, dragging the Peruvian vampire with her. Isabella pried the talons from her throat. The vampire's fangs flashed in the starlight. It was Fake Jane's ugly smile that warned him. "Isabella! Don't!"

The female vamp didn't heed him. She sank her teeth deep into where the femoral artery would be on a human. Except Fake Jane was anything but human.

A choked cry came from Isabella. She collapsed on the roadway, her body convulsing as gouts of oily black fluid sprayed from her lips.

Alex slashed at Fake Jane again. This time the tumi sliced her cheek. Human-looking skin peeled back to reveal yellow and green scales and scabrous flesh. She gave another high-pitched scream. Only his night-mares could invent something like her.

Before he could celebrate the fact the tumi had an effect, something walloped him from the side. Hard enough he flew through the air and slammed into the wrecked van. His ears rung as he rolled away from the follow-up that punched a hole through the wall of the cargo area.

Alex looked up and blinked. Fake Jane now sported a tail, a whip-like length of muscle with the same green and yellow scales as her cheek. Behind her, Isabella lay on the roadway. Far too still.

His vision shivered and blurred for a moment as he climbed to his feet. *Where the hell are Phil and Francisco?*

He leapt for the top of the van an instant before shrapnel exploded where his head had been.

The thing pretending to be Jane jumped as well. A standing jump that cleared the ten yards between her and the van as well as the ten feet straight up to the top of the vehicle. She landed on all fours with the screech of claws on metal. "Give me the tumi." From the grating stone-on-bone sound in her voice, she'd given up pretending she was Normal.

Fangs dug into his lower lip as he grinned. "Not on your life, bitch."

She returned his look with a scary alien-piranha smile of her own. "Then perhaps on yours."

He was definitely in deep shit. It had been an awfully long time since he'd been to church. That didn't stop the words from tumbling through his brain. *Dear Lord, Who art in Heaven . . .*

The delicate trace work of alien metal on the tumi began to glow. Both Alex and the imposter stared at the Incan artifact in his grip.

"No! This can't be! You're nothing!" Horror and fury filled the creature's eyes.

Alex was so startled whatever he'd been thinking tumbled away. The glow faded.

This can't be possible. He continued his mental recitation of the Lord's Prayer. The strange substance Phil's assayer couldn't identify started glowing again.

He was so busy figuring out this turn of events he didn't react fast enough when Marcus leapt on top of the van and tackled him. They tumbled over the side and landed with a bone-jarring impact on the packed earth.

The tumi flew from Alex's hand. Marcus's first punch connected with his face. Alex rammed a knee into Marcus's groin, shoved the bastard off him and rolled to his feet.

Fake Jane dove for the tumi. He'd never reach it before her, not with her speed. Switching directions, he lunged for the Normals. His first blow snapped one man's neck. The second goon slung his AK-47 off his shoulder.

Alex snatched the rifle. The base of his left palm smashed into the man's nose, breaking it and shoving bone shards into the asshole's brain. *Marcus really needs to hire a better class of thug.*

Bullets pinged against the side of the wrecked van. Alex whirled, dropped to one knee and fired.

A headshot took out the first vampire. The bullets must have been laced with silver because flesh slid off his bones before the body hit the dirt. The second dove over the embankment. Alex continued his sweep and squeezed off a shot at Marcus. The fucker disappeared into the foliage on the other side of the road.

By the time Alex completed his circuit, the tumi and Fake Jane were nowhere in sight.

Chapter 11

Adrenaline rattled Alex's nerves, spoiling his concentration. Foliage rustled as two large beings moved south, the pace steady and much faster than a Normal. Marcus and the other vampire.

One doesn't diss a master's blood relative, but Marcus Giovanni was yellow long before the asshole's defection. Good to know Alex's opinion didn't need to be changed.

It was the fact he couldn't hear a third body that troubled him. Fake Jane wanted the tumi and Phil. She had one, and she couldn't acquire the second one by sticking around. Assuming she believed his story that Phil was still stuck at the airport.

Which she probably didn't. Lord knew he wouldn't believe shit from an enemy.

But why did she want Phil? It made no sense. Fake Jane could have grabbed the Amazon in Los Angeles.

And why the hell use him as bait? Fake Jane would have discovered Phil's relationships over the course of the last two weeks. Kidnapping Tiffany would have been the more logical choice.

After the zombie attack at the poor girl's first wedding, maybe they all should count their blessings Fake Jane left the kid alone.

Alex stumbled toward Isabella, but the rotten meat odor warned him. Flesh melted from the poor woman's bones until only her clothing and a skeleton lay amid a sticky puddle of bloody goo.

He finally relaxed enough to realize Phil had been yelling at him telepathically for some time.

Don't come up here, Phil. He knelt to examine the rocks and soil near Isabella's corpse. The black oily substance that seemed to serve as the imposter's blood sizzled in the dirt. After what happened to Isabella, he didn't dare touch it. Maybe Huamán's eclectic might be able to use one of the samples on the rocks if Alex could find something liquid-proof to carry it in.

What's going on? Are you okay? Francisco says Isabella's dead.

Regret swam through his gloop of emotions. Isabella knew the risks of being a vampire enforcer, but her death was one more on Fake Jane's ledger.

Alex worked his way over to Isabella's vehicle, the engine still steaming from where the driver of the truck had ran her off the road and into a tree. With a grunt, he wrenched open the trunk lid. Nylon tarps and a couple of boxes of plastic sample bottles were inside, as well as other necessary investigative equipment he recognized from the toolbox in the bed of his own pickup. He ignored the crossbow and reached for the shovel and one of the tarps.

Yeah, she is. I'm serious. Don't come up. I was the bait to get you alone. I'll collect Isabella's remains and meet you at the main road.

The impression from their link said Phil would have laughed at the idea of him as bait for her. Would have if a fellow female warrior hadn't just died.

More brimstone filtered through their link. *Fine. We'll meet you at the turn-off.*

If collecting Isabella's remains, dealing with Phil's pissy attitude, and answering Chavez's constant interrogation on the drive back to Lima weren't bad enough, Alex would have given just about anything not to be in Master Huamán's audience room.

After Alex completed the recitation on how and why Isabella died for the third time, Master Huamán cussed some more. Even if Alex didn't know the local Native American tongue, he got the gist from the narrowed neon yellow eyes, the spittle and the fact that the vampire master whacked at the room's furniture with an antique Spanish cutlass.

Alex kept as still as possible. Phil did the same. At least the Lima Coven master hadn't started whacking at their necks with his sword.

Master Huamán whirled to face his chief enforcer, his long dark hair flaring behind him. "I want those rogues' heads on a platter!"

"I have sent a daytime team to track the culprits," Francisco Chavez answered calmly. He must be used to his master's tantrums. "The rogues will have to go to ground soon. Sunrise is in fifteen minutes."

Master Huamán tossed the sword on the scarred table. "What are these supernaturals you encountered?"

"We were hoping you might know." Phil's hands were clasped behind her back, her feet parted, as if she stood at parade rest. "The reptilian creature passed as my Normal assistant for two weeks that we are aware of. Scent, touch, mental impressions, you name it."

Francisco folded his arms over his chest and stroked his beard with one hand. "You said there was another demon in the shop?"

Alex nodded. "After the tumi was stolen, we caught a monkey-like being with glowing orange eyes in Phil's store. Gray, rotting, smelled like the devil himself. It was definitely looking for something in the debris." He spread his hands. "And the only thing missing was the tumi."

Master Huamán's eyes glittered as he watched Alex. "Did you destroy it?"

"No, sir. The damn thing committed suicide by touching Kiki."

The vampire master cocked his head. "Kiki? What is a kiki?"

"She's a Maltese." When Master Huamán continued looking at him in askance, Alex turned to Phil.

"A Phoenician holy dog," she clarified.

A malicious smile stretched the vampire master's mouth. "Then it sounds like you have a bigger problem than three murders."

Alex exchanged a worried look with Phil. "What do you mean, sir?"

"I mean, from your description, the tumi's owner has his minions looking for it."

"What? If you know who it is, you need to contact him—"

The vampire master started laughing, a mirthless, despairing sound. "Not even immortals such as ourselves want *his* attention."

"El Diablo?" Chavez whispered.

Master Huamán wiped the red-tinged tears from his face. "The entity the tumi belongs to is Supay." Another awful smile showed the vampire's full fangs. "The Incan god of death."

Chapter 12

Phillippa waited impatiently for the house's activities to die down for the day. While Master Huamán had been gracious in hosting them, she trusted the Lima Coven about as far as she could throw them. *No, I trust them as far as Tiffany's husband Max could throw them.* She smiled at her own joke. Besides, she'd already found the bugs in her guest quarters.

It was well after ten a.m. before she felt safe enough to approach Alex's room. She sighed before she tapped on the door. With her luck lately, Alex would think this was a booty call. Then she'd definitely have to hurt him.

No answer. She opened the door and slipped into his room. Sandalwood and Alex's clean evergreen scent mixed with soap filled the air. He'd taken the time to clean up before he collapsed in the huge colonial bed.

He lay on his stomach in only white briefs. Not even the sheet covered him. With the shiny red scars of healing silver burns, she understood why. He'd sucked down nearly ten pints of blood before their audience with the coven master.

She stepped silently across the room. Were his glossy gold waves as soft as she remembered? Her fingertips had barely touched his hair when she found glowing blue eyes staring into hers.

And his large hand wrapped around her throat.

Recognition flashed on his face, and he released her just as quickly. "Shit, Phil. Knock next time."

"I did." Her heart raced. "You didn't answer."

The glow in his eyes that had started to die flared again. "And you felt the need to waltz right in?" He climbed out of the bed and stomped over to his backpack, which rested on a nearby chair. "How long were you staring at me and my skivvies?"

"I wasn't—"

"Answer me." His voice was as low as a were's warning growl. What the hell was he pissed about?

A little twinge plucked at her. "Look, I knocked. You didn't answer. We're in another coven's territory with all this strange stuff happening. Stranger than usual, even for us. For all I knew, Lizard Girl was in here, cutting you into fish bait."

An evil smirk twisted his lips. "Answer my second question, Phil."

The compulsion twisted her nerves. Maybe death for reneging on her oath would be worth not having to deal with Stanton's arrogant attitude.

No, dammit to Hades! She wasn't going to die over something this stupid.

"I watched you sleep for a second or two," she ground out.

He quirked an eyebrow as her vow jerked her psychological tether. "All right. It was five. Five seconds max."

Alex sat and shoved his large feet into the legs of his heavy jeans. "Now what was so blasted important that you had to wake me?"

Phillippa laid a finger over her lips and pointed at the phone, a lamp and one of the paintings.

Alex pressed his lips in a hard line and nodded. He stood, zipping his jeans, and his usual cockiness appeared. "Well, darlin', if that's what you want, I'll be happy to accommodate you."

That drawl of his plucked at a whole different set of nerves. Ones she was determined to ignore. She opened her mouth, but he inclined his head toward the bugs.

Unfortunately, he was right. She needed a logical excuse to be in his room without arousing the Lima Coven's suspicions. Fine. She could play the game. "Oh, baby, it's just been so long."

A scowl appeared on his face. He reached out, took her hand and yanked her close. *Don't overdo it. That's just as obvious.*

I'm not the one who picked the excuse for me being in your room. She bared her teeth in a vicious smile. Even though his touch was a few degrees cooler than it had been a century ago, it still sent tingles through her body. She clamped down on the emotion, prayed he hadn't picked up on it.

If he had, he didn't show it. *So why did you come in here?*

There's a question we're not answering. Why would the lizard imposter want Supay's tumi?

Worry shone in his eyes. *I've been wondering about that, too. There's something I didn't want to say in front of anyone from the Lima Coven. When I was fighting Fake Jane, I got a hold on it for a moment. That strange stuff your assayer couldn't identify started glowing.*

She frowned. Alex had been Normal before his Turn. *Vampires can't activate magick unless they were a witch prior to their infection, and we both know you weren't. What were you doing?*

He grimaced. *Fake Jane is strong and fast. Way above an ancient vampire's abilities. She was about to hand me my ass, and I started reciting the Lord's Prayer in my head.*

That makes no sense. Why would a prayer to Jehovah activate Supay's object of power.

A shrug lifted his powerful shoulders. *You got me. But the tumi was the only thing that seemed to hurt Fake Jane. Could she be an Incan deity, too?*

Phillippa shook her head. *I didn't get that impression from Master Huamán. He was genuinely puzzled about her. The other thing that bothers me is Marcus allying himself with her.*

Alex grimaced. *That goes back to Sifuentes's theory that someone tried to use the Sunshine Believers as a decoy, and possibly strain Augustine resources further. Makes sense if Marcus is picking up where Selene left off.*

She nibbled on her lower lip as she mulled the possibilities. *Or we could have three different parties after the tumi. Supay's demons. The Sunshine Believers. Marcus and Lizard Girl.* She held up a finger on her free hand for each set.

Alex chuckled. *Lizard Girl? You've been hanging around Sam a little too much.*

Phillippa smiled back. *Oddly enough, I wish she were here. She has a natural talent for flushing out the enemy.*

He rolled his eyes. *And yet, you wonder why your insurance company is giving you a hard time.*

She groaned. *There's still our unanswered question. Supay obviously wants his tumi back, but we don't know why the other two parties want it.*

If the Sunshine Believers are involved, my guess is they're hoping to trigger an apocalypse by pissing off a god . . .

But what about Marcus and the creature he's allied with?

Alex shrugged again. *You've got me on what Lizard Girl wants, besides you.*

A chill ran through Phillippa. Lizard Girl's goal could be the same as any other foe. Make a name for herself by killing a daughter of Ares and Otrera.

Alex continued without any acknowledgement of her emotion. *Marcus' objective is obvious—fulfill Grandma Selene's goal and take down Caesar.*

Phillippa glared at him. *Maybe you should call him.*

And tell him something he already knows? Alex ran a hand over his hair. *He should return to Los Angeles by the end of the week. I'd like a little more evidence of Giovanni's real plan before I sound the alarm back in the States.*

Waiting gnawed at her, but she'd sworn an oath. *Fine. We'll play it your way, but I get to say, 'I told you so,' if this blows up in your face.*

Fine. Now let's go to bed and get some sleep.

Men. That's all you think about. She started to pull away, but he held fast to her hand.

I said 'sleep,' not 'screw.' We both need the rest if we're going to track Lizard Girl. He inclined his head toward the bug in the painting. *Besides, we need to keep up appearances.*

Every cell in Phillippa's body wanted to fight his suggestion. Well, not every cell. A few in the wrong places wanted to stay.

Alex, we're working well together. Let's not spoil it.

Another scowl filled his face. *I'm not the one thinking about sex, and I didn't sneak into your room to watch you sleep. Which, by the way, is considered stalking in the U.S., not to mention it's illegal*

He released her, the absence of touch so abrupt she reeled. He strode over to the bed, lay down and rolled onto his stomach, deliberately ignoring her.

Heat filled her, a strange mixture of embarrassment and want. Dammit, she hated to admit he was right. She had been projecting her own feelings on him, and that wasn't fair.

Was that her real problem over the last several decades? Had she blinded herself, assuming he still pined for her when it was just the opposite?

There was only one way to prove to herself and to Alex that any feelings were absolutely and completely absent. She stalked around to the other side of the bed and threw herself on the mattress.

One blue eye opened and peered at her. *Thanks for not breaking the frame.*

Shut up, Stanton.

Humor rode his mental words. *Sleep tight to you, too.*

Alex woke to warmth across his chest. Phillippa curled at his side, her arm hugging him. The mass of her chestnut curls spread over the pristine white pillowcase. Just like the memory that haunted him. He swallowed to get the lump out of his throat. Unfortunately, his erection would be a bit more of a problem.

Especially if she woke before he could make it to the bathroom.

It didn't help that he'd been dreaming about her and San Antonio again. Dammit, every time he thought he'd gotten her out of his system, she managed to wiggle her way back in.

But the longer he lay there, the more likely she'd wake up and discover his hard-on pressing against the ever tightening jeans.

With the greatest stealth he could manage, he held her wrist and maneuvered himself out from under her touch. Unfortunately, it meant contorting his body in ways even vampire abilities couldn't provide.

He crossed to his backpack when her sleepy voice murmured, "Alex?"

Shit. He snagged his backpack and held it in front of him before he pivoted to face her. "Yeah?"

"What time is it?"

"'Bout a half hour until sunset. Go back to sleep while I shower." *A very cold shower.* "I'll wake you when I'm finished."

"'Kay." She rolled onto her back. Soft snores filled the room. But underneath her t-shirt, her nipples beaded, tempting him to climb back on the bed and kiss her. Everywhere.

Make that two very cold showers. He stalked into the bathroom and gently closed the door.

Shortly after sunset, Phillippa jogged down the stairs on Alex's heels. It had taken an ice cold shower to get her dreams out of her head. She had woken up horny as hell, and she thanked the gods that her need wasn't quite as obvious as it would have been if she were a man.

Francisco met them at the foot of the staircase. "Our trackers lost both vampires."

"I'm not surprised," Alex muttered. When Francisco's eyes emitted a golden glow, Alex held up his hands. "It wasn't an insult. They planned last night's ambush thoroughly. I got lucky."

The Lima enforcer's eyes went from gold to neon yellow. "I lost my protégé because of your *luck*, Stanton."

"Now, wait just a damn minute—"

Phillippa stepped between them and placed a hand on each man's chest. She met Francisco's anger with a steady gaze. "Enough. Your peacock attitude will not avenge Isabella's death." She faced Alex. "Our mission is to deal with Lizard Girl, and by extension, Marcus if he was involved in Beatrice and Jane's murders. *Comprende*?"

The two vampires shot each other nasty glares before their postures relaxed.

Francisco grasped her palm and raised her hand to his lips. "Your wisdom shames me, my lady." A brimstone odor rose from Alex, no doubt the effect Francisco intended by kissing her hand.

To forestall another testosterone display, Phillippa said, "Unlike you two, I need some solid food. Why don't you fill us in while I eat, Francisco?"

Over her eggs and sausage and the vampires' blood, the Lima chief enforcer laid out the results of his daytime staff's search.

"Our werejaguars lost both of your vampire assailants at rivers."

Alex ran a hand over the stubble on his cheek. "Makes sense. Marcus may be a lily-livered turncoat, but he isn't stupid."

"What about Lizard Girl?" Phillippa mumbled around a mouthful of biscuit. She washed it down with coffee that made Tiffany's brew taste like flavored water.

Francisco smiled. "Ah, now she is an interesting one, no? She led our third were on a merry chase in her reptilian form. After much zigzagging over the mountains, she returned to human form near a rural road. Butchered a Normal farmer for his truck."

"Shit," Alex muttered. "She's racking up a serious body count."

Phillippa's heart jammed her esophagus. "So we lost her, too."

Francisco's smile widened to a full-fanged grin. "Do not despair, beautiful. Our eclectic had better luck with your foe's blood in a tracking spell. The one thing our young American enforcer did right was to cut the bitch." He waved a condescending finger in Alex's direction, who scowled over his mug of liquid breakfast in return. "She abandoned the truck, and a woman answering her description boarded the train to Cuzco."

Phillippa swallowed her last bite. "Why Cuzco?"

"It was the capital of the Incan Empire and their religious center. As to why she would take the tumi there—" He shrugged. "—that's anyone's guess, but I would say she plans to do something with it there or at one of the nearby ruins."

Something Alex said last night tickled her brain before it turned into full-fledged worry. She turned to him. His eyes reflected her concern. "I can't see her returning it. She didn't smell the same as Supay's demon monkey."

"So she's summoning the god himself?" Alex asked. "Controlling him through the tumi and using him to slaughter folks for some kind of blood magick ritual?"

Phillippa pushed her plate away. Breakfast no longer held any appeal as the ramifications danced through her head. "Or she plans to kill him and take his power, which she could do by using his own tumi against him. Either way, it doesn't bode well for the Normals."

Alex snorted. "Neither option bodes well for the rest of us either."

Even Francisco turned an extra shade of pale. "That settles it. We fly to Cuzco now." He rose. "Let me call our pilot and gather weapons. We'll leave the house in five minutes."

After Francisco marched from the kitchen, she turned to Alex. *What happens if we don't get there in time? And how in Hades' name are we supposed to stop her if we do?*

I don't suppose you'd be willing to ask your dad for help. Lord knows only another god would have any chance against Supay, and you're the only one I know who's acquainted enough with one to ask a personal favor.

Could she do it? Could she swallow her pride long enough to ask *him* for assistance? Not that he'd ever given it to her mother or any of her sisters. But what if the existence of his handful of followers were at stake?

Phillippa met Alex's eyes. *Let's hold that plan in reserve until we know what Lizard Girl's up to. Our best bet may be to contact Supay ourselves and broker a deal.*

And how do you propose to do that?

Through a priest or priestess of the old religion. She shrugged. *Assuming a few of the Incans managed to hide from the Inquisition and passed on their knowledge.*

That's some pretty long odds. Not to mention we're outsiders.

She raised an eyebrow. *You got a better idea?*

Alex shook his head. "No, but I've never heard a story where bargaining with Death ended well for the person idiotic enough to try."

Chapter 13

Phillippa dug her nails into the armrests. Since her first flying lesson before the Second World War, she'd loved the feeling of drifting over the terrain, of breaking the bonds of gravity and traveling as some of her cousins could.

Now, she sincerely wished her night vision wasn't that good. The pilot zipped the little twin-engine between Andes peaks as if the Erinyes chased him. Her stomach pitched when he passed a jagged cliff that couldn't be more than fifty feet below the wingtip.

"You okay?" Alex whispered.

She nodded, but her gut burbled its unhappiness. Another steep sweeping turn threatened to bring up the eggs and potatoes she'd managed to eat back in Lima.

Alex dug in a side compartment of his backpack and slid a little white sack onto her lap. "Just in case. I had them specially made for Anne."

At the mention of Caesar's head of household security, humor eased Phillippa's nausea. The tiny Amish woman was one of the fiercest fighters Phillippa had ever met, but when it came to air travel, Anne Levy was a total wuss.

Phillippa attempted a smile. "She would be having a rough time right now, wouldn't she?"

Alex chuckled. "Are you joking? She would have jumped out of the plane without a parachute when we climbed over that first ridge."

Another dark shadow whipped past the window. She swallowed the bile at the back of her throat. "I just wish he wasn't flying so near the mountains."

Alex frowned and bent over, his head practically in her lap. And while she remembered the experience the last occasion his head was in a similar position, now was not the time for pleasure. Not to mention, his attention was thoroughly engrossed by the window next to her.

Or what flew outside the window. A quick glance out the pane turned into a full-out stare. An oozing, yellow eye glared at them.

"What in Hades—?"

The creature rammed the plane. The little craft lurched toward a passing cliff. Both Francisco and the pilot yelled in Quechuan. Stone on metal screamed, and the floor shuddered violently beneath her boots.

Phillippa fully expected to see open air yawn beneath her feet, but the undercarriage remained intact from the glancing blow. She stared out her window. The thing was gray and black, perfect camouflage for nights in the mountains. Only its shadow passing between them and the stars gave away its position. And the shadow grew larger . . .

"It's coming again!"

Their pilot pushed the nose of the little plane down and banked to the left. The creature shot over them.

Alex looked over his shoulder. "It's gaining. How the hell is that thing keeping up with us?"

The pilot mumbled something in Quechuan. Francisco shouted, "Hang on!"

Gorge rose in her throat as the plane continued its plummet. Metal squealed. This time, it was her fingers digging into the armrests that caused the screech.

A quick glance at Alex didn't reassure her. His boots braced against Francisco's co-pilot seat. His fingers clamped around his own armrests.

"Do you see it?" The roar of blood in her ears muffled Francisco's voice.

Alex looked over his right shoulder again. "It's at five o—dammit! I lost it!"

Panic left the taste of acid and copper in her mouth. She stretched to see behind them. A wing covered the stars before it shifted. Another wave of shadow, bigger. "I see it. It's directly behind us and closing."

Granite loomed over them as they dove for the narrow thread of a river below. Rushing black water was only visible due to the spurts of foam as it crashed into and over jagged rocks.

The pilot muttered rhythmic words. *A countdown.* He yanked back on the yoke. The nose jerked up and left her stomach behind as the engines strained to climb in the thin atmosphere.

A scream of rage echoed against the rocks and through the cabin. The plane banked slightly to the right, trying to retrieve the altitude it had lost in the dive.

"Did it crash into the river?" Francisco yelled over the high-pitched whine of the engines.

Once again, she stretched to peer over her shoulder. Hundreds of feet below, baleful yellow eyes stared back. A huge wave of black water and white foam arched as the shadow leapt. Flashes of starlight on scales showed the heavy beat of its wings.

"Yeah, but it's back in the air and headed straight for us."

Damn, damn, damn. She couldn't use her powers. Doing so in a tiny metal box wouldn't just fry the plane's controls. It would fry the occupants as well.

A soft yellow glow filled the front of the cockpit. Francisco and the pilot conferred telepathically. But between their speed of transmission and her lack of knowledge of the Quechuan language, she couldn't make out a damn thing. The rising odor of sandalwood and ash in the confined cabin confirmed how frightened the local vampires were.

"What is that thing?" She had to shout to be heard over the laboring engines.

Francisco glanced at her before he faced the controls. *Something from nightmares,* senorita. *According to legend, the winged servants of Supay would take the sacrifices from the mountaintops.*

Why would it be after us?

That I do not know. We cannot outrun it, and we are too far from Cuzco. There's a small plateau nearby. We will slow and skim the ground so we may jump.

Phillippa swallowed hard. *Are you insane? On the ground, we'll be sitting ducks.*

Alex gripped her forearm. *We'll have better odds against the beast in a cave than we will in this plane.*

His eyes glowed neon, but his scent shifted to brimstone. The Texan was downright pissed. Something must have shown in her face because a fanged grin appeared on his face. *Like I said before, I'm tired of being someone's target.*

Unlatch your seatbelts. We're approaching the plateau.

At Francisco's words, Phillippa peered between him and the pilot. The flat space ahead couldn't have been more than a hundred yards long. This would be close. Metal shivered from another cry of the thing pursuing them.

Her fingers fumbled with the buckle. Soft clicks lay under the roar of the taxed engine. Metal on metal. A piston cracked or a bearing had come loose. The plane wouldn't keep them in the air much longer even if that prehistoric nightmare wasn't chasing them. She slid on her backpack. Alex did the same with his.

We're coming. Francisco voice whispered over and over in her mind. *We're coming . . . Now!*

Everyone bailed out of the plane. For such a small craft, the wash was incredible. Phillippa tumbled uncontrollably across the rocky turf.

Then nothing was under her legs. She scrabbled for a hold on the rocks. Granite cut into her palms. She swung from a ledge, her roll arrested. Far below her, the rapids flashed white foam.

"Hang on, miss!" the pilot shouted in Spanish. He crouched above her, cool hands on her wrists. With his strength, he easily lifted her back onto the plateau.

Phillippa sagged onto the mix of loam and rock, sucking oxygen. Any other time, she'd have been pissed at being rescued by a man. Now, she was glad not to be the monster's Happy Meal or mush at the bottom of the canyon.

The pilot stood and cupped his hands. "Mr. Chavez?"

The high-pitched whistle didn't give her enough warning. She grabbed the pilot's belt to yank him to the ground, but his head bounced past her and over the cliff.

She scrambled back as his skin and flesh fell from his bones. The rancid smell of rotten vampire flesh choked her.

The muzzle flash preceded the boom and echo of Alex's first gunshot as the monster snatched at the air where she had been. Four more shots from both Alex and Francisco followed in rapid succession. Each one scored the creature, but they had the same affect as the garlic-laced silver bullets had on the monkey demon in her shop.

None.

They were in the middle of nowhere. No civilians to get hurt or killed. No property to damage. For once, she could cut loose.

Phillippa stood and dropped her backpack. "Get down!" Her voice thundered across the granite spires surrounding them. Static prickled her skin, raised the fine hairs all over her body. St. Elmo's fire danced over her leather jacket.

Across the plateau, Francisco stared at her open-mouthed. Alex didn't question her. He tackled Francisco and dragged him into a shallow ditch, the lowest area available unless they tried their luck diving off the cliff.

In the distance, a boom echoed and rolled over the mountaintops. Their unpiloted plane came to its sad ending.

She scanned the sky, searching for the telltale shadow. There.

The creature aimed straight for Alex and Francisco. Too soon and its huge carcass would crushed them. Too late and its talons would shred them as easily as it had clipped the head from the pilot.

No more screams issued from the beast. Amid the quiet came the suppressed breathing of the two vampires, the high-pitched whistle of the creature's wings and the roar of her blood in her ears.

Electricity crackled between her fingers as the monster dove. With a scream of rage, she threw the giant bolt of lightning.

Chapter 14

Alex threw his body over Francisco's and covered his head.

When the bolt detonated above them, Supay's flying retriever bellowed, a horrendous noise. The flash. The electric sizzle that tingled over his skin. The world-ending tsunami of sound from the displaced air. Then, the acrid odor of a burning corpse filled his sinuses.

The ground shook when the monster crashed. They were far too close to the fiery remains. One ember blown the wrong way, and their deaths would be a lot more painful than their poor pilot's. He tried to pull Francisco upright, but the Lima vampire only stared at the fire lighting the plateau. Finally, Alex lifted him in a fireman's carry and stumbled away from the ditch that sheltered them.

Phil met them halfway across the football field-sized area. "Are you two injured?"

"I'm not." Alex swung Francisco to the ground. His gums tingled and his fangs automatically extended at the delicious odor coming from her. "You are."

"A few cuts on my hands." Phil shrugged. "Think you can control yourself, or do I have to fry your carcass, too?"

Good. If she was throwing snide comments, then she really was all right.

He grinned. "I'll try to restrain myself from drinking you. Unless you're offering?"

She snorted and turned her attention to the Lima vampire. "Francisco, are you intact?"

He blinked. "The rumors are true? You are the daughter of a god?" From the look on her face, she was seriously considering smiting him.

Alex shook the other enforcer's arm. "Francisco, we need to know if you're still with us. Are. You. Hurt?"

The other vampire shook his head. "Cuts, bruises when we bailed. They are already healing." He grinned at Alex. "We'll have to hunt tomorrow night, but wild game is plentiful here."

"What about—?" Phil nodded at the congealed mass on the rocks.

Francisco sobered. "The ground is too rocky to bury him, even if we had tools."

Alex laid a hand on her shoulder. For once, she didn't flinch at his touch. "Could you burn his remains? Then we'll build a cairn over his ashes."

His suggestion seemed to satisfy her from her curt nod. She strode back to the plateau, her hair whipping in the wind created by the altitude and the giant burning monster corpse.

Francisco elbowed Alex's ribs. "A woman worth fighting for, no?"

"Only if you enjoy electrocution, my friend. Why don't we gather some rocks?"

Phillippa winced. Even though Alex kept his words low, she couldn't help hearing them. Normally, she wouldn't give a gorgon's ass what anyone said, but this time, it bothered her.

In a way, Alex was right. If she'd wanted him gone permanently, she could have killed him and disposed of him with none the wiser. Officially, Alexander Socrates Stanton had died in a bandit raid in 1888. Who'd miss him?

Besides the entire Augustine Coven.

Electricity sparked along her fingertips, her emotional turmoil the fuel. With a flick, she ignited the oily remains of their pilot. The flame flared, miniscule compared to the blaze of Supay's flying demon.

So why hadn't she killed Alex if he truly vexed her? Because she'd cared enough to bury him all those years ago? Or bury what she thought had been him?

You loved him. There isn't anything wrong with that, but it does no one any good, least of all you, to stop living because he isn't here anymore. Now, why had Betsy Parker's words popped in her head?

Because the madam had been right when she approached Phillippa after she'd pounded an entire case of tequila the night the posse had returned to San Antonio. She wouldn't have been half as upset if Alex had simply broken his promise to return to her. She would have been pissed, would have hunted the bastard down, and would have kicked his mortal ass.

And to be honest, Caesar and Duncan wouldn't have let Alex return to her if he wanted to. Not a fledgling vampire. He would have been as much a danger to himself as to innocent Normals.

The realization burned brighter than their pilot's remains, brighter even than the pterodactyl corpse. She hadn't stayed in Los Angeles for nearly a century because of the dislocated nymphs or an orphaned Tiffany.

She had stayed because of Alex.

Pebbles crunched under Alex's boots as he trod down the path that paralleled the defile. The terrain made the trek on foot through the Rockies with Duncan over a century ago feel like a Sunday school picnic. If they didn't need to put as much distance between them and the burning demon as they could, he would have demanded they make camp over Phil's objections.

As if on cue, he heard the slide of her heel on loose gravel. He whirled and grabbed her elbow to steady her. Rocks bounced and rolled before splashing into the black water.

Dark circles smudged the skin beneath her eyes, standing out even under the night shadow of the mountain they circled. He let go of her as soon as he was sure she had her balance.

No sniping at him for helping her. No sarcastic comments about not needing any man's assistance. She was in worse shape than he originally thought.

"Hey, Francisco. We've got about an hour until sunrise."

The Peruvian vampire nodded. "My thought as well. We'll find shelter first. A herd of wild goats came through here not long before sunset. We'll hunt. How does that sound for dinner, senorita?"

"Fine," she said.

Francisco flashed Alex a look, but he shook his head. Their guide took the warning to heart.

Five minutes later, they stumbled across a cave nearly level with the river. Alex eased the backpack from his shoulders as he surveyed the interior. From the sand coating the floor, it flooded often. From the smell, they weren't the first creatures to take shelter here. But it was deep enough to shield Francisco and him from deadly UV rays, and no other animals were currently using it as a residence.

Phil insisted on helping scavenge enough dry brush to make a fire. Alex clenched his jaw to keep from saying something as she wobbled along the shore. As fast as the current ran, he wasn't sure he'd be able to fish her out before the rapids turned her into a bloody pulp.

When he and Francisco returned a half hour later with a field-dressed kid for her dinner, she was curled up next to the fire and dead to the world.

A sound jerked Phil out of a deep sleep. The stunt with the demon pterodactyl on the plateau had taken more out of her than she cared to admit. It had been centuries since she'd cut loose with all the electrical power she could muster. She'd forgotten what a toll it took on her body.

Real wakefulness seeped in and she became aware of the abnormally slow beat of a heart. She was nestled against Alex, her right arm slung over his back. Even on sand, he was a stomach sleeper, his head cradled on his folded arms.

On the other side of the dead embers, Francisco snorted, then settled into a steady snore.

An answering snort and muffled words came from outside of the cave.

She silently rolled to her feet and pulled her Glock from her backpack. The two vampires slept on, oblivious to the danger.

Okay, maybe it wasn't danger. Maybe it was the stupid goat herd doubling back to get water.

Except goats didn't talk to themselves in sing-songy voices. An odd language she heard in her demolished showroom four days ago.

She crept to the mouth of the cave and peeked out. Sharp sunshine lit the riverbed, turning last night's black depths into liquid crystal. In the shadow of a boulder downstream, a monkey demon shuffled down the path they'd followed last night, his nose to the gravel.

She considered waking Alex, but by the time he gained consciousness and realized he was throttling her, the demon monkey could be alerted and escape. The gun wouldn't do a damn thing to the demon, so she tucked it in the back of her jeans.

Too bad they didn't bring Kiki with them. The demon might answer some questions with the threat of the tiny Maltese.

Maybe this was the time for some old-fashioned brute strength and Amazon speed. Phil launched herself from the cave and raced for her target.

The monkey demon was so intent on sniffing their trail it didn't notice her until she was less than a yard away. It shrieked, the same nails-on-chalkboard sound its compatriot back at her store made.

She tackled it as it turned to flee. It twisted and squirmed, desperate for leverage to throw her off. She wrenched its arm behind its back and shoved its own talons into its gray half-rotted flesh. The demon squealed in alarm but stopped struggling.

"Phil!" Alex's shout came from the cave mouth.

"Stay inside! I'm coming." She climbed to her feet and yanked the demon upright. "My friends and I want to have a little talk with you," she muttered in the demon's ear.

It didn't respond.

She scanned the area but didn't spot any more unwanted guests. Ashy fear rolled off the demon and mixed with its odd animal decay odor while they marched back to the cave. The combination added to her nausea from her empty stomach, and she clamped her jaw in an effort not to dry heave.

Both vampires stood within the shadow of the cave mouth. They quickly moved back to make room for her and her guest.

"What the fuck?" Alex brows knitted into a puzzled line. Francisco stood next to him, his jaw hanging open.

"It was tracking us," she bit out before slamming the demon down on his knees. "Who's your master?"

The demon quivered under her grip, and the yellowish sclera shone around its orange pupils, their glow more pronounced within the dim interior.

"Answer me." She pressed its talons further into its flesh. The demon whimpered but said nothing.

"Phil, I don't think he understands you," Alex said.

Old anger and bloodlust swelled in her. She switched to Spanish. "Of course, he does. He just needs a little encouragement." She tightened her arm around its neck.

The demon choked.

"Miss, let me," Francisco murmured. The Peruvian vampire knelt next to it. Quechuan rippled from his tongue.

The demon rattled an answer in its sing-songy voice. It seemed to repeat one word she recognized. When Francisco said, "Supay," the demon cringed and nodded.

Francisco had the demon repeat whatever it was saying three times before he looked up at Phil. "It says its Lord sent him to track the Summoner."

She shot a glance at Alex, who shook his head. "What's he talking about?"

The Peruvian vampire spoke more Quechuan. The demon seemed to elaborate its story. It shifted, as much as it could with the joint lock and her other arm around its neck, and took a long, deep whiff of Alex. It babbled a few more words.

Francisco looked at Phil. "He says Alex tried to summon the Lord of Death. His mission is to track him down and kill him for his daring."

"Whoa, there." Alex held up his hands, fingers spread. "I did not try to summon Supay."

The demon hissed at Alex, who hopped backward.

Phil couldn't stop her chuckle. "I wouldn't mention you-know-who's name again. You've already pissed him off once."

The lightest sheen emanated from the vampire's eyes. "But I didn't—"

She rolled the possibilities through her mind. "You said the tumi—" The demon twitched beneath her grasp at the word. "—glowed when you touched it."

"Yeah."

"And you were saying the Christian Lord's Prayer?"

Alex threw his hands up. "You're the one who pointed out to Ray that gods respond to their adherents, not to non-believers."

Francisco looked at her before he turned his attention back to Alex. "His boss—" Francisco inclined his head toward the demon. "—should not have responded to 'Our Father, Who art in Heaven.'"

Irritation plucked at Phillippa. "Well, Alex sure as Hades did something to get on Supay's radar—"

The demon jerked in her grasp.

"Oh, shit," Alex murmured. His hands wiped down his face. "I thought 'Dear Lord,' not 'Our Father.' It shouldn't have worked that way either. Bebe keeps talking about intent . . ."

Phillippa tried to quell her humor at the incredulous look on the men's faces. In the end, the laughter won out. Not that she eased her grip on the demon. "But that was your intent. You wanted help from a deity to battle Lizard Girl. You were holding Supay's—"

The demon whined.

She ignored it and continued. "Object of power and you didn't specify a name. Using the word 'heaven' is the only reason he didn't come and kill you right then and there."

Alex stared at the cave ceiling. "Oh, fuck me."

"Yes, well and truly fucked, *mi amigo*." Francisco shook his head. "And not in the good way." He turned back to the demon and asked more questions in Quechuan.

Phillippa's stomach gurgled and growled as the conversation dragged on. It wasn't the first time she'd gone hungry, but the resulting irritability made her want to shove the monkey demon's claws through its rotten heart.

Finally, Francisco nodded in satisfaction. "You may let him go. He will not run."

"How can you be sure he won't do something else?" Alex drawled out the words. "I don't feel like getting shishkabobbed because an Incan god's pissed at me."

Francisco grinned. "As I explained to our friend here, you two were pursuing the actual thief, and you momentarily had regained possession of the tumi when you inadvertently thought the correct words to summon Supay. He has agreed to take us to the temple of his boss."

Phillippa looked at Alex. "That was one of the plans we talked about."

He rubbed his chin as he mulled over the possibility. "I know we did, but once again, I didn't know I'd ticked off a god when we discussed it. Where's this temple?"

"Cuzco."

The demon whined something in Quechuan, and Francisco gave her a pointed look.

She didn't trust the thing, but demons were usually bound by their word, assuming their guide had phrased the request carefully. She hoped to Aunt Athena that Francisco had. As soon as she released the creature, it skittered behind Francisco and glared at her around the vampire's thighs with its odd orange eyes.

Her stomach growled again, loud enough for the two vampires to grin. "I don't suppose you brought me back one of those goats."

Phillippa cut up the kid with the knife Francisco had provided her before they left Lima. By the time she started roasting the first haunch on a stick, the vampires had gone back to sleep.

Once Francisco was snoring, the demon edged closer to the fire she'd built at the mouth of the cave, but it kept to the opposite side of the flames. It seemed to be satisfied watching her, and for the most part, she ignored it as she skewered the second leg.

No doubt it knew exactly what she was. That may have been part of the reason it agreed not to run. Delivering her to Supay may be the one thing that would keep the demon from his master's wrath for failing to kill Alex.

Its attention flicked to the other half of the kid and back to her. An almost wistful expression appeared on its mottled face.

"Are you hungry?"

It cocked its head and stared at her. Damn, she forgot it didn't know English. She repeated the question in Spanish, but the demon still looked confused.

"Hungry." She mimed eating.

It nodded so vigorously that tiny chunks of hair and rotted flesh flew from its head. She toed the rest of the goat's carcass toward the demon. It snatched up the remaining meat, and peered inside the body cavity.

It looked back at her and chittered a question in its own language. She didn't need Francisco to translate. The demon wanted the internal organs. However, the vampires had field-dressed the kid before bringing it back to the cave.

She shrugged, pointed at the sleeping vampires and shrugged again.

It must have understood her meaning. It held up the remaining carcass in a type of salute before it tore into the raw meat.

She tried to ignore the way the demon cracked the ribs and sucked out the marrow before it nibbled on the bones themselves. Maybe parlaying with Supay wasn't such a bright idea after all, but they couldn't be worrying about demons tracking Alex while they chased down Lizard Girl.

Shadows filled the narrow valley as she and the demon ate in relative silence.

Jorge Sifuentes had seen some horrible and weird shit between his years as a homicide detective and marrying the beta of the Los Angeles werewolf pack. But the gibbering nutcase he and Siobhan tried to interview took the proverbial cake. Jorge stood in the corner with two orderlies as his wife had requested.

Matthew Kline, a member of the Sunshine Believers, knelt at Siobhan's feet and licked her shoes. The straightjacket didn't seem to matter to him.

"Matthew," she said as she gently cupped his chin and tilted his head to face her. "I need you to focus. Can you do that for me?"

"Unleash your beast. Please, Mistress. Show them. Show the non-believers what you can do. Rend their flesh!" His plea ended in a loud cackle before devolving into more sobs.

A shiver ran along Jorge's spine. The bastard knew. Somehow he understood Siobhan was more than human. Luckily, the two orderlies chalked up the Sunshine Believer's ravings to insanity from the amused look they shared.

"It's not time for that yet, Matthew." Siobhan's voice remained calm and soothing. "I need you to look at a couple of pictures for me. Can you do that?"

"I'll do anything for you." The mental patient gazed at her with adoring eyes as he rubbed his head along the leg of her jeans.

Even though Jorge knew she could more than take care of herself, the bastard's gross behavior made him want to beat the shit out of Kline.

She pulled the photos out of the manila envelope they'd brought and held up the one of Beatrice Madison. "Do you know this woman, Matthew?"

Siobhan repeating his name seemed to keep him focused on her questions. He examined the picture and shook his head. "No, Mistress. Shall I kill her for you? How slow do you want her death?"

"Someone already took her heart. Do you know who?"

A sick grin spread across Kline's face. "Do you want her heart back? Release me, Mistress, and I swear I'll retrieve it for you." He dropped his head and started licking her shoes again.

Siobhan sighed and glanced at Jorge. He shrugged. She was getting farther questioning the sick bastard than he had.

"Matthew," she snapped.

He flinched and cowered. "No! Please don't!"

"I'm not going to hurt you, but I need you to pay attention." She held out the second photo. "Do you know this woman?"

Kline glanced at the photo before he threw himself flat on the industrial tile. "The prophet."

"Prophet?" Once again, Siobhan looked at Jorge.

This was the first he'd ever heard of a prophet, but Kline obviously had met Jane or the woman impersonating her. Neither the LASO background check or Stephens's research had revealed a connection between Mann's dead employee and the Sunshine Believers. He tilted his head toward the now weeping Kline. "Run with it," he murmured.

Siobhan knelt next to the prostrate mental patient. "Matthew, she's a false prophet. I need to know what she told you and where she is."

It took a couple minutes of Siobhan stroking Kline's greasy hair before he could give a coherent answer. "She said she could bring back the Old Ones."

"How was she planning to bring them back, Matthew?"

"Sacrifice. But I couldn't catch any gods, so I brought her innocents." He looked up at Siobhan. The wild gleam in Kline's eyes stabbed fear through Jorge's heart. "Sometimes, they were still wrapped in their whore mothers, but I cut them out for the prophet. I can do that for you, Mistress. Please. Please take me with you."

Faster than Jorge would have thought possible for a Normal, Kline threw himself at Siobhan. He knocked her over and was on top of her before any of the men could react.

With her were strength, Siobhan twisted and wrapped Kline in a headlock. "That was a naughty thing to do, Matthew. You'll have to stay here for misbehaving."

"No!" Kline shrieked and struggled as the orderlies dragged him away from Siobhan and out of the interview room. Jorge held out a hand and helped her to her feet.

The psychiatric resident stepped into the room, a slight frown on her face. "I don't think I approve of your tactics, Detective Sifuentes."

"Like I give a shit."

"Encouraging his delusions—"

"Got us the answers we needed," Siobhan spat back.

He laid a hand on his wife's arm. Beneath his palm, the rough edges of sprouting fur faded. The last thing they needed was Siobhan giving the doctor a wolfie beatdown.

"He said nothing that cannot be attributed to his mental illness." Sadness lay behind the doctor's eyes. She may be Normal, but she didn't believe her words anymore than he did.

"Maybe," he acknowledged. "Or maybe I've solved a cold case that's been on my desk for ten years. Thank you for your assistance, Doctor."

He led the way through the maze of locked doors until Siobhan and he stood in pure California sunlight again. She shuddered, and he wrapped an arm around her as they trudged to their car.

"I need a shower," she muttered.

"I don't blame you."

"I'll need to burn these shoes, too."

"Of course."

She stopped and looked up at him. "Were you serious about a cold case?"

"Yeah. Anita Warren. She was my first case after I was promoted to detective." The mutilated body of the pregnant mother had made even Jorge's battle-hardened mentor lose his lunch. "At least, this discussion was slightly more productive than the ones at the prison."

"Maybe. I'm worried about the god thing. What happens if this imposter decides a demigoddess can be substituted in a pinch?" They resumed walking through the blistering parking lot.

"I'd put my money on Mann. You saw her barbeque-ing zombies at Stephens's wedding. Do you know what he meant by bringing back the Old Ones?"

Under his touch, Siobhan shuddered again. "According to pack legend, there were creatures that lived on this plane before the gods. When they were driven out, they swore revenge. But it's just a story."

"Yeah, well, I thought all werewolves looked like Lon Chaney before I met you." Jorge smiled at her.

"Asshole," she muttered, but she grinned back.

"There's a park not far from here. The stream's mountain cold, but it has some good trails if you need to run."

"Sounds great, but I don't know if I'll ever feel clean again."

Jorge kept his mouth shut. Siobhan was the one decent thing in his life, and he'd do anything to keep her that way.

Chapter 15

Tiffany winced as Miko Osaka slammed the phone receiver into its cradle. The noise bounced off the walls of Caesar's study. His mansion had been a second home for both women when they were growing up. "Not good I take it."

"No." Miko ran her hands through her straight black locks. "I fucking hate Latin men."

"I thought lesbians were supposed to hate all men." At Miko's nasty look, Tiffany held her hands up in surrender. "I was just joking."

"It wasn't funny."

"What's going on?"

"Alex and Phil got a lead on the imposter. They were flying to Cuzco with Huamán's chief enforcer when their plane crashed in the Andes."

Tiffany's heart threatened to choke her. This could not be happening. Phil had been the closest thing she'd ever had to a mom, Alex her big brother. "Are they all right?"

Miko stood abruptly. "The Lima Coven doesn't know yet. A fly-over spotted the wreckage, but their daytime enforcers haven't reached the site yet. There's no roads up there. They have to follow wild game trails, and even in jaguar form, that's going to take time."

She stalked over to Caesar's wet bar and poured a healthy tumbler of whiskey. "The asshole I spoke with told me not to worry my pretty little head. That their *men* would take care of things." She downed the contents and slammed the glass on the bar. "Times like these, I wish I were a vampire."

"I don't think your girlfriend would appreciate it, cuz."

A wan smile appeared on Miko's face. "No, she probably wouldn't." She eyed the glass decanter for a moment before she turned back to the desk.

Λ kick from the baby was all the encouragement Tiffany needed. She pushed herself to her feet. "I can head down to Peru. An unofficial visit."

"Oh, no, you don't." Miko was too fast. She planted herself in front of the closed door.

Tiffany ground her teeth and glared at her cousin. Stupid parasite. Four and a half months along in this pregnancy, and she was already slower than frozen syrup. Hell, she could barely bend over to reach her knife in its boot sheath. "Get out of my way."

Miko shook her index finger. "You are not leaving Los Angeles, and I'm not getting my throat ripped out for you doing something stupid."

Tiffany rolled her eyes. What a drama queen. They both knew their vampire relatives would do no such thing.

"Please, Tiffany." Miko's voice softened. "You are as much a sister to me as Mai. And after losing Grandfather and Jamal, I couldn't bear to lose you, too."

"Bitch. I can't believe you played the dead PawPaw card." Tiffany turned her head away to hide her tears from Miko. Losing their respective sets of parents twenty years ago in an attempted coup against Caesar had been bad enough. Their mutual grandfather Kensai and his husband Jamal had been killed during the stupid Seelie-spawned zombie crisis that had ruined her wedding.

Tiffany swiped at the wetness on her face. "Stupid hormones. I need some tissues, or are you going to stop me from getting those, too?"

This time, Miko stepped out of the way.

Tiffany marched down the hall to one of the first floor half-baths. She flipped the lock, lowered the toilet seat and proceeded to have a good cry. *Please, God. Let Phil and Alex still be alive.*

Phillippa had her fire extinguished and her backpack ready when Alex and Francisco woke shortly before sunset. The surrounding mountains shadowed the river valley so deeply that they could set out immediately.

The monkey demon hung close to Francisco as they climbed the game trail. Apparently, their companionable silence after their shared meal had been all in her head.

Within a couple of hours, they caught up with the same herd the men had hunted from last night. The two vampires and the demon made short work of the old dam they brought down. In all fairness, Alex did offer her some.

She shook her head. "I'll stick with trail mix and jerky for now. The last thing we need is for someone to spot my fire. Unlike our new guide, I can't do the raw thing."

Francisco grabbed a couple handfuls of the tough plants that passed for grass at this elevation and wiped the blood from his face and hands. "Our friend is with us. What else could be following?"

"Marcus Giovanni and his rogues could be looking for us," Alex said as he cleaned up. "Phil's right. Let's not make this easier for them than we have to."

Francisco nodded, and they set off in the general direction of Cuzco.

Despite their supernatural endurance, the high altitude and rough terrain took its toll on the little group. Phillippa couldn't remember being this out of breath since her childhood. Even the demon seemed to be lagging as they hugged a cliff-side trail that was barely wider than her feet.

The hours dragged on, and she was about to suggest they find shelter for the day when they rounded a rocky protuberance. Below them, lights from the city of Cuzco twinkled.

Francisco slapped Alex on the shoulder. "Told you we would arrive before dawn."

"Yeah, but getting a hotel room with a demon is going to be a mite difficult," the Texan said dryly.

Francisco conferred with Supay's servant. "He suggests going straight to the temple before daylight comes."

"Great," Phillippa muttered. "Trapped inside a deity's home for hours is a wonderful idea."

More chittering issued from the demon before it paused and repeated its words in Quechuan.

"He says his brothers will know he's nearby and will come to investigate if he does not return immediately."

Phil crossed her arms. "So we have a choice: be led into a trap or deal with a full-on assault."

Alex rubbed his chin. "Our buddy has a point. It's better to politely announce our presence. Otherwise, Supay may take it as another insult."

She stared at the stars for a moment before she sighed. Her breath rose in a frosty cloud. "Fine. Temple it is."

The trek down the mountain to the plateau holding the ancient capital of the Incan Empire took longer than the men anticipated. Their demon guide stuck to back alleys once they entered Cuzco proper. The eastern sky glowed pale pink when it led them to what appeared to be an old Spanish mission.

Phillippa gritted her teeth. After what Christians did in Ephesus, she wasn't a bit surprised that they would build overtop of an Incan temple.

The monkey demon bounced down steps that dipped below street level and opened a door set in the stone foundation. More chittering before it bounded through the opening.

"He wants us to follow him," Francisco offered.

"Thanks, but I didn't need the translation for that." Alex swung his pack off his shoulders and pulled out a flashlight.

She followed suit. Not even her vision or the vampire's would be much good in absolute darkness. "Any idea how far down these catacombs go?"

The Peruvian enforcer shrugged. "According to legend, all the way to Uku Pacha."

"What's Uku Pacha?" she asked.

Francisco gave her a devilish grin. "Hell, my dear."

Chapter 16

Alex groaned and flipped the flashlight switch. "I swear you both are worse than little children during a sleepover."

"Oh, and science solves everything, Mr. I-Love-Technology," Phil taunted.

"I didn't say that," he shot back. He ducked through the doorway.

The ceiling of the tiny room was equally low. Obviously, this place had been built with the size of the native population in mind. Barrels and boxes lined the walls. He tested the air. Wine and flour. Sacraments.

Another wooden doorway stood open. Through it came the demon's sing-songy voice along with a musty odor. The smell reminded him of the mummy of one of Caesar's relatives that Duncan and he had "liberated" from a San Francisco museum.

"This is where the Incans buried their dead?"

"Yes," Francisco murmured.

Alex crossed the room and aimed the flashlight through the open doorway. "Well, as long as no one reanimates them . . ."

"That isn't funny, *mi amigo.*"

"We didn't think so either when a necromancer raised half of the Hollywood Cemetery a couple of months ago," Alex said. Light reflected off the rough-hewn granite walls of the tunnel.

Phil shouldered past Francisco. "Want me to go first?"

Alex glanced at her, half-expecting a mocking grin, but the Amazon was totally serious. "No, I'm more concerned about this tunnel coming down on our heads than an ambush." He inclined his head toward her flashlight. "Let's just use one flashlight at a time. Just in case."

Instead of arguing, she nodded and slid the device into its sleeve on her backpack.

Francisco jabbed a finger at the closest barrel. "What if we take some of the blessed wine with us? An offering?"

Alex shook his head. "We want Supay on our side, remember? Wine already blessed as a sacrament to Jehovah would be an insult. Plus, whatever Lizard Girl is, she's not one of the Incan pantheon or the Christian. No offense, but I have a feeling we're going to need more local help than your coven. Taking a barrel with us would be more than rude to both sides."

The other enforcer grunted in acknowledgement, but he didn't look happy.

Another round of demon chatter echoed down the tunnel.

Alex plunged through the opening. His parents had raised him as a good Methodist, but for the first time in his life, he was afraid to pray. The possibility of what might answer scared the fangs out of his gums.

Alex checked the glowing numbers of his watch again. The manmade tunnel with its niches of quiet dead had given way to a system of natural caverns over three hours ago. Heat and thick air pressed against them as they followed the demon further beneath the mountain bordering the Cuzco plateau. The fading battery of his flashlight didn't bring any comfort.

"How close are we to the nearest volcano?" Phil asked.

"Too many miles to be concerned about," Francisco said.

"I'm more worried about ventilation," Alex added. "We're getting awfully deep here."

As if he'd cued the demon, it stopped in front of a blank wall. It reached out with a claw and scratched an intricate design on the granite surface. In response, the rock moaned and shifted as if someone were drawing back cotton curtains. The demon beckoned them before he darted through the opening.

Phil laid a warm hand on his shoulder. It was the first time she'd touched him since she curled against him in the cave yesterday morning. Of course, she'd been unconscious then. "You sure following the demon is a good idea? We may not be able to get back out."

He placed his hand over hers. "I think you're reading too much of your uncle's tricks into this."

Lines crinkled around Francisco's eyes. "No, Phillippa has a good point. In some ways, the Lord of Uku Pacha is more greedy than Pluto."

Alex's fangs extended, and an eerie blue light danced along the cavern walls. Traveling through the tunnels, pissed at his companion's cowardice, would produce the light he desired, but it wasn't the best of plans if he wanted to survive an audience with an Incan deity. "We've come this far. Stay here if you want. Or head back to the surface" He let go of Phil's hand and jerked free from her grip.

She grabbed his wrist, tight enough he could feel his bones creak under the pressure. "Dammit, Alex. Listen to me. Just because you don't believe in your god doesn't mean they don't exist."

What the hell? Since when had she noticed or cared about anything he did? No, this was another one of her I'm-so-superior ploys. "I'm not in the mood for your insults."

Her expression held no hint of mockery. "I'm stating facts. Sure, you go through the motions, but unless it's something you can touch and smell and measure, it isn't real to you." Earnest eyes stared into his. "If you don't treat Supay with respect, he won't just kill you, cowboy. He'll make you beg even after you're already dead."

She didn't get it. What really happened to him, Anne, Logan, and the rest of the supernaturals imprisoned and tortured in the basement of Mallory Labs. How they'd starved him. How they tried to break him by throwing him in the Pit with an innocent human. How close he'd come to giving in to the thirst.

"He can't do anything worse than what Selene and her cronies did to me last year, Phil," Alex said softly.

With an abashed look, she released his wrist. "Fine. Let's go." She marched through the parted rock.

Francisco chuckled. *You two need to sleep together and get it out of your systems.*

Alex snorted. "She prefers her men warmer than room temperature."

The odor of brimstone wafting from the opening had nothing to do with the Incans' hell and everything to do with an annoyed Amazon.

Phillippa clenched her fists to keep from turning around and cracking Stanton's jaw. *The nerve of that bastard.*

No, it was her own guilt chewing on her soul. She'd kept her distance from the rest of the supernatural community and their petty fights for so long she'd forgotten what mattered.

No, that wasn't true either. She simply couldn't bear the emotional pain of losing the people she loved any more. Not since that scorching afternoon in west Texas when she buried the corpse she thought was Alex Stanton.

As soon as the two vampires stepped through the demon's entrance, the stone shifted and flowed until it was a solid wall again. A trap just as she'd feared.

She whirled and strode toward the demon. It cowered and shrieked until her fingers wrapped around its neck and choked off its irritating noises. "Open that doorway, or I'll pop off your head and kick it to the moon."

"Let him go, Phil," Alex snapped.

"Make me," she snarled, but the compulsion tugged at her nerves. Involuntarily, her hand relaxed and dropped the demon.

The demon scrabbled away, babbling wildly as it put distance between her and it.

The urge to hurt someone, anyone, couldn't be ignored despite her pledge. She pivoted and grabbed Stanton by the collar of his leather jacket. "That thing will betray us."

His face remained impassive, though his eyes glowed neon blue in the suffocating darkness. "Release me, Phil. You will not attempt to harm me, Francisco or our demon guide unless I give you permission."

She tried to fight her oath, but the burning began deep in her belly.

Was this how she'd die for breaking her word? Not the Kindly Ones flaying her alive, but spontaneous combustion here in Uku Pacha?

With a wild cry, she released Alex's coat. Her legs gave out, and she curled into a fetal ball on the polished stone floor. She rocked herself until the agony in her midsection subsided.

Alex's touch and soothing words pierced the receding ache. He sat next to her, brushing her hair away from her face. "You okay now?"

"Yeah." She pushed herself upright, but couldn't meet his gaze. He knew exactly why she'd collapsed. The demon chattered softly as it peered around Francisco's waist.

The glow from Alex's eyes softened. "Phil, if you can't keep it together when we meet Supay, you need to stay here."

Francisco coughed discreetly. "That will be a problem as well, *mi amigo*. According to our friend, entry points are not exit points for Uku Pacha. Once our audience is over, we will be led to another place to regain Kay Pacha. The surface.

"Also, if we kill our demon guide in the underworld, we won't have to worry about finding our way out. We'll be kept here for his master's amusement until the end of time."

Phillippa sucked in a deep breath. The enormity of her screw-up threatened to overwhelm her. "I-I'm sorry. I let my father's pride and anger—"

"No, Phil." Alex's voice was stern, but the neon glow of his eyes had totally faded. Only his dying flashlight provided illumination. "You can't keep blaming your father. I don't know what went down between the two of you, and I don't care. But your behavior here, now, is you. Not him. And if you don't get your shit together, you're going to get us all killed."

Ire flared at the way he spoke to her, and it died just as quickly. He was being logical. If it were Caesar or Duncan speaking the same words, she wouldn't have reacted the way she had.

The muscle in her jaw twitched twice before she muttered, "You're right. I'll keep my shit together."

"Good." Alex climbed to his feet, then held out his hand. Swallowing the huge lump of humility in her throat, she grasped his palm and let him pull her upright.

The demon muttered something to Francisco before it bounded off into the darkness again. Phil brushed the sandy grit from her hands and followed the two vampires. Sometimes, translations were unnecessary.

Alex glanced at his watch. The digital display still hadn't changed since they entered the demon's domain. Something down here must be interfering with the circuits in the device. Based on counting steps, he estimated they'd walked another three miles.

The air in this tunnel was noticeably cooler. Clammy too. There must be an underground river nearby.

His flashlight flickered and finally died. Oppressive blackness closed in on him. He'd never had a problem with claustrophobia, but the weight of the rock overhead seemed to press against his chest.

"Phil, you got your flashlight?"

"Wait." The voice out of the darkness was Francisco's. After a moment, he added, "Do you see it?"

Alex blinked a few times. What first appeared as spots in front of his eyes resolved into the other vampire. A faint, sickly greenish glow showed Francisco ahead of him. The monkey demon's orange eyes were brilliant in comparison.

"Where's the light coming from?" Alex stared upward but the walls simply faded and disappeared into the distance.

"The stone," Phil said.

He turned to find her staring intently at the rock surface. A step closer brought him within touching distance of her, but he didn't dare. Instead, he examined the granite.

No, not granite. The crystal appeared to be quartz, but something else clung to the faces. "It looks like some kind of algae or lichen." Whatever the growth was, it was the source of the light, but the crystal wall refracted and amplified its glow.

He reached for the material, but once again, Phil grabbed his wrist. "Don't touch it. In fact, don't touch anything down here you don't have to."

"Why?" Curiosity rather than annoyance drove his question.

"Because you don't know what that—" She pointed at the lichen-like growth. "—will do to you, and this is not the time or place for one of your experiments." She sucked in a deep breath and released it. "And I really don't want to find out what Supay will do if you inadvertently harm something in his domain."

She was right, as much as he hated to admit it. They were guests, and it wasn't mannerly to insult your host or break his belongings.

"I promise. No touching."

That seemed to satisfy her, and she released his wrist. He slid his

backpack from his shoulders and stowed the flashlight. The extra batteries were in their holders, but no sense wasting them if they had light.

He swung the pack back in place, and they trudged after Francisco
and the demon.

Alex had lost count of his steps when the demon led them to the underground lake. The odor of rotten eggs and equally rotten chicken filled
the air. Black sand covered the beach, but the most unnerving thing was
how still the water was. No waves. No movement whatsoever. The surface was as smooth as polished obsidian.

The demon rattled something to them before it turned to their left. It
shambled at a faster pace.

"He says we need to cross the bridge, and we'll be in the city of the
dead." Francisco's whisper sounded too loud. His words echoed and re-
verberated against the crystal walls that disappeared into the distance.

Alex pivoted and followed the demon. Somehow, anything he could
have said seemed inadequate. Hell, he hadn't been this unnerved when
he'd been dying, and Duncan offered to Turn him. Seeing the bridge
didn't help his unease.

Bones. The whole damn thing was made of human bones. Femurs
and humeri composed the main parts of the structure. Ligaments tied
everything together. The worst part was the skulls that tiled the bridge's
walking surface. Every single one of them faced up, and soft groans issued from their parted jaws.

"Shit," Phil muttered next to him.

Alex exchanged looks with Francisco.

The other vampire shrugged and shot him a wan smile. "Your idea, *mi
amigo*. You go first."

On the other hand, the demon practically skipped across the grisly
bridge.

Alex stared across the water. The bridge led to an island about a mile
away. The buildings on the little slice of land were brightly lit compared
to the faint glow of the lichen-covered crystal walls. Someone, or some-

thing, was on that island, waiting for them. The alien sense of expectation permeated every cell of his body.

He stepped onto the bridge. It shifted under his weight, similarly to a rope and wooden plank construction. The movement sent ripples through the black water. Resolute, he followed the monkey demon.

The bridge swayed as Phil and Francisco followed. Alex didn't want to touch the finger bones that comprised the railings, but he had to in order to keep his balance. He frowned as he trailed after the demon, who had begun to sing in its own language.

The groaning skulls jerked under his boots. Something more than the four of them acted on the grotesque structure. He looked over the edge. Pale flesh breached the black water before disappearing under the skulls. The bridge jerked again.

"*Madre de Dios*," Francisco whispered. "What was that?"

"Something we don't want to get acquainted with," Alex answered. He glanced at their guide, and even the demon's bright orange gaze watched the lake with unease.

It chittered something in Quechuan. Alex didn't need Francisco to translate. He ran after the bounding demon. The clatter of boots on bone said Francisco and Phil raced after him.

Pillars of black basalt anchored the island end of the bridge. Alex leapt for the ebony sand beyond. Francisco landed with a grunt beside him.

A sharp *crack* ricocheted through the humongous cavern. The end of the bridge tore from its moorings. The skulls flipped straight up, launching Phil into the air. With his heart in his mouth, Alex could only watch as she plunged into the ebony water without even a splash.

Chapter 18

Frigid water swallowed Phillippa. Something heavy wrapped around her ankle, dragging her further into the lake's depths. Something stronger than her. Something that felt dead and rotten beneath her fingers.

Its grip was so tight she couldn't pry the tentacle loose. She was rapidly running out of air and options.

Despite her warning to Alex, she summoned the little electricity she could muster. The water would dampen the effect, but maybe it would be enough to startle the creature into releasing her.

Her lungs burned as she tried to concentrate. Lightning flashed from her fingertips.

For a moment, she wished she couldn't see the thing that held her. Ghostly flesh surrounded a crimson mouth with a multitude of jagged teeth. Too many tentacles to count waved in the water.

She felt rather than heard the creature's shriek, but the tentacle around her ankle blackened under the electrical discharge.

The pressure on her boot disappeared, and she tumbled in the monster's wash as it fled deeper into the lake. For a split-second, panic threatened to consume her. She blew a bit of her air into her cupped hands.

The bubbles floated past her mouth and chin. She turned herself around, blew a bit more air to confirm her orientation, and arrowed for the lake's surface. Maybe, she'd get lucky, and her captor would remain discouraged.

Dizziness swept through her. Her arms and legs felt leaden. How deep had the creature dragged her?

Maybe she should ditch her backpack. Even as the thought travelled through her mind, she knew it was too late. Each stroke, each kick, became more difficult until she couldn't move. Her lungs were on fire.

All she had to do was breathe in the lake, then everything would be over. No more battles. No more fighting to survive. No more Alex.

The image of the blond vampire roused her out of the threatening stupor. Dammit, she had an oath to uphold, and she wasn't giving him the satisfaction of seeing her fail.

Three strokes later, she passed out.

"Phil!" Alex's throat was raw from screaming her name, but the lake remained as smooth as glass. "Phil!" Water dripped from his hair. He slapped the surface, but it barely moved. His dive where she went down had produced nothing. Where had that damn thing carried her?

"It's been too long." Francisco's voice carried the anguish Alex refused to let himself feel.

He shouted her name again. She was a fucking Amazon. She was too tough to die from a stupid lake monster of Hell.

Ripples erupted in the lake, several yards from where Alex tread water. He struck out in that direction. Francisco shouted in Spanish, tore off his boots and raced into the lake.

Alex reached Phil first. Her skin was ghastly under its normal olive sheen. Her lips were dark purple, nearly blue.

He wrapped his arm around her and towed her toward the shore. Francisco helped him drag her onto the black sand.

"Dumbass," Alex muttered as he felt for a pulse. Nothing. No breath either. "Why didn't she ditch her backpack?" Adrenaline made his hands shake as they yanked the soaked bag off to lay her flat.

"She may not have had a chance. Look at her boot."

The brown leather looked as if someone had dribbled acid around Phil's ankle. "Get it off her," Alex said.

Francisco stripped off his own jacket and used it to pry the damaged boot from her foot. Whatever was on the leather immediately began eating holes in the insulated nylon. The Huamán enforcer tossed both the footwear and his coat away from them.

The monkey demon danced around them, babbling in its own language, but Alex ignored it. CPR. He needed to start CPR.

Airway clear. Pinching her nose shut, he pressed his lips to hers and blew. Her chest rose and fell. Five breaths. Nothing.

Francisco crawled back to her chest and started compressions. Was he as anal as Duncan about learning Normal first-aid techniques?

The idle thought couldn't keep Alex's fear at bay. "C'mon, Phil. You are not doing this to me."

More mouth-to-mouth. In all the ways he imagined touching her lips again, this was not it. A pause. She remained still. Too still.

"We are too late," Francisco murmured.

"Shut up. Just shut the fuck up and keep pumping her chest." Alex blew into her mouth again. *This can't be happening. It's all my fault. I made her swear on the Styx.*

He couldn't go home and face Tiffany. Couldn't tell the kid that her foster mother was dead because of his own stupidity and pride. Why the hell had he insisted that they come down here?

"Stanton . . ." Francisco voice was too sad to bear.

Alex sucked in another lungful of air. Beneath his hands, she jerked. Water vomited from her mouth. He grabbed her and rolled her onto her side.

She convulsed, bringing up more and more gouts of clear liquid.

"Phil?"

More vomiting, then she coughed and sputtered a few times before she muttered, "I need to kill that thing."

Squeezing his eyes shut, Alex gathered her in his arms and hugged her tight. "Don't ever scare me like that again, Phil."

"Alex?" she whispered.

Underneath the sulfur and rot smell of lake water, her clean sea grass scent reassured him. He rocked her in his arms. "I'm here. I'm not letting you go ever again."

"Alex," she hissed. "We have company."

He opened his eyes. Pale, translucent shapes surrounded them. Adults and children, male and female. They were dressed in the clothing of many different eras of Peruvian history, though the majority wore Native American garments.

Interspersed between the ghosts stood gray, decaying animals with orange glowing eyes. Monkey-like apes similar to their guide. Jaguars. Condors. Even a few llamas and alpacas.

They stood silent and still until they parted like a wave. The figure that emerged from the crowd of the dead and the damned looked exactly like something out of a Sunday school primer.

He easily stood fifteen feet tall. Yellowish horns rose from his head. Eyes as black as sin stared at the intruders. The complete eye was black, not just the iris and pupil. Red skin merged into shaggy hind-quarters that ended in cloven hooves. In one hand, the newcomer held a staff. It glowed with the same white light as the unknown material on the tumi had.

In his peripheral vision, Alex caught Francisco crossing himself. Not a good start.

He gently released Phil and climbed to his feet. A little respect could go a long way in remaining alive. Keeping his eyes on the figure, he bowed. "Lord Supay."

"Your name?" The bass voices made even the sand on the beach quiver.

He's speaking in several languages at once. Maybe I won't have to worry about something getting mistranslated. That didn't mean the god wouldn't take offense at something innocuous either. "Alexander Socrates Stanton, sir."

"Why did you presume to attempt to summon ME!"

The thing in lake moaned in response to its master's displeasure, a low note similar to the song of a male humpback.

"I apologize, sir. At the time, I had reason to believe the item I held was a fake. If I'd known it was yours, I would have returned it immediately."

"Where IS it?"

At least, the god was listening and not smiting him.

"A demon unfamiliar to me took it. My companions did not recognize my description either. When we encountered your servant—" Alex waved at their demon guide. "—we asked that he bring us to you that we may offer our apologies for not recognizing your property. That we may serve you in recovering what is rightfully yours to rectify our error."

Something touched his mind. He didn't dare resist the god's probe. With the incredible power behind it, he couldn't if he wanted to.

Supay's form wavered and shifted. Instead of the image of Lucifer, a Native American stood before them, matching Alex's six-four. Only his eyes remained completely obsidian. He was dressed in finery, gold and feathers styled in the tradition of an Incan ruler except the cloth was black with only scarlet embroidery. "Come. We will discuss your service to me."

Chapter 19

Phillippa climbed to her feet. Black sand clung to her wet clothes, but she didn't dare brush at it and bring attention to herself. Alex was showing the god the proper amount of respect, and he focused on the Texan. If Supay mistook her for human, the element of surprise might work in their favor if they had to fight their way out of Uku Pacha.

"Before we speak of your service, I would know why you brought a godling from the Middle Sea to my domain, Alexander Socrates Stanton." The unsettling black eyes rested on her.

Shit. Don't be an idiot and give him my name, Alex.

"She's helping me track down this unknown demon. It murdered—"

"And why would one such as she assist you?"

Alex glanced at her before answering. "She has pledged herself to my quest, Lord Supay. A human girl under her protection was killed by the unknown demon who took your tumi from me."

Supay's attention on her didn't waver for an instant. "And why would a Middle Sea godling's protectorate have anything to do with my possession?"

"It is a convoluted story, Lord Supay," Alex interjected. He was smart enough not to step in front of her. "We are not sure of how the puzzle fits together as yet. We ask that you would be gracious—"

"Answer my QUESTION, godling." The multitude of Supay's voices rattled her very bones.

Phillippa lifted her chin. Hopefully, the god would only punish her and not the two vampires. "Your tumi was in my possession. The demon murdered my assistant Jane in order to steal it."

He continued to stare at her. Pressure filled her head as he read her thoughts. She dropped to her knees at the agony in her brain. There was no way to prevent it, to fight him. This wasn't going to be like crashing a plane or drowning. Her death was going to hurt, and the agony would continue for eons.

The pain abruptly stopped, and she fell to her hands at its absence.

"Phil?" Alex knelt next to her. Blue neon smoldered in his eyes. Brimstone and ash rolled off his skin.

She took his hand and squeezed it. "I'm fine."

Supay cocked his head as he continued examining her. "You are not the newborn who has disrupted the balance."

Phillippa winced when Alex helped her to her feet. Her muscles quivered from the god's probe. Needing Alex's assistance to remain upright was disconcerting as well. It had been a very long time since she'd met an entity she couldn't fight.

"What newborn, Lord Supay?" Damn, even her voice shook.

"The one I smell on you and Alexander Socrates Stanton." Supay pointed at Francisco, who paled noticeably under the wan green light of Uku Pacha. "He does not carry the scent." The god frowned and asked something in the demonic language of their guide.

The monkey demon chittered on for several minutes before Supay motioned for him to stop.

Phillippa shivered, but not from the chill air. From the monkey's gestures toward Alex and her, it was trying to justify to its master why it hadn't killed them.

"Come," Supay repeated. He whirled on the heel of his gold sandals, his ebony cloak flaring behind him, and he marched toward the large black building that dominated the center of the island.

Phillippa exchanged looks with the two vampires. "Any idea what he's talking about?"

Francisco shook his head.

Alex rubbed his chin, a contemplative expression on his face. "If I had to guess, I'd say there's more to Lizard Girl than we realized." He trailed after Supay.

She looked at Francisco and shrugged. The three of them collected their gear and followed the god down a street literally paved with gold. The ghosts and demons trailed behind them. The *squishing* noises from her one remaining boot were the only sounds as they walked through the city of the dead.

Tiffany tapped her toe impatiently. The security line at LAX moved forward with excruciating slowness, and she really had to pee. Stupid baby had been playing bongos on her bladder for the last half-hour. Dammit, they should have a separate screening area for people with medical conditions.

Some middle-aged cowboy wannabe tried to walk through with a gigantic silver belt buckle still attached to his designer jeans. Then he decided to argue with the TSA agents.

She groaned. Maybe she should run to the restroom before she wet herself. A glance at the people behind her said if she got out of line, she'd never get through the security checkpoint before her flight to Lima left.

An elderly woman couldn't get it into her head that she couldn't take her walker through the scanner. The stupid agent couldn't get it into his head that the woman was going to fall flat on her face if she tried to pass through without it.

Tiffany checked her watch again. Fifteen minutes until boarding started.

Thank Murphy, the next three people had a clue. She stepped through the scanner and reached for her bag.

"Mrs. Howell?" A stout middle-aged woman in a TSA uniform stood next to her. Short, gray hair made her look grandmotherly, but her eyes said she would kick ass if pushed.

"It's Stephens," Tiffany automatically corrected.

The security agent gave her a toothy grin. "My apologies. If you'll step this way, please." She waved toward one of the screening booths.

"My flight leaves in a few minutes. What's the problem?" Tiffany be-latedly added, "Ma'am."

"This way, please." The agent balanced on the balls of her feet, and her hand dropped to her baton.

Tiffany swallowed her irritation. This was someone who knew how to fight. She couldn't risk the baby even if she wanted to take on the bitch and spend the night in jail. "Fine."

She entered the screening cubicle the agent indicated. It was already occupied.

A shitass grin showed Siobhan Sifuentes's white teeth. Miko had a perturbed expression. But worst of all was the fury on Max's face. Gentle, sweet Max.

"Just what the hell do you think you are doing?" her husband roared.

Chapter 20

Relief swept through Alex when their escort didn't separate Francisco, Phil and him when they reached Supay's palace. The monkey demon who had guided them to Uku Pacha escorted the three of them to a room on the second floor of the building. It pointed at various devices and explained them to Francisco in Quechuan. At least, the palace was toasty compared to the atmosphere outside.

"All right, folks. He wants our clothes," the Huamán enforcer relayed in Spanish.

"Why?" Leave it to Phil to be suspicious.

Alex unbuttoned his shirt. "Because if we were Normal, we'd be dead. That damn lake is contaminated, or couldn't you tell?"

"I was a little more worried about the monster wanting to eat me," she said dryly, but she didn't argue further and started peeling off her own soaked clothing.

Francisco pointed at the tiled section in the corner. "That's the shower. Press the lever to dispense the water."

Alex paused. "If the water comes from the lake . . ."

"I asked as well. Our friend assures me the source is a separate underground aquifer."

Two more of the monkey demons came into their room with fresh clothing. Their guide bounded around and collected everything, including their backpacks. He said something else to Francisco before the three demons bowed and left.

A very gorgeous and very naked Phil started after them. "Wait a minute!"

Alex grabbed her upper arm. It took monumental effort to keep his eyes focused on her face. "They're going to clean our belongings."

"They took our weapons," she hissed.

"And the only thing we have that can take out one of Supay's demons is probably sprawled on Tiffany's couch getting her belly rubbed. So let it go."

She yanked her arm out of his grip. "You are too trusting, Stanton."

"I can admit when I'm in over my head, and I have no problem going to a higher authority for help. Now, behave yourself and get in that shower."

Pain flashed across her face. Dammit, he didn't mean to give her a command, but if that's what it took to keep her from doing something stupid and getting them all killed, so be it. She gave up fighting her oath, pivoted and stomped over to the little bathing facility.

Alex deliberately turned away. The last thing he needed was the wrong portion of his anatomy showing its appreciation for the nude woman.

Francisco joined him in studying the mural on the wall. "A strange welcome, no?"

"Why would the god of death have accommodations for mortals?"

"Our friend says his lord kept this room for the occasional hero who'd come to retrieve a loved one from Uku Pacha. If I understand our friend correctly, it's been a century or two since anyone living has ventured down here."

"Any idea why the non-lethal reception?"

Francisco shrugged. "We're not trying to take something from his realm. And how often does a mortal offer to assist a god? It may be curiosity."

Behind them, Phil said, "Or he plans to use us as bait to flush Lizard Girl and the tumi out of hiding. Shower's free."

Alex turned to find her already dressed in a calf-length tunic. She was unsnarling her hair with a wide-toothed wooden comb the demons had provided. He squelched the urge to help her and crossed to the odd little shower. To his surprise, the water sluicing from the spout overhead was the perfect temperature.

✻

Their demon guide appeared in the doorway of their room at the same time Alex figured out how to belt the colorful embroidered shirt he'd been given. Their monkey demon led the three of them further into the labyrinth passages of Supay's palace, but each twist and turn added to Alex's disorientation. He didn't want to admit he was lost in front of Phil.

Francisco?

Yes?

Is your internal compass screwed up?

Has been since our friend led us through his secret passage from the main catacombs.

"What's wrong?" Phil whispered.

"Nothing," Alex responded. "Use your company manners while we're here."

She glared at him, but wisely remained silent.

The demon led them into a banquet room. At the head of the polished basalt table sat a raised dais with a throne that looked like it was solid gold. Gray demons sat, stood or crouched at all the places along the table except four chairs nearest to the throne. A llama demon stood next to a golden gong behind and to the right of the dais.

Their escort led them to the four empty places. It indicated that Francisco and Phil take the chairs opposite of itself and Alex. Once they were seated, the llama head-butted the gong. All of the demons rose. Alex gestured at Francisco and Phil to follow suit.

Francisco's expression held curiosity. Thank goodness, he was taking this whole thing in stride. But Phil made a face like she was sucking on the sourest lemon ever grown.

The llama made a long drawn-out speech in the demon language. Alex only caught the god's name before he shimmered into existence, already seated on his throne. With his gesture, the demons settled themselves.

Alex sat. Francisco and Phil followed a beat later.

The shades brought in huge platters of raw meat. Alex studied how they carried physical objects. A couple of ghosts accidentally passed through his shoulder as they set a goblet of blood on the table for him and a plate for the guide. His skin puckered at the proverbial cold ectoplasm. Maybe they used some kind of telekinesis. Or maybe they depended on memories of how their muscles used to work.

Supay held up his own jewel-encrusted cup. "To our honored guests."

The demon horde responded, but Alex had no idea if they were repeating the god's words or asking formal permission to eat the visitors.

Maybe not eat them because the demons ripped into their bloody meals. Even those in llama and alpaca forms devoured the flesh set before them.

Alex eyed his goblet. His stomach growled in displeasure. With no idea of how long they've been in Uku Pacha, it was difficult to judge his hunger. He and Francisco had drained the old dam about twelve hours before they reached Cuzco.

Supay's chuckle brought Alex's attention back to the god. "It does me little good to keep you here if you are to serve me on Kay Pacha." He took a long drink from his cup. The liquid he licked from his lips was obviously not wine.

Alex raised his goblet in a salute and drained it. The blood was nothing he'd consumed before, but it had the same underlying hints as the goats he'd drank during their hike through the Andes.

"Alex," Phil whispered. Her hands covered her mouth, and her eyes widened until whites surrounded the storm gray irises.

Supay sniffed. "Unlike your Uncle Aidoneus, I do not need to resort to trickery to populate my realm."

Alex examined the plate before Phil. The gold dish held lightly roasted fish, olives, grapes and bread. He didn't recognize the spices used on the seafood, but he suspected it was something native to the eastern Mediterranean region. "It's okay, Phil."

"No." She shook her head wildly. "No, it's not. This was a mistake. I should never have let you come down here."

The odor of ash coming off her was so thick he couldn't stop from coughing. All the demons at the table stopped eating and stared at her. Their orange eyes glowed a little brighter.

A sharp bark of laughter erupted from Supay. "I do my own collecting of souls. I don't rely on psychopomps like many other lazy asses I could name. And if I wanted Alexander Socrates Stanton's or even yours, little Amazon, I would have taken it the moment you stepped foot in my domain." His eyes narrowed as his attention swiveled between Alex and Phil. "But then I would be justified for the loss of two of my servants, no?"

Great. Just great. Between an annoyed god of death and an Amazon on the verge of a panic attack, Alex's day, night, whatever, was getting crappier by the minute. Despite the tightness in his neck, he tried to appear nonchalant.

"With all due respect, Lord Supay, your demon chose to destroy itself rather than speak with us after we caught him in her domain." Alex inclined his head toward Phil. "If it had simply told us you wanted to retrieve your property, a lot of unnecessary grief could have been avoided."

"And the other?"

Alex sucked in a deep breath. "We defended ourselves when we were attacked. If your first servant had simply talked to us, again both deaths could have been prevented."

The god leaned back in his throne and folded his hands beneath his chin. The gesture was so similar to one of Caesar's it sent a chill down Alex's spine. "Tell me your story from the beginning and leave nothing out."

Supay's request didn't make sense since the god had already read his and Phil's minds when they were by the lake. Maybe it was a test to see if they would lie.

Alex started with the initial phone call from Jorge about the break-in at Seven Wonders. Phil and Francisco added their details. Supay interrupted occasionally to clarify an issue. He didn't have lines in his skin as a human would, but with each question, the god's frown sagged a little more.

When everyone was silent, unease tickled Alex's nerves. Never in his life did he think he'd see a worried deity.

"May I show my servants the image of the beast you encountered on the road outside of the new city?"

Alex nodded. He'd have to ask Phil for the details later, but he rather had the impression that gods did not ask permission from mortals.

This time the touch to his mind was delicate, careful. A three-dimensional image of Fake Jane appeared in the center of the banquet table. His memory of her morphing into the lizard creature played out amid the bloody scraps of dinner.

Three-quarters of the assemblage appeared confused. The rest shrieked and babbled in the demon language. If he thought the smell of Phil's fear was bad, the demons' made it down right impossible to breathe. The shades shimmered out of sight or passed through the walls of the room. But the monkey demon who guided them to Uku Pacha regarded him with new respect.

"This is a minion of the Old Ones." The furniture shivered under Supay's multitude of voices as he explained Lizard Girl to Alex and his friends as well as his younger demons. "With the birth of the new god weakening the ancient seals, it managed to squirm past them. Its mission is to break one of the seals completely, to allow its masters back into this dimension. The newborn is not ready for its test."

"There's more than one seal to keep these Old Ones out?" Alex asked.

Supay laughed, a horrible, bitter sound. "Since your godling companion referred to my tumi as being made from leftover space shuttle parts, I shall continue with that analogy. The openings of your craft have special doors. More than one, correct? What happens if an abnormal amount of energy is released? Say a stick of dynamite. Near enough to crack the non-titanium section of one of your shuttle's doors."

Alex could feel his already low-temperature blood freeze in its veins. What Supay described was exactly how fourteen astronauts had died. One small opening, a frozen seal on the *Challenger* and a missing heat tile on the *Columbia*, resulting in catastrophic failure. Except the god was talking over eight billion Normals and supernaturals.

Alex stood and held out his hands. "How does she plan on destroying these seals and where? And how do we stop her?"

"Where? There are any number of sacred places she may do the deed. As for how?" Supay gave a mirthless laugh. "To open the portal, she will use my tumi to kill another god."

<h1 style="text-align:center">Chapter 21</h1>

Phillippa's heart lurched in her throat. From Alex and Francisco's expressions, they understood a disaster of this magnitude, but the determined set of Alex's lips said he thought the mission was something he could accomplish. His "save the world" determination was what attracted her to him all those decades ago, but this situation was more than he could handle.

Hades, it was more than she could handle.

She mulled the possibilities through her mind. Something didn't make sense. Lizard Girl needed a full god to pull this off.

Phillippa tapped her fingers on the smooth stone table surface as she tried to sort out the logic. "Lord Supay, do you know who she has targeted?"

He snorted. "If I knew that, I would also know where my tumi is."

"Then why would she need me? Killing me isn't going to provide the amount of power you're talking about."

"No." The god barked something in the demon language only, and half the horde scattered in all directions as fast as they could run or fly. "They go to warn my brothers and sisters," he added in the strange way he spoke Themiscyran, Ancient Greek and several other languages at once.

Phillippa shoved her untouched plate aside. "No, she's going to use someone from another pantheon. On the off-chance she can't break the seal now, she'll make sure she starts a war to keep the gods distracted while she searches for another way."

Supay's eyes narrowed. "And how would you know that?"

"It's what I'd do. I'm more powerful than Normals and most of the supernaturals . . ." *Hera help us!* Everything dropped into place in her mind.

From the look on Alex's face, he'd put the pieces together as well, but wanted to deny the picture they formed. "No." He shook his head vehemently. "Selene's bullshit started before this latest crack in the seal formed."

"But what if she's not a servant who slipped through the crack? What if she's been here since the last breach? Immortal. Biding her time. Staying out of sight. Setting things in motion to prepare for the next occurrence. If she keeps the demigods, the vamps and the fae distracted, anyone with a lifespan longer than a century or two, anyone with enough experience to see the pattern, keep them at each other's throats..." She stared at Alex, could practically see the wheels of his brain turning through her logic.

He turned to the god. "Lord Supay, I mean no disrespect, but how could someone get your tumi out of Uku Pacha without your knowledge?"

The god's countenance darkened. Dammit, leave it to Stanton to piss off the gods themselves.

She leaned forward and rested her elbows on the table. "Think about it. She passed herself off as human, which means she can probably pass for other races. Lord Supay collects his own souls. All she'd have to do is wait for him to leave on a business trip. Then she pretends to be one of his demons, slips into Uku Pacha, grabs the tumi and is out before any of the other demons catch on."

"There's something you two are forgetting." Francisco jabbed at Alex's memory still replaying over the table. "If your Lizard Girl stole the tumi from here, how did it end up in a Normal's hands on a flight to America? And better yet why?"

"Shit." Alex frowned as he watched one more replay. "We're not getting anywhere sitting around the table." He bowed to the god. "With your leave, Lord Supay, it would be best if we return to Kay Pacha and resume tracking her. We're already a day behind."

The demon beside the vampire leapt to his feet and bowed as well. It chittered something to the god.

"Yes." Supay leaned forward and touched the monkey demon's forehead.

"Thank you, my lord," the demon replied in clear Spanish. He turned to their little party. "I will accompany you on your hunt."

Phillippa couldn't resist a smile. "Understanding you without a translator is going to make things easier."

The demon grinned back, an awful thing full of rotten, jagged teeth. "For all of us, my lady."

Her smile tightened. "As long as you realize I'm never going to trust you."

It barked with laughter. "It goes both ways, Amazon."

A thread of relief wound around her heart. An honest enemy was preferable to the conniving bitch who stole Jane's life. Maybe, just maybe, she would be able to extract her revenge before this was all over.

Tiffany tried not to shrink under Max's four-letter tirade as they drove down the highway. When he paused for a breath, she said, "You're beginning to sound like Sam."

"Leave my sister the fuck out of this. She's in Ohio, not traipsing off to South America. And she's not pregnant with my child!"

"Phil's in trouble!"

"She's an Amazon, not to mention she's the daughter of the Greek god of war. She can damn well take care of herself!"

"They found remains—"

"Which the Lima Coven already identified as their own pilot. *And* they discovered the cairn on a different mountain than the plane. Someone built that cairn, which means the others survived. The searchers are probably right, and Phil, Alex and the Lima enforcer are hoofing it to Cuzco." He sucked in a deep breath before he hit the hazard lights on their minivan and pulled onto the berm.

Once Max shoved the gearshift into "Park," he took off his wire-rims and reached past her into the glove compartment. He carefully cleaned his glasses with one of his special cloths before he replaced them and faced her. "Tiffany, I know you're worried, but Phil and Alex are after a murderer." His voice was super calm compared to the tirade of a minute ago. "Miko told me about Phil's assistant Jane. None of you know what that thing is. I don't want—" He inhaled again. "I don't want the same thing to happen to you."

She folded her arms over her stomach. The baby kicked at them because she hated anything on top of her. Tiffany could only imagine how much harder the butterfly movements would become over the next few months. But Max's Neanderthal attitude since the wedding was getting on her last nerve. "I can take care of myself."

"Under normal circumstances, I'd lay my money on you any day, honey. But yesterday morning, you had trouble tying your own damn shoes."

Helplessness overwhelmed her. She dug her fingernails into her palms. Dammit, she was not going to be one of *those* women. She was not going to cry. "You don't understand—" The words backed up behind the snot clogging her throat.

"I don't understand what? That Duncan and Phil are more than foster parents to you. That you came damn close to losing him during that zombie attack at our wedding. That you're already upset Phil's planning to leave Los Angeles after the baby's born. That you're pissed because your parents will never see our baby."

Bastard had to hit every single one of her hot buttons. She swiped at the one tear that managed to escape. "You're a fucktard, you know that?"

"Yeah." He stared at the passing traffic before he turned back to her. "But I'm your fucktard, and you're stuck with me."

He leaned over the console and waited a moment before his lips touched hers. His kiss was gentle and sweet and calming. When it ended, neither of them said anything. Max shifted the minivan into gear and merged with the Los Angeles traffic.

Alex tucked his t-shirt into his jeans. "How long will it take to get back to the surface?" When they returned to their room, their clothes, including the spares, were clean, dry and folded on three different chairs along with their backpacks. The demons had even fashioned new boots for Phil and replaced Francisco's coat.

Demon John shrugged. Alex had suggested the nickname because not even Phil could wrap her tongue around its public name. "Time is different down here than on Kay Pacha. We will walk and climb for a day, but when we reach the surface, less than two degrees of the sun's rising will have passed since you entered my lord's domain."

Alex ran the calculations through his head. If he understood Demon John correctly, it would be just after sunrise *yesterday*. "Are you going to be okay in full sunlight?"

The demon grinned. "Better than you."

"Alex." Phil frowned as she sorted through her belongings. "My gun's missing. So's my flashlight."

Demon John turned to the three female monkey demons standing near the doorway and chittered something to them in their language. The differences between the male and female demons weren't very obvious. Recognition turned more on little quirks of behavior.

Sheepish expressions appeared on all three faces. The middle one answered.

Demon John looked abashed as well. "They had trouble reassembling your equipment. And one device was ruined by the lake water."

Francisco snorted as he obviously tried to stifle his laugh. When Alex glared at the Lima enforcer, he found a sudden interest in pulling on his socks.

Alex swallowed his own irritation, faced the women, and said patiently, "Where are they, ladies? I'll take care of it."

A quick question and answer, then Demon John said, "In a room down the hall. She can take you." He pointed to the middle demon.

"Alex." Phil laid a warm hand on his forearm. She shot a concerned look at the demons. "We shouldn't split up."

For a brief instant, he wished she was truly concerned about him. But with her, everything came down to stopping Beatrice and Jane's murderer. "Nothing's going to happen. He needs us to find Lizard Girl, remember?"

"But—"

"Let it go, Phil."

Muscles in her jaw twitched. She was trying to fight her oath again.

He laid his hand over hers. "Finish getting dressed and packed. I'll take care of the guns." He lowered his voice. "You'll be fine. I promise."

She yanked her hand back. He didn't understand most of what spewed from her lips, but "conceited" and "asshole" were prominent in a couple of the languages she used.

Dammit, he didn't have time to deal with soothing her precious ego. He turned back to the center demon. "Show me, please."

Even if she didn't understand his words, she understood his tone. She beckoned him past the curtain covering the doorway. He followed as she bounded down the hallway. She stopped and indicated a room on the opposite side of the hallway three doors down from their room.

Alex ducked past the curtain. Sure enough, his and Phil's Glocks were laid out on the table along with Francisco's sidearm, all oiled and in pieces. Ammo and clips had been cleaned as well. Batteries lay next to the disassembled flashlights. A few quick, easy motions, and everything was back together. But Phil's smartphone was officially DOA.

He couldn't blame the demons for that. For all he knew, her stunt to bring down the pterodactyl-like thing fried the circuitry and Phil hadn't wanted to admit it. Bless the demon's hearts though, they had provided little bags for the ammo since the lake water had destroyed the cardboard boxes.

He smiled over his shoulder, then whirled around searching. The female demon hadn't followed him into the room. He took one step toward the doorway when he caught movement from the corner of his eye.

The eerie twisting wasn't caused by the little oil lamp hanging over the table. Shadows twisted and stretched before coalescing in front of him.

Alex took a precautionary step back. *There's a rational explanation.*

But the tiny hairs on the back of his neck rose anyway when the shadow resolved into the humanoid form of Supay.

The god held his index finger to his lips. *You will be my eyes on Kay Pacha, Alexander Socrates Stanton. In return, I will give you some of my sight, but you cannot reveal my gift. I'm not so much a fool. Someone here in Uku Pacha has betrayed me. Betrayed all of Creation. You must find the traitor.*

Anger, not fear, flooded Alex. Being used as everyone's pawn was getting damn old. But he was frozen in place, couldn't lift a hand, couldn't speak as Supay raised his other index finger and touched Alex's forehead.

When Phil found out about this, she would never let him forget that she said not to split up. Except Supay's power already wrapped around his soul, and he knew this compulsion wasn't like Phil's voluntary oath.

Agony ripped through his mind, and his eyeballs felt like they wanted to explode in the sockets. *Phil is going to be so pissed at me* flitted through the pain as he fell toward the floor.

Chapter 22

Phillippa couldn't shake the feeling something was wrong. She charged past the demons by the doorway. "Alex!"

"What?" Not his usual teasing response. He sounded almost . . . angry. But he always took her tantrums in stride. Had she pushed him too far when she cursed at him? All he'd done was show concern.

But he was a male showing concern. Irritation and embarrassment mixed oddly in her gut.

She followed his voice down the corridor and discovered him in a room on the opposite side of the hall. He stood next to a table, shoving bullets into a magazine cartridge with enough force that it was a wonder he didn't dent the casing.

"Those aren't the ones I brought. Where's the silver and garlic ones?" She stepped to his side. "I'll load those."

He paused and frowned. "They're not here. Demon John!"

The demon bounded through the doorway. "Yes?"

Alex's eyes flared neon blue. Phillippa prayed that the demon knew what the glow indicated and that he wouldn't lie about the ammunition.

"Where's the bullets we brought with us? The count's right, but these aren't silver." Alex shook the casing under the demon's flattened snout.

Demon John retraced his steps and poked his head out of the doorway and asked one of the other demons. When he bounced back, a frown twisted his thick lips. "Our Lord ordered the others to replace your armaments with these." Demon John pointed to the bullet.

"We're going to need something stronger than steel," Phillippa pointed out. "We know that other vampires are working with Lizard Girl. Our ammo was designed with them in mind."

He nodded. "Yes, yes, but he said you also required something that will work against the Old Ones' minion as well."

Francisco strolled in to join them. "I clarified things with the lady demons. The jacket's titanium, but the core is filled with that strange material in Lord Supay's staff." He shrugged. "Don't ask me what it is because the demons' word for it doesn't translate into Quechuan."

"How does it work?" Phillippa picked up another bullet and stared at it. The little piece of metal felt lighter than it should.

"Invoke Supay's name when you fire." Francisco's fingers stroked his mustache. "Or smear it with blood."

Phillippa collected her bag of bullets and Glock. "It always has to be blood, doesn't it?"

"You don't seem to mind shedding it," Alex snapped.

Francisco and Demon John stared at him. Good to know she wasn't the only one who thought he'd lost his mind.

"Hey, I'm sorry for lashing out at you a few minutes ago, but I don't need you to babysit me."

"Yeah, because I might give you too much soda pop to drink."

Oka-a-ay, maybe this wasn't about their earlier tiff. "What in Hades has gotten into you?"

"Nothing," he muttered. "A bit of a headache. We've been down here too long. Let's get going. We have a lot of ground to cover."

The llama who had acted as Supay's major domo during the aborted feast accompanied them to the bridge. In the few hours since they had arrived, the span of bones and ligaments had been repaired. Or maybe this was a different bridge. Alex wasn't sure. The llama sang in the demon language as she trotted ahead of them. Occasionally, a flash of milky white tentacles appeared close to the mirror-smooth surface but never broke it.

When they reached the other side, Demon John hugged the llama. They whispered for a moment in their language before she wheeled and headed back to the island.

"Girlfriend?" Francisco asked.

The look Demon John gave the enforcer indicated he thought the vampire was insane. "No." The monkey demon bounded to the right and entered a tunnel that could have been the one that brought them here.

Or maybe not. *This is why no one escapes the underworld. Even if you avoid the monsters and demons, you would get lost.*

They could have been walking for a day. It could have been three. Either way, Alex breathed a sigh of relief when Demon John led them through a metal doorway. The return trip had been blessedly uneventful. They found themselves in the basement of what could be a school. Pint-sized desks and chairs were stacked on the opposite side of the room from an ancient boiler.

The familiar tug on his skin warned him. "The sun's already up."

Francisco chuckled and pulled a smartphone from his shirt pocket. "No problem." His fingers flew across the touchscreen. "Our ride will be here in twenty minutes."

Alex leaned over to look at the device. "How's that still working?"

The Huamán enforcer's grin widened to show his elongated canines. "I did not play with underworld sea monsters like Phillippa, nor did I sit on mine as you did."

Alex let his lids droop and leaned his forehead against the tile wall. The shower in his suite didn't wash away his bad judgment or the images replaying through his mind.

What the hell had he been thinking? Even worse, how did the witches and Sam deal with seeing ghosts all the time?

Part of him had wanted to gouge out his eyeballs during the short ride from the school to the Huamán safe house. The ghosts of the native children nearly sent him over the edge. Starved, mutilated wisps that peered at him from doorways and shadows.

When Alex had asked Demon John about it privately, he'd shrugged his shaggy shoulders. "Not all of the dead wish the peace our Lord has to offer. Some because of fear. Some are desperate to live the life they feel they were robbed of." He shook his head sadly. "A great many of the people were so traumatized by the invaders from the east they cannot escape the nightmare. They continue to wander the streets where they died."

Alex turned off the water and reached for a towel. Phil had been right about not trusting Supay, and now, he couldn't even tell her that. Every time he tried, it felt like someone super-glued his tongue to the roof of his mouth. Luckily, Demon John hadn't questioned him about his new "gift," and Alex had been a little surprised that he could articulate the words when they were alone. If Phil or any of the Lima Coven were present, forget it.

He ran the towel over his hair as he walked back into his bedroom. Sea grass and sand hit his nose. He dropped the thick cotton from his face. Phil stood in the middle of the room, her arms wrapped around herself and an odd look on her face.

"Did you talk to Tiffany?"

"Yes." She sounded like she was choking on Uku Pacha lake water again.

"What's wrong? Did something happen in Los Angeles?"

"No. I—" She stared at him. Her gaze dropped south.

And damn if his cock didn't like the attention.

He quickly wrapped the towel around his waist and reached for his backpack. "So what did Tiffany say?"

"Siobhan got the same story from one of the committed Sunshine Believers that Supay gave us." Her body shuddered. "Lizard Girl needs a god to sacrifice in order to open that seal."

Not that he blamed Phil. This whole mess scared the shit out of him, too. "Is she sure? The man's in the nuthouse."

"Jorge taped the interview, and Tiffany played it for me. Your 'nutcase' recognized a photo of Jane, and he's been locked up since December."

No wonder Phil was upset. The Believer's story totally changed the timetable for how long Lizard Girl had been masquerading as the Seven Wonders assistant manager.

Phil looked so damn miserable. His hands itched to hold her. Comfort her. He wanted to apologize for acting like a prick in Uku Pacha, but if he did, she'd demand to know the reason for his behavior. And he literally could not go there.

Instead, he focused on business. "A Lima Family member spotted Lizard Girl boarding this morning's train to Machu Picchu. There's no other way off the mountain except on foot, and we both learned how difficult this terrain is."

She frowned. "Why?"

"Why what?" He pulled the extra jeans and shirt from his pack.

"Why wait four days before taking the train to Machu Picchu? It's almost like she was waiting for us to get to Cuzco."

"She only waited a day and a half at most. Remember, time doesn't flow the same way in the different planes."

Phil rolled her eyes. "You know what I mean. Why wait?"

He considered her point. "Summer solstice is in two days, and both Francisco and Demon John said the Hitching Post of the Sun, an Incan sacred stone, is up there."

She dropped her arms. "Supay sent out warnings to the rest of his pantheon. Would the sun god Inti show up knowing it's a trap? Not to mention, the site will be packed with tourists. So why perform the ceremony at Machu Picchu?"

"Additional sacrifices? Food for her masters when she breaks through?" He wiped a hand over his scratchy eyes. "Look, can we drop this for now?"

Her mouth opened and closed a couple of times before she ground out, "The world hangs on what we do next."

Irritation made his eyes itch even more. Why did she have to turn everything into a fight? "And neither of us has had any sleep in three days. We aren't thinking straight. Why don't you go to your room and catch a nap?" Her jaw dropped, but before she could say anything, he added softly, "Don't make me command you, Phil."

Her cheeks flared dark red. "I-I can't."

He tilted his head and waited. This was the first time he'd ever seen her embarrassed, and he planned to enjoy every second of it.

She couldn't meet his eyes. "After our stunt in Lima, Francisco assumed we'd be sharing a room here."

A number of choice obscenities ran through his mind, but he was too tired to give them voice. "Please shower first. You still smell like Uku Pacha."

Outrage appeared on her face. Whatever she wanted to say, from the click of her teeth, she decided against it. She marched for the bathroom.

Alex was pulling his skivvies out of his backpack when the ghost of the little Incan girl passed through the west wall.

Phillippa leaned her head against the tile, letting the cool water wash away the scent of decay from their visit to the Underworld. Things had changed between her and Alex again. She couldn't even put a finger on exactly what.

The person with her now seemed some strange combination of quiet, somber human Alex and boisterous vampire Alex. She had to give him credit for not abusing her oath. Not that Alex in any version would. Honor was too important to him.

But then she could say that of any of Caesar's people. It was part of the reason she bothered to associate with any of them.

However, a teeny part of her wished Alex would order her to take off her clothes.

For the love of Gaea, you are pathetic. If she wanted to sleep with him, all she had to do . . .

The low sound of Alex's voice melded with the hiss of the spray hitting the ceramic. Did he even realize he talked to himself when he worked through an issue? Apparently, she wasn't the only one having a debate with themselves about sharing the bed.

Maybe she needed to get him out of her system once and for all. Then she could leave Los Angeles with a clear mind.

Assuming they survived the next few days.

Clean ocean traveled on the water vapor. Alex kept his eyes closed. Once Phil crawled into bed, he would head into the bathroom and get dressed. As exhausted as he was, he'd given up on the hope of a quick nap. Questions churned in his mind with the ghost's assurance that Inti wouldn't go near Machu Picchu in two days.

The mattress shifted. Hot skin touched his thighs, and deft hands unwrapped the towel he wore.

His lids snapped open, and he grabbed Phil's wrists. She straddled him, gloriously naked. Damp curls fell over one shoulder. With the heavy drapes pulled shut and the lights off, her skin glowed with a faint white light. With Supay's gift of Sight, he now understood what Sam meant by Phil "looking different" than any other supernatural.

"What are you doing?"

"Francisco's right. We need to get this—this *thing* between us out of the way."

Alex could feel his right eyebrow crawling toward his scalp. "Excuse me? Since when have you ever taken a man's suggestion seriously?"

She sighed. The rise and fall of her perfect breasts sent the wrong signals south. "Our attraction is interfering with our job. We've got some time before the next train leaves, and we can catch up on our sleep on the ride south."

He should push her off, but his other brain was taking over. The one that had imagined her naked and in his bed again for over a century. "This is not a good idea." Somehow, he shoved the words past the desire clogging his throat.

She deliberately stared at his growing erection. "I think you're lying to yourself, Stanton."

He glared at her. "One of Supay's demons could give me a lap dance and the same thing would happen."

"Do you really want a demon doing this?' She leaned forward and kissed him lightly on the lips. Her breasts pressed against him. Blood throbbed through his body.

Their lips parted, and deep purple eyes stared into his. Waiting . . . for him to do or say something.

He released her wrists and cupped her cheeks. "I'm sorry, Phil. I can't do a one-night stand. Not with you."

The expected fury didn't materialize. Instead, she pushed herself off him and rolled to her feet. "I understand." She grabbed her clothes from the back of the chair. "I'll go downstairs and let you get some sleep."

Her voice had never sounded so . . . flat. She was always so passionate even in her anger at him over the last century.

He climbed to his feet. "Phil, wait."

She paused, her hand on the antique iron handle, but she wouldn't look at him.

"Why didn't you write back to me?" He sounded pathetic, but after all this time, he needed to know. The realization that this trip was the first time they'd been alone together since that night in San Antonio struck his chest like a sledgehammer.

"What?" Her startled expression said it all.

"You never got them." A sad chuckle forced its way out of him. "I broke every rule. And I thought I was so fucking clever sending them to Samantha Norris at Betsy's place, but Caesar must have known."

Phil released the knob and took a step closer to him. "No, don't blame him. After I—" Her throat bobbed and she stared at a blank spot on the wall to her right. "I left Betsy's employ shortly after I—after I—thought I'd buried—"

She turned away, trying to hide her emotions, but the scents rolling off her were obvious. Fear. Grief. Self-loathing.

He eased forward a bit, desperately wanting to hold her. Why hadn't he kept his fool mouth shut when she climbed on top of him? "So you're the one who dug the graves? Duncan and I doubled back after I recovered from my Turn . . ."

He didn't want to mention what they'd done to the bandits. What he had done. Drinking human blood was a major offense in the Vampire Nation, but he'd been a fledgling then. And Duncan had never told a soul. After what those bastards did to his friends and colleagues, Alex didn't regret one drop he'd drunk. Even he had only told one other person in his life what really happened, and it took him over a century to do that.

He would have confessed to Phil first if she'd written back to him.

She tried to subtly swipe at her cheek. "Not just me. When your captain didn't check in at the telegraph station in Uvalde, they sent out a posse to search for all of you." She snorted softly. "They didn't appreciate a woman riding along, but Betsy pointed out I was the best tracker available."

"But why did you believe you—" The memory hit him hard. "You never met Jamie Frazier."

She sniffed and wiped at her nose. "Let me guess. About your height and blonde, too."

"Yeah. A little green as well. Got his horse shot out from under him in the first round of gunfire from the bandits."

She faced him. Her eyes shone with unshed tears. He'd hurt her, and she hated him for not letting her know he was alive. That knowledge tore at him. If only he'd ignored Duncan and headed back to Texas—

God only knew how many more corpses would be on his ledger if he'd done so.

"I'm sorry," she whispered. "I know better than trying to recapture something from the past."

Shit. She's about to launch into the "let's be friends" speech. He just couldn't handle that. Not with everything else going on.

He ran his hands through his hair. "Why don't we get dressed, find Demon John and rustle up something to eat and drink? You're right. We can sleep on the train."

Dammit, he should have stuck with his original plan and walled up his heart when it came to Phillippa Mann.

The tension in Jorge's neck eased a bit when Siobhan broke out into a big, toothy grin.

"Thanks for letting us know," she said and thumbed the "End Call" icon on her phone. She leaned back in the passenger seat of their sedan.

"Alex and Phil are okay." He knew he was stating the obvious, but the last thing he wanted was to see the vampire and the demigoddess dead. Stanton was one of the few enforcers with real peace officer experience and the easiest to deal with in Augustine Coven. As for Phillippa Mann, she went out of her way to keep a low profile over the last seventy-five years she lived in Los Angeles, which was more than he could say about other supernaturals. Especially a certain zombie.

"Yeah, the Lima Coven's chief enforcer too," Siobhan confirmed. "They made it to the outskirts of Cuzco right at dawn this morning." Worry replaced the initial relief in her voice. "Tiffany said she'd fill us in on the rest when we get to the Augustine mansion."

"You're shitting me." He smacked the steering wheel. "This is the first date night we've had in over a year."

"It's not my fault your mother has issues about the baby."

"Only because she couldn't keep a diaper on a pup."

"If she wouldn't get the kids hyped up on a sugar high, she wouldn't have a problem with them shifting. Therefore, there would not be wolf diarrhea on her precious carpet. How many times do I have to tell her you can't give tres leche to baby werewolves?"

"Hey." He reached for her hand. "I don't want to fight. It's just that I can think of better ways to spend an evening with you."

The setting sun illuminated Siobhan's wan smile, and her hot palm wrapped around his. "If it helps, Tiffany is having Max pick up dinner for all of us from Anthony's."

Jorge snorted. "Buying us dinner is the least she could do for ruining our romantic evening." He checked his rearview mirror to change lanes and frowned. He eased his hand out of Siobhan's grip and placed it back on the steering wheel.

"What is it?" Siobhan twisted to look over her shoulder.

"A tan FJ Cruiser. It's been trailing me since I left the office."

"I see it. Five cars back." A low growl rumbled deep in her throat. "The man in the passenger seat looks familiar."

Adrenaline pulsed through Jorge's veins. "From where?"

She turned to face the front again. "Lunch. I met with a clean-up specialist to discuss the bid for renovating the apartments where Phil's assistant manager—" She blew out a deep breath. "The building was on the schedule for renovations next year, but Dad wanted to move it up after what happened. The guy following us was at the restaurant sitting four tables behind the contractor."

Jorge ran through scenarios in his mind. Given this whole mess started with the Incan god of death's weapon, the two men following them may not be Normal. The last thing he wanted was his people in the crossfire of a supernatural battle.

"Are you calling for back-up or shall I?" Siobhan asked.

A quick glance showed his wife's full-toothed grin. Anyone else would be pissing his pants at her feral expression. It turned him on. Always had.

He flashed her a matching smile. "Neither. Call Tiffany and tell her we're coming in hot. The vampires dragged us into this mess. They can damn well cover our asses."

Punching the accelerator, he wove between vehicles. Sure enough, the Cruiser raced after them.

Chapter 23

Tires screeched as Jorge whipped the sedan around the corner and down the quiet Brentwood street. The men following had given up on discretion. A second bullet shattered the rear window of the sedan.

"Slow down and let me out."

He shot a glance at his wife as they slid around the corner for the next street. "Are you crazy? These idiots want to get up close and personal. And I'm sure as hell not taking a chance that they're packing silver."

This is Augustine Enforcer Leona Alvarez. Keep going, Detective. The estate gates are open.

"We've got an escort," Siobhan said at the same time.

"Damn, I hate it when they do that telepathic thing." Despite his grumbling, relief flickered through him. Two shadows ran along the estate walls, matching the vehicles insane speed. He should have known the vamps wouldn't take a chance of destroying their alliance with the wolves by letting something happen to Siobhan.

The steering wheel jerked in his hands before he heard the actual shot that blew the left rear tire. In the side mirror's reflection, metal on pavement blasted a flurry of sparks in their wake, but he managed to keep the sedan on the road.

Do not stop, Detective, the female voice said inside his head.

"No, shit!" But the Cruiser was closing on them.

The ornate iron sphinxes came in sight. Jorge yanked the wheel hard and slid to a stop inside the walls. Both he and Siobhan scrambled out of their car. The smooth grip of his side arm comforted him as he drew the weapon and took cover.

Their pursuers screeched to a halt in front of the estate entrance. They must have sensed a trap because the driver slung the SUV into a J-turn.

And slammed into air with a horrendous crunch.

No, not air. The illusion shimmered for an instant, then dropped. Their fender was firmly embedded in a Hummer. And not one of the civilian H2s, but Augustine's personal fully-loaded military version.

More vehicles popped into existence. Under the security lights, he could see the resignation on their pursuers' faces.

"Are you two okay?"

Jorge stared at the empty spot next to him. "Bebe?"

"Yes." The witch dropped her illusion. Wild curls framed her round face. "Are you two okay?" she repeated. "No injuries?"

"We're both fine. Just pissed," Siobhan growled.

"Keep your hands were we can see them and get out of your vehicle." A thin wisp of a woman stepped from the shadows of the wall.

Miko Osaka's normally bright countenance was stern, unyielding. She may not look like much, but she could be just as dangerous as the supernaturals. Jorge rubbed his jaw. He'd learned that the hard way when he sparred with her at the gym.

The two in the Cruiser carefully climbed out and immediately collapsed to the pavement.

"No!" Bebe charged forward, but one of the vamps grabbed her.

He bent his dark head to her ear. "It's too late, Doctor. Arsenic."

"Oh, Goddess," she moaned. She turned away and buried her head in the vamp's chest.

Gorge rose in Jorge's throat. Whatever Bebe saw frightened her, and living with the vampire master of the western U.S., there wasn't a whole lot she hadn't seen.

He stalked over to the closest body, Miko matching his pace, but when he knelt to examine the man's effects, he almost felt relieved. On the man's collar, a coiled eight-legged lizard-snake superimposed over a star winked at him in gold.

"Jorge, where are your kids?" Miko's soft voice replaced the relief with terror.

Jorge calmed his mother over his cell phone while Siobhan relayed their problem and worries to her father on hers. When they both ended their calls at the same time, he noticed the perturbed expression on his wife's face.

"How soon can a pack member get over to Mama's?"

Pink flared in Siobhan's pale cheeks and she paused for a moment.

"John is sending someone, isn't he?" He stared at her. He couldn't imagine his father-in-law showing no concern over his grandchildren.

"Um, there's already a pack member there." The pink in her cheeks shifted to bright scarlet.

The implications sank in. Blood pounded in his temples. "He doesn't trust my mother."

"It's not a question of trust, honey. It's a question of protection."

"He doesn't think us poor Normals can take care of our own," he snapped. Deep down, he knew it wasn't Siobhan's fault. Sometimes though, his father-in-law's arrogance really made him want to hit something.

Or someone.

"No, he's worried that if someone tries to purge the Los Angeles supernaturals again, they won't ignore the pack. Or the fae."

Jorge snorted. "The fae have made their decision."

Siobhan shook her head. "Not exactly. Too many ears here, and I promised Dad I wouldn't say anything until he's ready." Her eyes pleaded with him to let it drop.

He sighed. She was right. The vamps and Bebe would have to concentrate to read Siobhan's mind. His would be easy pickings. But dammit, he'd definitely get the truth out of her when they got home. This political bullshit was for the birds.

Loud voices erupted from the kitchen. They exchanged looks and headed in that direction. As Siobhan hit the swinging door, a masculine voice bellowed, "You are supposed to be on maternity leave!"

Tiffany jabbed a fork in the direction of her husband. "I stayed inside the mansion like everyone told me. Ask Melissa." She pointed to the nymph huddled on a chair. "Why the hell am I getting bitched out?"

"Because you shouldn't even be here!"

"It's the safest fucking place in the city!"

"No, it isn't if the bad humans are coming here," Melissa said.

"You're not helping," Tiffany shot back.

Bebe Zachary lifted two fingers to her lips and blew a piercing whistle. "Enough! From all of you."

Siobhan slapped her hands over her ears, but at least, Tiffany and Max stopped arguing.

Melissa stood. "Thank you for your hospitality, Doctor Bebe, but I would just as soon stay in my own tree than remain here with all this negativity." She whirled and stomped out the back door.

Tiffany glared at Max. "Now see what you did."

Max didn't back down. "I did not—"

"Yes, you did." Miko poked her head above the refrigerator door and looked at Jorge and Siobhan. "Beer, soda or water."

"Soda," he and Siobhan answered at the same time.

The acting chief enforcer set two cans of cola on the island before them. She shoved two boxed dinners in their direction as well. "Tiffany, tell them about your news from Phil."

Tiffany spoke so fast that Jorge had to wave her to slow down a couple of times. Finally, his jaw dropped and he stared at her a few moments trying to collect his thoughts.

"Are you telling us they went traipsing down to Hell and back?"

Tiffany had taken the pause to cram a forkful of linguini alfredo into her mouth. She mumbled around the food. "Uku Pacha. There's more than one area for the dead in the universe, and in Incan lore, everyone goes Uku Pacha, not just the damned."

"Since when are you an expert, cuz?" Miko grinned.

"Been researching the last few days. Trying to find out more about Supay and tumis." Tiffany speared a shrimp. "Point being, the Incan god of the dead confirmed the story you got from that crazy Sunshine Believer asshole."

"Oh, Goddess." Bebe buried her face in her hands.

Everyone else around the kitchen island exchanged looks. Miko rested a hand on the witch's shoulder. "Doctor, if you know what's going on . . ."

"When Selene and her eclectic Lucien were trying to kill me—" She swallowed hard. "When Lucien died, his ghost didn't simply pass through the door between worlds. Something came and tore his soul apart. Devoured it." She shook her head. "Don't ask me what it was because I'd never seen anything like it. I've been doing my own research over the last two and a half years, but I haven't found a word.

"Then tonight, when those two Sunshine Believers committed suicide, the same thing happened."

"Scarlet teeth?" Siobhan whispered.

At Bebe's slow nod, Jorge's blood turned to ice. "What are you talking about?"

In the fifteen years he'd known Siobhan, he'd seen her furious, passionate and grieving. But he had never, ever seen her truly terrified. "The Sunshine Believers have sworn their souls to the Old Ones."

Chapter 24

Tiffany shifted her stare from Siobhan to Bebe and back. Her hands automatically covered her slight bulge, and Max wrapped an arm around her shoulders. The baby took a good solid kick at her palms. "So we're talking about the Apocalypse?" *God, please tell me I'm wrong.*

"Spill. Everything," Miko commanded.

Siobhan bristled, and for an instant, Tiffany feared she'd go wolfie on Miko.

Jorge laid a hand on his wife's arm. "You said something about the fae. Do they know anything about this?"

From the nasty look Siobhan gave her husband, Jorge was looking at an up-close and personal vasectomy.

Except the detective's expression looked entirely too somber, not his usual black humor or sarcasm. "I don't think this is the time for secrets, honey."

They stared at each other for a long minute, almost as if they were telepathic, before Siobhan nodded.

"You have to understand that the relationship of our pack and the Seelie go back to the old country. Unlike the other packs, our legends say we were wolf first. The original alpha fell in love with a human maiden. He bargained with the Seelie queen for the ability to become human in order to woo her."

"But there's always a catch when it comes to the fairies," Tiffany muttered.

Siobhan nodded sharply. "Yes, and the details are irrelevant. What matters is that Duke Millanthropas came to Dad shortly after your reception."

Muscles tightened under Tiffany's skin. That fairy bastard had manipulated a necromancer into launching a zombie attack that nearly killed her and the baby at the first farce of a wedding. She struggled to keep her hands on her abdomen and not reach for the silver knife tucked in her boot sheath. "And why didn't your father kill him?"

"There's a civil war brewing within the Seelie. Millanthropas believes Sam's creation heralds a return of the Old Ones. That they are the real danger, not Sam, but his queen refuses to listen."

A sound somewhere between laughter and disgust came from Max. "Do you blame her? My baby sister can be a one-woman demolition expert."

Bebe stomped over to another cupboard. "I need something stronger than tea." She pulled out a bottle of Jack Daniels and a tumbler.

Tiffany eyed the healthy portion of alcohol. "Think that's such a good idea, Doc?"

"Probably not." Bebe's weak smile didn't reach her eyes. "But if we're going to talk about fairies, the Old Ones and the end of the world, I want to be good and drunk while we do."

Tiffany took a swig from her bottle of water. Concern nibbled on her gut. Both Bebe and Miko acted shell-shocked by this turn of events. She'd been so busy rebelling over the last eight years, it never occurred to her that there was anything the older folks couldn't handle. Dammit, she would not go down without a fight.

She turned back to Siobhan. "What exactly did Millanthropas want from your dad?"

The werewolf sucked in a deep breath and released it. "When his coup succeeds, he wants Dad to act as mediator in negotiating a truce with Caesar."

"'When his coup succeeds'? Cocky little bastard, isn't he?" Tiffany sipped her water. Her gaze dropped to the unopened can of Coke next to Siobhan. Maybe she was just as bad in the addiction department as Bebe if she craved caffeine this much during her pregnancy.

Siobhan lifted the lid on her box and poked at her prime rib. "He's scared."

"I would be too if I were insane enough to take on the Seelie queen," Tiffany shot back.

"That's not what he's afraid of. When Dad asked Millanthropas what would happen if he failed, he said that death would be preferable to being consumed by an Old One."

Tiffany eyed Bebe. "You mean like our buddies in the street." She turned back to Siobhan and pushed her dish of shrimp alfredo away. "So what does this truce involve?"

"An alliance between all the supernaturals, including the demigods. He claims we're the only thing standing between the Old Ones and the annihilation of *all* the races, including the Normals."

Tiffany tapped her nails against the granite countertop. What she wouldn't give for some bubblegum right now. Anything to calm her nerves, but she chewed her last piece while pacing inside the living room and listening to all the action she missed in the driveway. "What about the Unseelie? Both queens have a price on Sam's head."

"He thinks that once the Winter Queen sees the portents, she will side with him."

"That's taking an awful fucking chance with all our lives. Anything else?" Tiffany could see the possibilities of this going wrong, but if Millanthropas was right . . .

Siobhan popped the tab of her can and took a huge gulp of cola before she spoke. "This is the part I don't get. Millanthropas was absolutely sure the Old Ones would break through the dimensional planes on the North American continent. The closest estimate he could give Dad was somewhere in the U.S. along the Pacific Coast."

Tiffany tilted her head. "That doesn't make sense. Why is Fake Jane heading south for a seal where the Old Ones originally broke through?"

"I don't know. The Rockies and the Andes lay along the same edge of the Pacific plate. Maybe Millanthropas got his coordinates reversed."

Tiffany's brow stretched her eyelid as it rose. "Do you really believe that?"

Siobhan exhaled sharply. "No."

"Probabilities. That's all precognition is. Calculating probabilities." Tiffany stood. "I need chocolate."

Miko popped open the freezer door. "Plain chocolate, chocolate almond, peanut butter chocolate, and cinnamon chocolate."

"I'll take door number four." Tiffany grabbed two spoons out of a drawer. Miko handed her the pint carton of cinnamon chocolate ice cream as she handed Miko a spoon.

She held up her own spoon and stared at it. Time was the key to the calculations. "Has Millanthropas looked into the future since Lizard Girl headed south with the tumi?"

"Not that I know of," Siobhan answered.

"So his fortune was only accurate as long as Supay's property stayed in California. Your dad needs to ask him for a new reading." Tiffany shoveled a large bite into her mouth. She swirled the creamy goodness around and swallowed. "Once Caesar's back in town, we'll inform him. Peace talks will have to be someplace neutral."

"Of course."

Miko glared at Siobhan and Tiffany in turn. "Aren't you two overstepping your titles?" Despite her annoyance, there was a hint of relief in her voice.

Tiffany held up her hands. Best not to step on any more toes than she had. "You got a better idea?"

The acting chief enforcer's lips pursed in a grimace more suited to her sister Mai. "No."

Another kick from the baby had Tiffany rubbing her stomach again. If Phil and Alex didn't get themselves killed by this servant of the Old Ones or whatever the hell Jane's imposter was, then everything would be just peachy.

A glance at the normally imperturbable Doctor Bebe Zachary swigging whiskey like it was Kool-Aid didn't reassure her.

Not one bit.

❖

Sunlight warming Alex's cheek jerked him out of the strange dream he had. The brief instant of panic subsided as the railway car he rode filtered into his consciousness. Outside, the sun hovered above the western mountains as the train climbed.

Francisco said the Huamán Coven had commissioned the observation car, with its bullet-proof glass and UV coating, for those members who kept to the old religion despite the conquistadors. He laughed and said it also came in handy for vampire tourists.

Heat caressed the other side of Alex's body. Once again, Phil curled up against his chest, sound asleep. She'd bound her hair in a braid, but a few curls escaped to tickle his neck. If he didn't know better, he would say she did this to tease him, except that wasn't her style.

No, she was far more direct, like straddling him while she was naked.

Damn idiotic conscience. He should have taken what she offered. It was better than nothing, wasn't it?

No, he didn't want to be someone's stress relief. Except . . .

He gazed at her upturned face. The fact that she had come after him all those years ago meant he was more than a one-night stand to her, didn't it? She'd buried poor Jamie, thinking it was him. She'd left her job as bouncer for Betsy Parker's brothel shortly afterward. He'd tasted her grief in the air as she related the story.

Yet decades later, after the molasses backfire, she had blatantly told him in no uncertain terms that he'd been nothing more than a stick to scratch her itch. So, which was the truth?

Her soft lips were parted, inviting. He could kiss her and find out.

He might also discover that the bullet-proof windows could not withstand a lightning bolt.

Really? Was he that cowardly to resort to stealing a kiss from a sleeping woman?

If she offered herself to him again, his answer would be a most definite "yes."

If she offered again, that was.

Phil blinked and looked up at him. Dark lashes framed blue-green eyes with recognizable need in their depths. As he watched, the irises shifted to purple.

He remembered that look all too well. "Good morning." He couldn't help grinning. She was so damn beautiful.

"Morning, cowboy." She wrapped her arm around his neck and kissed him.

Chapter 25

This dream was like every other dream Phillippa had concerning Alex Stanton. Bright sunshine turned his golden hair into a halo. His skin was warm again, not vampire cool. He was so close, so kissable. Dream Alex never told her "no."

Their lips met, and hers parted automatically. Inviting him in. Wanting, welcoming his invasion.

And as always in her dream, he responded with his old enthusiasm. Their tongues tasted and tested. He pulled her close and pressed her against his muscular chest. The kiss grew more passionate, and she knew how this would end.

Until a sharp edge pricked her tongue.

His teeth. No, not a tooth. A fang.

She jerked away from him. The sun nearly swallowed the neon blue glow of his eyes, but the elongated canines were unmistakable.

This wasn't her dream Alex.

A stream of curse words rushed through her brain, but the only one she could utter was "Shit."

She pulled away and buried her face in her hands. "Shitshitshitshitshit."

"I don't recall you complaining about my kissing last century." A hint of his old humor tinted his words.

"I'm sorry. I shouldn't—" She jumped to her feet. "I've gotta pee." She raced down the aisle, past Francisco conversing with the young Normal porter.

She slammed the bathroom door shut and locked it, then sank down on the toilet lid. How could she make such a fool of herself twice in one day?

Hell, she shouldn't have been sitting next to him to begin with, but they'd been discussing strategy with Francisco and Demon John.

She couldn't even blame him. Not once had he abused her pledge. Everything she'd done was by her own choice. She climbed to her feet and used the facilities, just in case he asked, so she wouldn't have to fight the stupid oath.

When she exited the bathroom, Demon John crouched in her old seat, whispering intently with Alex. As she approached, they both clammed up.

"What's the big discussion?" she said as she slid into the seat across from Alex. It seemed the safest option.

Alex opened his mouth, and nothing came out. What the Hades was wrong with him? He'd been acting weirder and weirder since her tantrum in Uku Pacha. Her gut said something happened to him down there, but he refused to discuss it any time she broached the subject.

"He asked about my service to my lord," Demon John interjected. Now that he spoke in a language she knew, he didn't seem quite so alien. Kind of like her cousins who had wings, fins or hooves.

She was even getting used to his smell. Hades, she wanted to hug him for bringing up a relatively safe subject so Alex didn't question her own odd behavior.

"He didn't create you?"

This was the first time the demon didn't seem quite as afraid of her. She was even getting used to the odd cough-chitter sound of his laughter. "No. If we choose to enter his service, this is what we become."

"As opposed to being a ghost?"

Demon John nodded.

Francisco nudged her shoulder, and she scooted over. He passed around bottles of a local brew before he sat next to her. "Did it hurt? The transformation?"

Demon John shrugged. "No." He took a swallow of beer. Liquid leaked from cracks in his lips, but he merely swiped it away with the back of his hand. "I can't tell you what it was like. It's hard to remember that far back."

"When my assistant was investigating the tumi, the tests said it was twenty thousand years old. Did Su—" She corrected herself at Demon John's wince. "Did your master create it that long ago?"

"Possibly. You must remember time moves different here than below or above. I remember when he forged it. It was long after I entered his service."

Alex's sharp intake of breath matched hers at the demon's admission. "Are you saying you're over twenty thousand years old?"

Again, Demon John shrugged. "Possibly. Does it really matter?"

"And you were human before you served your lord?" Excitement raced in Alex's tone. His curiosity was showing.

"Yes."

She could have sworn Demon John's orange eyes twinkled.

"But the Incan civilization only dates back to the 1300s."

Demon John cocked his head and looked at Francisco, who rattled something in Quechuan. "Ah." Demon John turned back to Alex. "Why do you believe no one lived here before the ones you call the Incans?"

"Well, of course, someone was living here before, but if your lord is . . ." Alex frowned as he pieced things together.

Phillippa tried not to laugh at his perplexed expression. "Do I need to spell it out for you?"

Alex shook his head. "I think I get it. He first appeared to us as Lucifer, which was the identity forced on him by the conquistadors. But we acknowledged who he was. His form changes depending on our perceptions or treatment of him?"

She shrugged. "Pretty much. Doesn't your treatment of a person depend on your perception of him or her? Back in Los Angeles, we view Tiffany as the baby Duncan rescued twenty years ago. And it causes problems."

He grinned. "Especially when Duncan gets into one of his overprotective kicks."

"Exactly." She waved a hand. "The Greeks didn't respect my father, but the Romans did. It had a big effect on his disposition."

Alex gave her an odd look. Something yanked deep inside her. This was the first time she'd spoken about her father in objective terms in a very long time. She realized she was just as guilty as the Greeks in her regard for him. Had that been the real source of their friction over the millennia? She didn't respect her father?

Alex turned back to Demon John. "So your lord has been worshipped in this region for thousands of years under different names?" His question brushed aside her twinge of guilt.

The demon nodded. "The names change, but Death is a constant in mortal lives."

The two vampires grew silent. She understood why. While their lifespans were increased by the V-virus, they could be killed.

Just like she could be.

The knowledge sombered their little group as the train chugged up the mountainside.

Something nagged in the back of Alex's mind as they waited in the rail car for sunset, and he desperately wished he could figure out what. There was a piece of the puzzle they were missing.

Moments before the train was to leave for Cuzco, Francisco deemed it safe to exit. A lone mournful whistle echoed against granite outcroppings as the engine began its descent. Alex tried to quell his unease. It was the first time in a century he felt isolated from any help.

They skirted the base camp for a group of Normals hiking the Incan Trail. No sense alarming the poor souls with their demon. Not to mention, they didn't need anyone questioning why they were doing something as insane as hiking the mountain track at night.

They followed the Lima enforcer when he headed up the path at a steady gait. The moon was two days past full, but it gave more than enough light for them to see.

"Do you think we can pick up the pace?" Phil grumbled.

Francisco chuckled. "While you and our demon friend may not be affected, Alexander and I need to be concerned about altitude sickness.

Granted, it may not be as bad for us as it would a Normal, but still, it can happen."

"We'll get there in time, Phil," Alex added.

She snorted, but otherwise said nothing.

It wasn't worth arguing with her. Alex dropped back to match Demon John. "Is there a particular reason the servants of the Others would use the Hitching Post of the Sun as the place for their sacrifice?"

The creature shrugged. "Defiling a sacred place in such a manner would weaken the deity in question. Disrupt his power. Why do you ask?"

"Something your lord said has been sticking in my head. Why attack a point where your enemy's the strongest? Why not go for the weakest point?"

Demon John frowned. "I do not understand."

"Supay said—" Demon John winced, and Alex blew out an exasperated breath. "Sorry, your lord said that there were portals that he and the other gods had sealed. Why not break through one of those points?"

Again, Demon John shrugged. "I am a lowly servant. You ask me to understand the motives of the gods themselves."

Alex grinned. "I'm talking about common sense. The tumi's the key to this whole mess. I think Lizard Girl's using the tool of the god who banished her masters for a reason. Where did your lord seal a portal? It couldn't have been the Hitching Post if that's the sun god's sacred spot."

Demon John stopped and stared at him with those disconcerting orange eyes. "You're asking me to remember my own death."

That wasn't the answer he was expecting from the demon. John turned and continued up the path.

Alex jogged to catch up with him. "Wait. I'm sorry. I didn't mean to upset you."

Demon John halted again, but didn't look at Alex. "I remember a time when Death was a woman."

"When you were still human?"

"Yes." The demon began walking again. Phil and Francisco had already rounded a bend in the path and were out of sight. "But that was long ago. When she was both Life and Death."

"Life and death," Alex murmured. "Was there only one god then?"

John chuckled. "You want to place everything into the context of your belief."

"No, I don't." When John looked at him in askance, Alex shook his head. "Honestly, I'm not. I'm trying to understand Lizard Girl. To stop her, I need to anticipate her next move. We've been one step behind this whole time."

He rested a hand on John's shoulder. It felt hot and powdery beneath his palm. "You're the only one here who has fought her or her kind before. I know it's difficult to talk about, and I don't mean any disrespect to you, but anything you can tell me might help."

The demon remained silent, and Alex dropped his hand. Disappointment tasted like ash, but he couldn't blame the poor soul. He didn't like thinking about his Turn, the reason for it, or the immediate consequences either. Best to keep focused on the future.

They walked another quarter of a mile before John said, "Nazca."

"I beg your pardon?"

"Where I died fighting the Old One at my lord's side. It was Nazca."

Chapter 26

Alex was afraid to breathe. He waited for John to add to his story, but they continued climbing the trail for another hundred yards before the demon spoke again.

"I was a hunter for our tribe back then. One day, my sister and I tracked a herd of goats. We came across a spot where the land was bare. The soil was an odd color, almost silver. And it moved.

"I warned my sister not to touch it, but she refused to listen. She dug into the bare patch, and found a baby." John pursed his lips, or tried to. "The child was barely alive, wrapped in a burial skin. I thought we were better off killing it. Back then, there were many other species that hunted humans, some through trickery. But my sister refused."

"You thought he was a changeling?"

Again, John gave him a puzzled look. "You mean a shapeshifter?"

"Could be." Alex grinned. "But according to my people's stories, a changeling was a non-human child exchanged for a human baby."

John grunted. "Yes, we had similar stories. When we returned, our shaman had no idea what to make of the child. He performed tests to determine if the baby was as you said, a changeling. To all appearances, he was an abandoned human baby. My sister took him to raise as her own." A rough bark of laughter erupted from the demon. "Oh, that boy could eat!"

Alex smiled. "Most kids can."

John held up a hand. "Not like this one. He was hunting with me by the time he reached five summers. He could take five bucks himself by ten summers. Our people prospered, or so we thought." The demon's good humor vanished.

"The ground shakes started during the boy's twelfth summer. He scaled the Mother Mountain for his rite of manhood. When he came back, he said the Goddess commanded him to go to the southern desert."

"You mean the Nazca Plain?"

John paused on the trail and bowed his head for a moment. "Yes, my sister and I accompanied him on his journey. He was, after all, family, but something was terribly wrong with my nephew. After quieting for years, his hunger was back. It was a terrible thing to behold. Nothing could ease it, no matter how much the three of us hunted. He soon became a walking skeleton."

Alex waited for the demon to compose himself. After a moment, they continued their hike.

"We reached the desert. The plain smoked and rumbled as if Mamapacha herself was giving birth to a volcano. The thing that broke through the soil—" John shook his head and sucked in a deep breath of frigid air. Mist wreathed his head as he exhaled. "There are no words even in the language of Uku Pacha to describe it. All I can tell you is that the portion I saw was the size of a small mountain, and I could sense there was more of it behind the dust and fog and light.

"When he beheld the monster, my nephew's skin turned as black as obsidian. His eyes gleamed red, and he lunged for the abomination."

They walked another mile. Alex cleared his throat. "Wh-what happened?"

"My sister died from the strange air in the space of a heartbeat. I tried to fight, but to the monster, my spear might as well have been a blade of grass. Something pierced my chest. I couldn't tell you if it was a talon or a tooth."

John blew out another deep breath. "When I awoke, my sister and I were in Uku Pacha. And my nephew was a god."

"Were you like—" Alex waved a hand toward John's gray decaying pelt. "Like this?"

John shook his head. "We were spirits as you might expect. Our lord felt so guilty over our deaths he tried to restore us to life, but this was the best he could do." A soft chuckle rumbled from his chest. "Death cannot even cheat himself."

Silence reigned as they continued their climb to Machu Picchu. Alex mulled over the demon's story. Strength, speed and an insatiable appetite. Supay's story sounded terribly like what Tiffany's sister-in-law Sam was going through, and he didn't like that implication. Not one bit.

Phillippa slid her backpack off her shoulders and stretched. They had made good time, reaching the ruins a couple of hours before dawn. The guards hadn't even seen them. Moonlight created sharp shadows as they passed through the dead city.

Francisco crossed the square. Close to a set of terraces that rippled down the other side of the mountain sat two round stones layered like wedding cake. A third, cylindrical stone topped them. The vampire circled the object. "The only recent scents are Normals."

"I will scout around," Demon John said, and he bounded off through the ancient stones.

She didn't trust the monkey demon. Maybe it was old habits.

"You need to lighten up," Alex murmured as she stared in the direction the demon had disappeared.

"Yeah, I noticed you two getting chummy on the trail." She retrieved her water and took a healthy swallow.

"Knowledge is power."

She expected a teasing grin with those words, but the vampire looked far too somber. "What did he say that's got you all depressed?"

His scowl would have been more fitting on Duncan's face after one of Tiffany's escapades in high school. It didn't work on Alex at all. "Supay's childhood sounds an awful lot like—"

Stones ground together, the noise so slight she would have thought she imagined it if the two men hadn't also frozen and cocked their heads toward the direction of the sound.

The same direction in which Demon John had bounded.

A second later, orange eyes gleamed in the darkness of an alley, and the monkey demon shuffled into the square.

Only to have Alex unload three shots into the demon's head. The bullets that Supay had given them worked. John collapsed into a heap. His left foot twitched a couple of times before it stilled.

She whirled to face the enforcer. "What the fuck is wrong with you?"

"That wasn't John." Alex's expression was grim. He scanned the area. Francisco pulled his own weapon and sniffed the air.

"What do you mean it's not—"

Alex held up his left hand. As pissed as she was about his non-explanation, she remained silent, and not because of the compulsion of her oath. Alex wasn't the shoot-first type.

Do you smell it, my friends?

Alex nodded at Francisco's question. An instant later, Phillippa picked it up as well. She pulled her Glock from her waistband. Under the rot and mildew of an Uku Pacha demon lay the faintest hint of the scent she'd detected at Jane's apartment.

The demon's body started to jerk. Gray flesh sloughed off to reveal blue and red scales under the moonlight. Whatever had been disguised as John rose and shook itself. Dust and hair flew in all directions.

"Interesting." The creature wiped at the black oily liquid on its forehead. It resembled a gecko with a severe orthodontic problem. Just like Alex's description of the thing that had been hiding in Jane's form.

It flung the fluid it had wiped off at the Hitching Post of the Sun. The rocks sizzled as if he'd dumped a flask of acid on them. Its lips stretched, showing row upon row of razor-sharp teeth. "I believe you forgot to add your blood to your little projectiles." Its whip-thin tail jabbed in the vampire's direction to emphasize its point.

"Where's John?" Alex ground out.

The lizard brushed at the dust settling on his hide. "Digesting." It sucked on its teeth for emphasis.

Phillippa took a step forward. She didn't like or trust the monkey demon, but no one should die as some monster's snack. The flicker of anticipation in the lizard thing's flat black eyes made her pause. Fake Jane had indicated she used Alex to lure her to that isolated road where Isabella died. They needed to discover the imposter's plan. Losing her temper guaranteed she and the vampires would die.

She kept her weapon focused on the lizard's head. "Where's your partner?"

"And Marcus Giovanni," Alex added.

"Why should I give them to you?" The lizard thing sounded far too smug.

They're close by. Leave it to Stanton to state the obvious.

Phillippa matched the creature's grin. "So we don't tell Supay what you did to his uncle."

The lizard thing's grin faltered. She felt Alex's jolt of surprise, but she didn't dare break eye contact with Fake Jane's partner. *Did you really think I wouldn't keep an eye, or an ear, on Supay's minion?*

Forgive me. Sarcasm ran thick in Alex's thought.

"So do we have a deal?" Phillippa said.

The horrid, wide smile spread across the lizard thing's face once more. "You can have my sister if you can catch her."

A high, thin whistle sliced the frigid air. Phillippa was jerked backward before she realized something had wrapped itself around her neck. Her lungs screamed for air. She caught a glimpse of yellow and green as she clawed at the tentacle strangling her.

Not tentacle. Tail.

The bitch who killed Jane lifted Phillippa into the air by her neck. Obsidian eyes glittered under the waning moon. "Looking for me, boss?"

Chapter 27

Alex raised his gun, but Lizard Girl swung Phil between them.

"Drop your weapon or I snap her head off."

A bluff. She'd obviously forgotten how much she had divulged when she and Marcus had kidnapped him. He gave her a mocking grin. "Go ahead. The whore deserves it."

He pivoted to face Francisco and swung to his left to keep both her and the red and blue bastard in sight. The Lima enforcer backpedaled to do the same. Marcus and his cronies had to be nearby as well. From this position, the two of them could watch each other's back.

From the slow swing of her head, Lizard Girl realized her predicament, but she didn't release Phil. The Amazon's struggles grew weaker by the second.

"You have nowhere to run, vampire." Somehow, Lizard Girl managed a sibilant hissing sound among those hard English consonants.

"Seriously? That's the best line you can come up with?" he mocked. "Any Bond villain can do better than that."

Phil's feet stopped kicking and her hands dropped from the tail wrapped around her throat. *Dammit, woman. You were underwater longer than this in Uku Pacha. Hold on.*

Lizard Girl released her hold, and Phil dropped bonelessly to the ground. Black, soulless eyes met his. "I owe you."

Her tail lashed out, but he was out of range. Still, the movement made him jump back.

A rhinoceros plowed into him from behind. Not a rhino from the fists pummeling him. He twisted and swung. The butt of his Glock connected with Marcus Giovanni's temple.

The respite was short-lived. More vampires poured down the sides of the buildings surrounding the plaza. Even worse, some of Supay's demons were scattered among Marcus's followers.

Why the hell hadn't they been able to smell the vamps and demons? Alex could understand not detecting the lizards after Fake Jane's performance in Los Angeles.

Giovanni hit him again. He thrashed and struggled in his attempt to get the traitor off him, but two vamps piled on top. One of them slammed his wrist against the paving stone, and his bones cracked. "Francisco, run!"

Time seemed to drag. The Lima enforcer eyed Lizard Girl. Alex could see him analyzing the situation. Phil still lay unconscious at the bitch's feet. He couldn't shoot at the rogue vampires without hitting Alex in the process.

Francisco spun toward the red and blue lizard who had tried to replace Demon John. "In Lord Supay's name!" He pulled the trigger. The muzzle flashed.

White filled Alex's vision.

Phillippa woke to a low throb, as if the planet itself was screaming. Rocks rained down, and she wrapped her arms over her head. Agony pulsed in her throat, but she was breathing. *Thank Gaea for small favors.*

When the shower of stones stopped pummeling her, she felt around her, but in the blinding cloud of dust, she couldn't find her gun, much less Lizard Girl. *What the Hades happened while I was unconscious?*

She heard a shout to her left. *Francisco?*

Run, Phillippa! A man's scream followed the warning.

"Don't leave jussst yet, bossss." Lizard Girl's voice came from her right.

Phillippa reached out mentally for Alex, but she met a wall of pain. She'd never run from a fight, but if both vampires were down, she was badly outmatched.

The memory of poor Jane chopped into pieces and stuffed into her refrigerator flared. No, this was definitely not a fight she'd avoid. Death would be worth it as long as Lizard Girl went down with her.

Her fingers curled around a decent-sized rock, and she climbed to a crouch. "Now, why would I leave? We were just getting started." Her voice croaked and wheezed.

An odd hissing chuckle came in reply. She focused on the sound and launched her missile. Another rock was in her hand before the dull *thunk* and a muffled cry of rage filled the dust-laden plaza.

"C'mon, sweetheart," she mocked. "You can't handle a little love tap? We have so much more dancing to do."

Lizard Girl said something in her own language. The sibilant syllables literally made Phillippa's stomach rebel, but she locked onto the noise and threw the second rock.

Another curse, this time a familiar voice in Italian.

She grinned as her hand wrapped around another chunk of dusty granite. "Maybe you should get a better class of henchmen."

"Maybe you should stop throwing rocks like a child if you wish to keep your lover alive."

Phillippa arrested the swing of her arm. Did Lizard Girl really have Alex? The only thing she could feel from the cowboy was agony.

She waited.

Lizard Girl said nothing, but Phillippa heard the scrape of boots on stone. Interspersed with the vampires' sandalwood, there was the distinctive rot and mold odor of Supay's minions. Had Demon John sent word to his master before Lizard Girl's partner ate him?

Gradually, moonlight filtered through the settling dust. The tableau didn't reassure her. A group of demons and vampires held Francisco. A flap of his scalp partially covered one eye and blood oozed from myriad cuts. One of his legs was dislocated at the hip.

Alex was in far worse shape. Bruises covered his face, one hand hung at an unnatural angle, and his sternum caved inward. From the wet rasp of his breathing and the blood leaking from his mouth, he had severe internal injuries. Lizard Girl's tail encircling his waist was the only thing keeping him on his feet. Her talons rested against his neck. A quick slice would take off his head.

Marcus Giovanni and more vampires stood behind Alex. From the well-placed swelling and scrapes around their jaws and eyes, the cowboy had dished out plenty of damage before they took him down.

Between each group, a crater smoked right about where Lizard Girl's partner had stood. What the Hades had Francisco and Alex done?

A chill went down her spine. Blood or invoking Supay's name, Demon John had said. While suicide wasn't her first choice and the little bag of bullets in her backpack would obliterate the ancient city, it may be their only chance to stop Lizard Girl.

She glanced around wildly. Where was her backpack? She had taken it off to stretch when she first entered the plaza.

"Don't think about it, darling Phillippa, or I kill lover boy here."

Giving up her life was one thing. Francisco and Alex were another. The men were involved in this mess because of her. Because she hadn't paid closer attention to the items in her store. Because she was so anxious to get away from Alex, two innocent women had been murdered.

Or one not-so-innocent woman. Everything clicked in her head.

A sad, ironic laugh erupted from her abused throat. "You were using the Sunshine Believers to obtain the tumi, but Dennis and Beatrice Madison had a change of heart."

Lizard Girl snarled. "I don't know how but they managed to hide it from me."

Despite the dire situation and his obvious pain, Alex's eyes twinkled, and Phillippa couldn't stop her own grin. Kiki had put a major crimp in everybody's campaign for the tumi. Her presence as a heavenly companion had masked the weapon while it was at the Madisons' house.

"But why take the tumi to the U.S. if you were going to sacrifice me down here?"

Lizard Girl laughed. Her cackle would put the late Margaret Hamilton to shame. "Who said anything about sacrificing *you*?"

Some perversity made Phillippa ask the next question. "Then what do you need me for?"

"You'll find out soon enough." Lizard Girl glanced at Marcus. "Chain her."

"What makes you think I'm going to stand still for that," Phillippa spat. Dammit, where was her backpack? There was too much debris from the vampires blowing up the other lizard.

"Because you don't want me to slice off your precious vampire's head. Any fool can see you love him." Lizard Girl turned to Alex and smiled. "Well, maybe not every fool."

Phillippa's heart ached. This wasn't the time and place for this conversation. She watched his blue eyes glow neon. Whether he was furious with her or Lizard Girl she couldn't tell.

"Don't do it, Phil," he said from between clenched teeth.

He was right. Lizard Girl would kill him out of spite once Phillippa was securely manacled.

"Let Alex and Francisco go, and I'll come quietly."

"Then I have no guarantee of your good behavior, do I?"

Despite her best efforts, anger snuck into her soul. "You have my word."

"On the River Styx?"

Phillippa stared at Alex.

"I command you not to obey Lizard Girl," Alex said. "Avenge Jane."

For an agonizing moment, no one breathed.

Lizard Girl's jaw dropped.

Phillippa could feel a feral grin split her own face. Apparently, it never occurred to the Old Ones' servant that she'd swear an oath to a vampire.

The second of shocked disbelief shattered, and everyone jumped into motion. Lizard Girl tossed Alex to Marcus. Her tail shot toward Phillippa's neck.

This time she was ready. Her forearm intercepted the whip-like appendage. Using momentum, she slung the lizard head-first into the Hitching Post of the Sun. The sacred rocks rang from the impact, and Lizard Girl screamed.

Phillippa smashed a jagged shard of granite into the section of tail still wrapped around her arm. Black oily ichor leaked onto her jacket before the tail section dropped to the flagstones, and the leather started smoking. She shed the garment and flung it in the face of a charging monkey demon.

A strangled cry came from the demon before it exploded into flames. Phillippa scooped up the still-wriggling tail tip, careful to avoid Lizard Girl's blood, and threw it at another approaching demon. Same results, but now she was down to fists, feet and rocks.

A brief glimpse showed Alex and Francisco taking advantage of her distraction, but Alex was too badly injured to do much damage.

Green and yellow scales landed between her and the cowboy. Flesh and teeth on one side of Lizard Girl's head had literally melted in their contact with the Hitching Post.

"I may not be able to kill you just yet, but I'll relish it when I do," she hissed.

Phillippa didn't bother to reply. It still hurt to talk. Besides, she'd always let her skills speak for her. A jumping back-spin kick drove the lizard toward the Hitching Post. The monster's talons dug into the flagstones to stop her momentum. Phillippa caught a flash of re-evaluation in Lizard Girl's eyes.

Two accurately aimed stones took care of two more of the rebellious demons. The rest hung back, and Marcus's vampires weren't stupid enough to take her on after the stories from Tiffany's wedding last spring.

Electricity crackled along her fingertips, but Lizard Girl was already moving again. Phillippa might be able to get in one shot, maybe two before they were back to hand-to-hand.

I hope Inti doesn't take this the wrong way. A running leap carried her to the top cylindrical rock of the Hitching Post. Even through the soles of her boots, she could feel the power in the sacred rocks. She pulled on it, adding it to her own.

She twisted to face the pursuing Lizard Girl. Talons screeched as they dug furrows in the granite flagstones. For the first time, the monster showed real fear.

The hum of electricity reached a crescendo in Phillippa's head. She raised her hands and released the bolt.

Machu Picchu lit up with the discharge. The subsequent crack of thunder deafened her. Displaced air blew her off the Hitching Post. She smacked into a wall before crashing to the flagstones.

Head still ringing, Phillippa climbed to her hands and knees. If she survived this insanity, she would have to make a huge donation to the World Heritage Foundation for the destruction she caused the historical site.

The rotten meat smell of dead vampires and smoke from their corpses filled the night air. Her own panting created a cloud of steam. Where in Hades was Lizard Girl? *Please, oh, please let her be dead.*

Sharp hooves caught her on the shoulder. With nothing but a long-sleeved silk t-shirt to protect her, skin and muscle parted beneath the blow. She gasped and clutched the injury as she dodged the next strike.

"Whore!" Brilliant orange eyes glared at her from a decaying llama's face. "You've ruined everything! Now I'm trapped in Uku Pacha forever."

Phillippa darted left. "What the Hades is this? Monster-pick-on-Amazon week?"

"You should have stayed in your own land!" The demon llama lashed out and took a chunk out of the wall where Phillippa's head had just been.

"Let me get my friends, and I'll be happy to depart your lovely country." Not that she would before exacting her revenge.

"And leave me with what? To be tortured for the rest of eternity by the child I was foolish enough to raise?" The llama danced to the right and cut her off.

Phillippa's heart sank. Demon John's sister stole the tumi from Uku Pacha. "How could you do this to someone you regarded as a son? How could you kill your own brother?"

The llama's lips peeled back to display wide, jagged teeth. "Look what they did to me!"

Phillippa wasn't fast enough to avoid the furious demon. Hooves caught her in the temple and jaw. Her head snapped back, and blackness claimed her.

<h1 style="text-align:center">Chapter 28</h1>

Alex couldn't get enough air to scream out a warning to Phil. All he could do was watch helplessly as the Amazon went down. Considering the claws of the monkey demons could cut through steel, his imagination filled in what those nasty hooves would do to someone's skull. The only saving grace was that Lizard Girl wanted Phil alive.

A kick from Marcus broke the last two intact ribs in Alex's right side and drove him to the ground. It was Mallory Labs all over again. Outgunned and outnumbered, and he couldn't do a damn thing to stop any of it.

Except this time, he'd dragged Phil down with him.

There has to be a way out of this. Think! But thinking was getting harder to do through the waves of dizziness. Not enough oxygen getting to the brain.

Green and yellow coated his blurry vision. Lizard Girl crouched over him. "You cut me, vampire."

He forced himself to focus on her. If only he had something to trade for Phil's life . . .

Lizard Girl's tongue flicked out, up and over one of her solid black eyeballs. "As much as I desire to return the favor, I do not have the time."

She looked up at Marcus. "Stake them on one of the eastern terraces." Her piranha smile widened as she regarded Alex again. "Do it in such a way that my darling cutie here watches his companion burn first."

Pain intruded into Phillippa's cocoon, prodding and kicking her to wakefulness. It was accompanied by heat and thirst. She opened her eyes.

Or thought she did. Not even Uku Pacha had been this utterly black.

She experimented, closing and opening them a few times. Nothing. Had that last blow to the head destroyed her vision?

Her head. Someone was stroking her hair. The last time someone had done so she had been a girl. A centaur had tried to kidnap her, but she'd fought him off. The price had been a broken wrist. Hippolyta had set the arm, then sang to her and stroked her hair to help her sleep.

Where in Hades's name was she? And who was touching her?

The scent was masculine, but not Alex's evergreen and sandalwood. No sandalwood at all, so it couldn't be Francisco either. Or Marcus and his rebels. No rot and mold so it couldn't be . . .

Her heart lurched. Demon John had been eaten by Lizard Girl's partner. She had an ugly feeling the red and blue monster hadn't just been talking about the demon's body.

She remained still and concentrated. Clean mountain air and steel. Sweat and leather. And something familiar from her childhood.

The hand stilled and fell away from her. A soft clink of links. Chains.

"How's your head?" A voice she'd never thought she'd hear again. Not after the three thousand-plus years since their last fight.

"Father?"

Alex twisted his left side, trying to find some purchase to pull free. No luck. The titanium posts were too long, sunk deep into the rich terrace soil and the bedrock beneath. From the hint of ozone the chains exuded, spells reinforced the links and manacles.

On top of being tied down on one of the lowest terraces, he was having more and more trouble breathing. The virus was barely keeping him alive with all of his injuries.

And he was so damn thirsty.

Francisco wasn't in any better shape. The one thing Marcus did right was staking them out of each other's reach.

They were running out of time. Venus had crossed the horizon, a silvery dot above the mountaintops, and the sky slowly brightened.

But not slowly enough.

Francisco blew out a wet breath. Blood bubbled from his lips and trickled down the side of his face. "Well, my friend, it has been fun, but I believe it's time for the next stage of our adventure."

"We can't give up." The words were pathetically futile in his own ears. He'd survived Selene and Mallory's torture chamber for Chrissakes!

Alex grunted and strained at the pole holding down his left ankle. The planet clicked, a sub-audible sound-feel every vampire recognized. Their time had run out. A thin slice of red popped above the eastern ridge.

The shadows withdrew from Francisco as deadly ultra-violet radiation flooded the land. Alex watched the Lima enforcer's skin turn a darker brown and gradually to black. The tiny wisps of smoke came next.

Francisco whispered the Twenty-Third Psalm. The first lick of flame at his collar heralded his first scream. Worse, a scent reminiscent of frying bacon flavored the air.

Alex thrashed against his fetters. Blood slicked his arms and hands. The skin on his ankles tore, but he couldn't free himself much less get the other vampire out of the patch of sunlight.

The same patch that crept toward him.

Anger overrode the fear just as it had when those bandits had shot him over a century ago. But this time, Duncan wasn't going to fall out of a wagon as some *deus ex machina* to save his ass.

The titanium pole warmed under the sun's rays. The fingers on his left hand turned brown. Underneath, his blood sizzled. Pain shot through him, and he renewed his efforts to escape.

A thin wail came from Francisco now. Ash flaked from his cheeks and forehead, temporarily displaying gleaming white bone before that too darkened.

The frayed, torn edges of Alex's shirt started smoking as the skin at his wrist literally caught fire. It wasn't the agony that was the worst part.

Failing Phillippa again tore at him. For all her confidence, she was in deep trouble because he couldn't get past his own desire. He wanted her with him down here in Peru. He could have just as easily ordered her to remain in Los Angeles.

Now, they were both going to die because he couldn't let go of her.

Alex.

It hurt to turn his head. He could feel the skin on his neck crack and ooze. Francisco was silent now, but something sat next to the body. A blurred image he couldn't quite make out.

Help is coming. Hold on a few moments longer.

The voice sounded like Francisco's, but the other vampire was dead. Alex nearly choked on the blood running down the back of his throat when he realized the thing he was looking at was Francisco's ghost.

Hands, or possibly paws, burst from the thick terrace sod, surrounding Francisco's body. They latched onto the liquefying corpse, and it disappeared into the earth.

Here we go! Francisco's ghost sounded gleeful as it grasped another hand, this one red with black glyphs etched into the skin. A very familiar hand.

More brown hands erupted around Alex. He kicked and screamed obscenities but they grabbed him just as they had Francisco. Dirt covered his face as he felt them pull him downward.

I'm not dead! But whatever had ahold of him ignored his telepathic shouts. Out of the darkness, a red face appeared. One framed with yellow horns, and its eyes were solid black.

"As I told you before, Alexander Socrates Stanton, I do my own soul collecting."

Chapter 29

They strapped Alex down on one of the examination tables again. No clothes. He was nothing but an animal to them, so he fought them like an animal. It was almost worth the scent of their terror when he tried to bite them.

One of Mallory's so-called doctors, the short one with the Adolf mustache, had aimed a UV lamp at his chest. The asshole turned it off as soon as his skin blackened and split, then recorded the time it took for the virus to knit his flesh back together.

And they did it repeatedly, all over his body. Then came the day they deliberately fried his balls off.

The guard thought he'd tasered Alex into unconsciousness. It was the only other time since his Turn he drank human blood, but he didn't regret this incident, not deep down in the darkest places of his heart, any more than he had regretted drinking from the bandits who killed his fellow Rangers. He'd been so damn thirsty. He almost made it out of Selene's chamber of horrors that day. Got as far as the elevator before she caught him.

She dragged him into another cell. Tiny, delicate Anne was in there. Marcus Giovanni held a sword at her throat. Alex stared at her as she mouthed, "Don't do it."

He hadn't, and she had suffered for it. They both did, and he still didn't understand why she forgave him.

If it had been Phil, he would have done whatever Selene wanted.

He blinked. Sickly green light filled his vision. "Kane must've blown another transformer." His mouth didn't work right, but what could he expect? They never fed him properly.

He was so fucking *thirsty*.

"Good to see you awake, *mi amigo*. But who is this Kane you speak of."

A familiar voice. Alex tried to concentrate but his chest ached and his skin . . .

It no longer burned, but he had the sensation of dried mud cracking along his flesh. *This is very, very bad.*

Alex blinked again. More recent memories settled into place. The tumi. Phil's client and assistant manager murdered. They were in Peru.

No, he was under Peru.

His vision was clouded thanks to the UV-induced cataracts, but he could recognize outlines. One of Supay's monkey demons squatted beside him. The orange eyes cast a soft light in the dimness. It was the voice though that made gooseflesh attempt to crawl along his burned and peeling skin.

"Francisco?"

The demon nodded once.

Shit. Shitshitshit. "No. God, no." His chest ached and not from the beating Fake Jane had given him. Phil, a prisoner. Marcus, crazy enough to help raise something even worse than Ole' Scratch himself. And now . . .

"We're dead?"

"I am." The demon with Francisco's voice grinned. The twisted, rotting teeth didn't look any better with cataracts.

"Francisco." So much pain and regret lay behind that one word.

"Do not mourn. Alexander," the demon said, switching from English to Spanish. "I made my choice of my own free will."

"You call this—" Alex raised a burnt hand in Francisco's direction. "—a choice?"

Rotten teeth parted and chittering laughter issued from the demon's throat. "Yes, I do. There was a moment when the three of us were separated in Uku Pacha. Supay appeared to me. He said my time on earth was rapidly coming to a close."

The demon glanced away before the orange gaze returned to Alex. "He said I could go to the Christian heaven when I died, and our mission would fail. Or I could swear allegiance to him, and he would make sure

I could continue with you." Another twisted grin lit Francisco's altered face. "But I was not the only one who made a deal with our lord of death."

"I didn't—"

"Alexander, you offered to serve him in his court." Francisco's words were gentle, but the truth in them was harsh. "Phillippa and I were there when you offered to find his tumi and destroy Jane."

"I was just trying to keep us alive, and it was for nothing." The bitter words were garbled because he could feel his tongue literally coming apart.

"Blood is coming." Demon Francisco reached for Alex's shoulder, but hesitated.

He didn't blame Francisco. His body was barely hanging together. The funny thing was he didn't feel the pain anymore. What would happen when he died? Had he inadvertently sold his soul to Supay by offering to help the god?

Phil. He closed his eyes. She'd blame herself even though there wasn't a damn thing either of them could have done differently.

No, that wasn't true. He could have used her oath on the River Styx and forced her to remain behind. But she really would have hated him forever, so he'd done the chickenshit thing and let her come to Peru with him.

For all he knew, she was already dead. His heart squeezed at that thought.

"No, she is not dead yet."

He opened his eyes at the single voice speaking in a multitude of languages at the same time. A woman stood next to the pallet on which he lay. An impossibly beautiful Native American woman. Unlike Phil, the white light emanating from her was almost blinding.

Her black hair shimmered in the mix of her white and Francisco's orange light as she sank down to sit next to him. She wore an Incan dress in colors he couldn't begin to name. Animals and people seemed to dance across the handspun fabric. Brilliant green eyes regarded him. "What are you willing to sacrifice to save her, Alexander Socrates Stanton?"

"Everything. I love her."

She seemed to understand his garbled words. "To you Easterners, only death resides in the dark, but here life begins as well. Are you willing to be reborn?"

"What—" He tried to clear his throat, but it didn't help. He could feel the tissues breaking down. "What will I become?"

The woman smiled. "You will still be yourself. Simply more."

"Better. Faster. Stronger."

From her frown, she obviously didn't get his pop culture joke. "Of course."

He sighed. The death rattle was all too familiar. That exhale was the same one he made right before Duncan offered to Turn him all those years ago. Whatever the price, whatever he'd become, it would be worth it if Phil lived. "Do it."

She picked him up as easily as an infant and settled him on her lap. He was in no condition to fight her even if he wanted to. A slender arm held his head to her throat. "Drink."

Horror engulfed him. "No!" He struggled to get away from her, but his efforts were pathetic at best. Inconsequential.

"You cannot harm me, Alexander Socrates Stanton."

"I won't drink from a human." Her scent tormented him. Fresh corn tortillas dripping with butter and honey.

He was so damn *thirsty*.

He'd resisted drinking from Sam when Mallory threw her in the pit with him. Back when she was Normal and she smelled like Mama's apple pie. He'd resisted then, but he'd been just starving, not on the edge of death. And this woman . . . no, this goddess smelled so much better than Sam had.

His canines automatically elongated at the nearness of fresh blood. *God, help me.* Revenge on those who'd wronged him was one thing, but drinking from an innocent . . .

The woman's laughter sounded so beautiful, so ethereal, he would have cried if he were able. "Can't you tell I'm not human? Supay said he gave you the gift of Sight."

"Who are you?"

"You may call me 'Mother.'"

Mother. Mama. Mamapacha. Mother Earth.

"Please forgive me," he whispered.

More of her laughter filled the little cavern. "There is nothing to forgive, child. What I offer, I offer freely."

The hunger overwhelmed him. Canines sliced into delicate flesh. A cornucopia of tastes exploded in his mouth. Icy stream water. Mellow passionfruit. Smoky mountain trout. Fresh ground corn. Honey. Sweet grass. Roasted potatoes.

The rush was incredible. With each swallow, energy pulsed through him. The agony of his burns, broken bones and internal injuries roared back to life.

It hurt. It hurt too much to endure.

He tried to pull away, but she cradled his head, holding it close. "Not yet, my son," she whispered. Her hot breath tortured his delicate, new skin. "Remember your love."

Phil. Out there. Above. Somewhere. Alone. At the mercy of Lizard Girl. A blood sacrifice to break the seal. Nazca. Where Supay fought the Old Ones.

The blaze inside him burned hotter than the interior of a star. *Phil.* Surviving was the only way to get back to her. And so he drank and swallowed and suffered.

"Why can't I see you?" Phillippa murmured. Ares wasn't surrounded by his usual nimbus. All of the gods she'd ever met had a glow about them. In fact, Sam was the only non-deity she'd ever known who could see Phillippa's own faint shine as a demigoddess.

"Sorcery." He grunted, and chains rattled. "The Chaos servant's spell pulls my power to fuel my bonds."

"How—" She hesitated.

"A trap."

Was that embarrassment she detected in his voice? Not that she blamed him. She'd practically been caught with her pants down around her ankles by Lizard Girl. The realization of how he had been caught made her chuckle.

"What's so funny?" Ares growled.

"Don't sweat it, Father. She fooled me, too." Phillippa pushed herself into a sitting position. The wave of nausea would have made her vomit if she'd had anything in her stomach. "How long have I been out?"

"If my estimate is correct, a third of a day since they locked you in here with me."

Eight hours. Gaea only knew where they could have taken her. Or they still could be near Machu Picchu. She couldn't detect anything outside of this damn prison.

"Well, she can't teleport, or she would have done so before now. Have we moved since I arrived?"

"Yes." Another grunt from Ares. "Do you know where we are?"

"I was in Peru, fighting Lizard Girl and her merry band of assholes in the middle of Machu Picchu when I got suckerpunched by a demon." She felt around her. Metal bottom and sides. Her ankles were manacled together. Cuffs and chains on her wrists shackled her to the floor.

"What in Hades' name were you thinking challenging a Chaos servant?"

She bristled at his tone, the same combination of irritation and disappointment he used when she was a little girl because she wasn't as good a fighter as her sisters.

"If I'd known that's what she was, I would have gotten more help when I followed her to South America," she said dryly. "The bitch killed a mortal under my protection."

Alex? Francisco? Nothing but silence answered her. The cowboy could be clever when he wanted to be. The possibility he and the Lima vampire might be nothing more than oily sludge in the middle of Machu Picchu's plaza didn't bear thinking about.

"Don't do that again, Phillippa." Pain laced Ares' voice.

"What? Why?"

"This box is designed as an echo chamber aimed solely at me."

"Oh. Sorry." She had to contort her body to reach her boots. Her injured shoulder screamed in protest. But the knife sheathed there was gone. No surprise, but it didn't hurt to check.

"What are you doing?"

"Checking to see if they left me with anything to pick the locks with." She chuckled again. "I'm impressed they left my boots on—"

The boots. Her footwear had been made by the demons of Uku Pacha. She'd thought about buying new boots in Cuzco, but Alex pointed out that Supay might take offense to her rejecting the gift.

If Supay had known about the monkey demon who destroyed himself by touching Kiki, then he might know about John being eaten by Lizard Girl's partner. He'd send another demon, or two, or a thousand, to keep an eye on the vampires because he wanted his tumi back.

And if Lizard Girl was nearby, she'd have the god's object of power. The bitch may be shielding the weapon and Ares, but if anything Phillippa did reflected on Ares, then odds were she didn't have any type of spell cast to hide her own presence. Not when her supposed surviving allies were vampires.

Bleached bones flashed through her mind. No, she wouldn't believe Alex was dead this time. She couldn't. If she did, she would be a massive ball of grief, and she needed to keep her wits about her.

"Father, tell me if this hurts you." She shifted until her feet were flat on the metal floor. *Tap-tap-tap. Tap. Tap. Tap. Tap-tap-tap.*

"Well?" she asked.

"Nothing."

She couldn't help grinning to herself. It seemed Lizard Girl wasn't so clever after all. Passive communication slipped under her spell. Phillippa continued tapping her message with her demon-made boots.

Ares' deep voice penetrated the darkness. "What are you doing?"

"Calling for help." The big question was whether Supay would deign to answer.

Alex woke to green leaves dappled in sunshine rustling above him. He lifted his head. A dream. A very old dream, except the spot where his bare foot lay in a puddle of light grew very warm.

He was naked, lying in the middle of a section of torn soil. Like the earth had vomited him out of itself.

His tongue flicked over the tips of his canines. Still as sharp as ever. His right foot remained lily-white. No blackening. No smoke. No pain.

He laid his head back down. Everything seemed so fuzzy. Phil, Francisco and he had made it to the ancient ruins. Lizard Girl and another servant of the Old Ones had beaten them there. Everything dissolved into a haze of pain.

Phil.

Alex jerked upright. Phil had been kicked in the head by Demon John's sister. Mamapacha had said the Amazon was still alive. Why did Lizard Girl need Phil alive? She needed to sacrifice a full god to break the seal at Nazca.

Then the Incan earth goddess had given him her blood. He took a deep breath. Ribs were healed. Lungs inflated properly.

None of that explained why he was sitting buck naked in sunshine and not burning to death.

Grunts and crashing brush came from his left. He rolled to his feet, ready for what he wasn't sure. A monkey demon appeared, carrying three backpacks. Backpacks he recognized, but it wasn't Demon John carrying them.

The creature dropped the packs. "How are you feeling?"

"I—" Recognition came slowly. Alex's muddled head felt like his days as a Normal when he'd used opium and cocaine to self-medicate his melancholy. "Francisco?"

The demon paused his search through the bright scarlet pack that had belonged to the Lima enforcer and peered at him. "Don't tell me I have to explain everything to you again?"

"I—" Alex rubbed his temples, willing the fog to go away. "I think I'm still drunk on Mamapacha's blood."

"It's entirely possible."

Alex held up his arm and watched the play of light and shadow along his skin.

"She said you'll be immune from the sun for only three days, so don't get used to it." Francisco grunted as he examined a pair of jeans. "I'm definitely not going to fit in these again."

"Where'd you find our backpacks?"

"We're about an hour's hike from where we were staked out to burn. I took a chance that your Lizard Girl left our equipment there and retrieved it while you were sleeping off the goddess's blood." He tossed Alex's pack across the torn earth. "Besides I didn't want to look at your naked ass for the next couple of days."

"Thanks for leaving me passed out and helpless." Alex couldn't help the sour words. He was in over his head, and he knew it. Worst of all, Phil had tried to warn him more than once. Another pang hit his chest. *You'd better keep yourself alive, Phil.*

"You have the goddess of creation's blood in you. Nothing natural would touch you, and our unnatural friends are making a beeline south." Francisco chuckled. "Your lady love remembered where her boots were made. She's been signaling for a day now."

"Wait! It's already the Solstice?"

Francisco held up a hand. "The Summer Solstice had nothing to do with Lizard Girl's plan. That was her ploy to grab Phillippa. Her kind isn't dependent on any astronomical sign, so don't get your underwear in a twist. Oh, wait! You're not wearing any."

Alex grimaced and fished a spare out of his pack. "Like I really want to see a free-balling monkey demon either."

Francisco made a disgusted sound low in his throat. He held up a little hand-woven bag. From the metallic rattle, it held the bullets they'd been given in Uku Pacha. "These are useless. My gun was crushed by a falling wall in the plaza, and my body's fire ruined my knife."

Alex glanced at the demon as he fastened his jeans. "We could probably throw the bullets with the same effect, but they won't have the same range. Besides, you don't need them with those new claws of yours. They can slice through reinforced steel."

Francisco held up his hand and examined the razor-sharp tips. "You don't say?" A wicked smile full of rotten teeth flashed. "I'm looking forward to putting them to the test. Here." He tossed the bag to Alex. "Nick yourself and coat these with blood. It'll save ourselves some time, and I don't have to worry about you invoking the wrong deity."

"I'd still prefer something to shoot them with." He tucked his t-shirt into his waistband. Funny, but even at this altitude he didn't feel cold.

Francisco reached into Phil's backpack and held out a Glock, butt first. "Here. Sorry but this is the only one I could find."

Alex accepted the weapon. "Thanks. I—" He raked his hands through his hair. "I'm sorry for getting pissy earlier."

Francisco shrugged. "It's nothing." He surveyed the little copse. "As much as I'd like to stay and enjoy the sunshine myself, our foes have a day's headstart, and we have a maiden to rescue."

"She's hardly a maiden." The words popped out before he could stop them.

The odd chitter-cough laughter of a demon filled the glade. "I knew there was a history between you two. Before or after you were Turned?"

Well, the proverbial cat was out of the bag. "Before." The memory triggered his fangs, and Alex nipped his little finger and started smearing blood on the Underworld bullets.

"She didn't accept your Turn I take it." Francisco transferred anything they might need into Phil's backpack.

"She didn't know. She thought I'd died in a bandit raid and left San Antonio before—" Realizing what he was about to admit, Alex reached for his shirt.

"Ah, you broke the rule of silence for naught." Francisco shook his head, and bits of hair and dried skin spun off into the brush. "I will not reveal your secret. As you might have noticed, I'm no longer a vampire. Therefore, I am not bound by those laws anymore."

They repacked the backpacks in silence. What could either of them say? The game had changed, and their objectives and roles along with it.

Alex stared at his bare feet. "Seems a shameful waste of Mamapacha's blood for me to go traipsing through the desert without boots and a coat."

Francisco plucked at the threads of his backpack, muttering in the sing-song demon language, before he tossed the bright red nylon into the turned bed of earth. Immediately, the backpack was sucked down as if someone, or something under the ground yanked on its straps. A minute later, the soil churned. Brown leather boots and a matching jacket appeared.

Alex grinned at Francisco. "Neat trick."

Francisco grunted before he said, "The gods have taken an interest in us. I'm not sure this is such a good thing."

"It's a little late now, don't you think?" Alex shook the dirt from the boots and slid them on. Perfect fit. Just like the ones the denizens of Uku Pacha had given Phil after the underworld lake monster's acid slime had ruined hers. He tried not to think about Lizard Girl's talons digging into the Amazon's pristine flesh.

Alex bundled the jacket into his backpack and zipped it. He was too warm to need the coat now. Maybe it was effect of the blood Mamapacha had given him. Maybe it was the fact he stood in sunlight for the first time in over a century. Either way, he'd need the jacket when night fell in the high desert they would be traveling through. "Let's get moving."

Tiffany poured her first cup of real coffee in nearly five months. The cravings refused to go away. She'd just have to be careful. If Max found the fresh-ground pound she'd picked up this morning, he'd go ballistic.

But dammit, she needed the caffeine after getting almost no sleep last night. Max hadn't fared much better. They'd both finally dozed off while watching a season of an old sitcom on Netflix.

She savored that first sip before she waddled over to the kitchen table and booted up her laptop. Many of the European universities had digitized their libraries. Maybe she could find *something* regarding these "Old Ones."

Her phone chose that moment to buzz. She checked the caller ID. *Seven Wonders.* Was Phil back from Peru? She thumbed the icon and said, "Talk to me. How was South America?"

"Tiffany?"

"Melissa?"

"Yes. Lady Phillippa told us to call you if we had a problem at the store—" Her voice sounded nervous and furious at the same time, which was definitely wrong for the happy-go-lucky nymph.

Tiffany slapped a palm on her forehead. "I've told you guys a million times. No magick around the computers. Shut everything down and re-boot the system."

"It's not the computer this time. We have a prisoner, and Io said I should ask you before I kill him."

"A prisoner?" The one drink of coffee churned in her stomach. "What species?"

"A Seelie disguised as our mortal contractor."

Shit. Could things get any worse? "I'm on my way. Melissa, swear on the River Styx you and the other girls won't do anything before I get there."

Melissa must have had the phone on speaker because the other nymphs chimed in when she said, "We swear on the River Styx that we will not harm our prisoner until you arrive, Tiffany."

"But I make no promises after that," Melissa said. "He stole my mortal lover."

"Okay." Tiffany thumbed off the call and scrolled through her contact list. The girls were supposed to keep their hands off anyone Phil did business with, but obviously, hormones had gotten the better of Melissa. Something really stunk if Millanthropas was manipulating the weres with one hand and attempting to send in spies with the other. And dammit, she was supposed to be on maternity leave!

Tiffany got up from the table and scrounged a travel mug to dump her coffee into as she waited for Bebe to answer.

"Hello?" From the mumbled reply, the witch was sleeping off her Jack Daniels binge.

"Sorry for waking you, Doc, but you're never going to believe what type of vermin the nymphs caught at Phil's store this morning."

Chapter 30

Miko and Bebe pulled into the Seven Wonders lot right behind Tiffany. She parked and waited for the other two women.

"So this alleged truce was a scam?" Miko asked. With her suit and sunglasses, she looked like an agent from *Men in Black.*

Tiffany grinned. "We don't know anything for sure, cuz. Don't go blowing off fairy heads just yet."

Bebe eyed the store's façade from behind her own shades. A sign in turquoise and pink on the boarded up front doors proclaimed, "Closed for remodeling," in beautiful calligraphy. "Those jokers did a number on the building, didn't they?"

"You haven't seen the inside." Tiffany waved them to follow her to the back.

At least, the nymphs had been smart and replaced the rear entrance door first. Bright California sunshine bounced off the polished stainless steel. It made Tiffany wish she'd brought her sunglasses as well.

At her rap on the door, Apollonia opened it and gestured for them to come inside. Multi-colored glittering scales covered her face and arms. If the sweet, dreamy butterfly nymph was on the verge of losing it, Tiffany could only imagine the state the rest of the girls were in.

"What happened?" she asked.

"You mean besides fae suck at casting glamours?" Apollonia closed and locked the door behind them and led them to the showroom.

The smell of burning flesh made Tiffany's extreme morning sickness feel like a walk through a bakery. A male fae sat cross-legged in the middle of the bare concrete floor. The nymphs had bound him with steel wire. Heavy denim and boots protected his lower extremities, but his wrists were raw, bleeding and smoking. Io held a nail gun on him, and the rest of the girls held every kind of steel tool imaginable. Even worse, bark, leaves and branches poked from the nymphs' skin and hair, displaying their anxiety and anger.

The stupid idiot hadn't stood a chance.

Tiffany shook her head and *tsked*. "Now, what do we have here?"

"Two humans and a witch." The fae sneered. "Am I supposed to be quaking in fear?"

"I'd be more worried about the ten pissed-off nymphs if I were you, dumbass." Tiffany smirked. "Because I brought them my knife collection to play with if you don't cough up some answers."

"They don't have the fortitude." But there was a little glimmer of doubt in his eyes.

"You just don't get it." Tiffany forced down the nausea and crossed her arms. "My cousin and I don't really like you either. We both ended up in the hospital because of a certain necromancer and his zombie hordes attacking my wedding. Your queen gave said necromancer shelter. And then there's the matter of both queens putting a bounty on my sister-in-law."

She inclined her head in Bebe's direction. "In fact, the only one here who's neutral on the subject of your continuing existence is the witch."

"Well, I don't know if neutral is the right word . . ." Bebe drawled. She peered over the top of her sunglasses at the fae. "Honorable combat is one thing. Baby killing is another." She inclined her head toward Tiffany's bulging belly.

His face blanched. If the fae had one button to push, it was children.

"So here's the deal." Tiffany smiled at him. "You're going to answer my questions, or I let the nymphs chop you into fish bait. You've got five seconds to decide."

She silently counted to herself. When she reached "Four Mississippi," the fae quietly said, "I will answer your questions."

Demon John's story and its similarity to Sam's creation nagged inside Phillippa's achy head. "Father, may I ask you some questions about Great-uncle Aidoneus?"

Ares sighed. "Have you given up already, my little filly?"

Her heart jolted at the use of her nickname. He hadn't done that since her first moon blood.

She coughed to cover her nervous laugh before she said, "That wasn't what I meant."

"What do you wish to know?"

"Out of the six children of Rhea and Kronos, who was really born first?"

He was silent for so long that she didn't think he was going to answer her. "Why?"

"It's a theory I'm working on concerning the Old Ones. The Chaos lords."

More silence. She continued her toe-tapping Morse code. The master of Uku Pacha and his minions may not understand its actual meaning, but it should give them something to follow. She hoped.

"Hestia was born first, but I overheard Father and Mother talking once that Aidoneus was swallowed first."

"So the first to die becomes the ruler of death?"

"Your great-uncle did not die, little filly."

"Maybe not in the conventional sense, but he was restored when Grandfather rescued his siblings."

"Yes." The silence dragged a little more before he said, "Does this have something to do with the newborn god I smell on you?"

Fuck. The one time in over five millennia Phillippa wished she was wrong.

Everyone, including Lizard Girl, must be able to detect Sam's scent on her. They had spent a lot of time together because of Tiffany and Max's wedding. Which was natural as the foster mother of the bride and the maid of honor/sister of the groom.

So, there really was no point lying about it to her father. "Yeah. She's a friend of mine. Some pretty horrible things were done to her, and she doesn't realize the full extent of her abilities yet." Another thought occurred to her. "Why did Lizard Girl capture you? Why not go after Sam? If she's really a baby god, wouldn't she be easier to manage?"

Bitter laughter erupted from her father. "Their lack of knowledge and inexperience is precisely why they are so much more dangerous. It is very difficult to predict what they may do."

"So why grab me?" Phillippa asked. "I've been trying to figure it out. I thought maybe I was bait to get Sam into her clutches. Lizard Girl doesn't need me to open the portal."

His laughter died and sorrow crept into his voice. "Oh, little filly. So wise, but you cannot perceive the truth in front of you."

This would be so much easier if she could see his face, but the dark seemed to make it easier for him to talk. "I don't understand."

"She needs a god's blood willingly given."

His meaning twisted her gut. "You mean I'm a hostage to ensure your compliance?" Then she burst out laughing. "Oh, that is rich! She should have grabbed one of your other children, or resurrected Hippolyta, or, or—" She howled and pounded on the metal floor.

"Phillippa—" From the tight sound, Ares gritted his teeth. "Don't strike the box."

"Sorry." When she could catch her breath, she swiped at the tears rolling down her cheeks. "Hades, even Aunt Aphrodite would have been a better choice."

"You don't understand. The Chaos servant knows me too well." Grief bled into his voice, and the air filled with the mixed scent of lilacs and ash. "You were always my favorite, child."

Chapter 31

Demon John's sister could have kicked Phillippa in the gut, and she would be able to breathe easier than she could now.

"I'm sorry I never told you," Ares continued. "It was simply too dangerous to admit my feelings for you. There are those that would—"

"My sisters? Give them a little credit."

"Not your sisters. Aphrodite."

What he was saying didn't make sense. Phillippa mulled it over, and well, it still confused her. "Why would she care? It's not like—" He may be chained, but that was hardly a reason to throw his multiple trysts, and her anger concerning them, in his face.

"We were faithful to each other?" Bitter laughter rolled through their little prison. "I'm under no illusion of what I am. Don't worry about sparing my feelings."

"I was more worried about getting smited. Or is that smote?" Her own self-deprecating humor joined his.

When their laughter died down, his next exhale carried a burden of weariness. "She threatened to destroy your mother if I didn't leave her."

"Why didn't you just tell us? We could have—"

"No, you couldn't," he snapped. "If you and your sisters raised your hand against her, what exactly do you think would have happened?"

"But we—"

"Would have had your asses smote. If not by her, then by your grandfather for daring to challenge a god. While you may have his ability of throwing lightning bolts, you would have died, Phillippa." In a quieter voice, he added, "I couldn't have borne that. And yet . . ."

"And yet what?" she whispered. It simply had never occurred to her that he'd left to protect them.

Another heavy sigh. "Your mother made her own damn choice, no matter how idiotic it was. But if I could prove Aphrodite was responsible for your sisters' deaths, I would rip her fucking head off."

"What-what are you talking about?"

"Think about it, Phillippa. Hippolyta fell in love with Heracles and died because of it. Antiope fell in love with Theseus and died. Penthesilea and Achilles. Didn't you ever see the pattern?"

"It was war. All those Greeks just wanted to prove themselves." Which was true, but what if Aphrodite had influenced the situation?

Ares snorted. "The smartest thing you ever did was to keep your head down and disappear."

Was it intelligence? Or was she a coward? Father wouldn't fling accusations at his long-time paramour for no reason. Why hadn't she noticed the pattern he pointed out?

Because you wanted to survive. It's the real reason you kept Alex at bay all these years, her conscience whispered. The anger burst the damn she'd shoved it behind, and she pounded against their prison walls until her father screamed.

Alex raced after Francisco along an old game trail. The terrain was jagged, dangerous. Their slog from the plane crash to Cuzco was a walk through Golden Gate Park compared to this. Yet, he didn't feel tired or thirsty.

Even at the incredible speed they were traveling, he didn't understand how they would reach Nazca before Lizard Girl, Marcus and their crew. He said as much to his companion as they ran.

"With Phillippa as their prisoner, they had to backtrack to Cuzco," Francisco replied. "Even Lizard Girl and the rebel demons would have difficulty dragging a furious Amazon over this terrain, so they're stuck using conventional travel. They don't dare take shortcuts through Uku Pacha or Hanan Pacha." He flashed a grin over his shoulder. "Phillippa remembered her boots, and we're tracking her progress."

"Her boots?"

"Yes, the ones gifted to her in Uku Pacha." Francisco let loose a raucous laugh. "She's been tapping out a signal for some time now. My fellows from the Underworld have been initiating landslides to slow their progress as well."

She's alive! Mamapacha hadn't lied. But a worried thought crossed Alex's mind. "Please tell me the demons are not killing Normals."

A derisive sound issued from Francisco. Not quite a raspberry because that would probably shred his lips. "Only my lord may take a soul, Alex, and only when it's that person's time."

Relief that Phil was okay bled into his natural curiosity. "What are the lines in the desert really for?"

"The original lines are not *for* anything. They are the magnetic scars on the land where my lord fought the Old One. The rest were added for decoration."

"But you can only see them from the air."

"Alex, when were you born?"

The abrupt change in subject knocked him off his stride. He slid and caught himself before he plunged off the nearly sheer wall of basalt they traversed. "1855 A.D.," he said as he caught up with Francisco.

"So you recall your country's Civil War?"

The memory of his father arguing with one of the neighbors over the secession issue sprang into his mind. And Momma had died without seeing her sisters again due to the disruptions in rail travel. "Yeah." Where the hell was the demon going with this?

"Didn't the armies spy on troop movements from the air?"

"Are you telling me the Nazca people had hot air balloons? There's no evidence they had that kind of technology!"

"Just because you haven't found the evidence doesn't mean something did not exist." Francisco glanced over his shoulder as he bounded over a boulder blocking their path. "Did you bring any evidence with you that you've been to Uku Pacha twice?"

"Point taken." No evidence except the disconcerting impression that Supay watched everything through his eyes.

Once the fae barfed his information, they retreated back to the mansion for a war conference with the other ranking enforcers. But not until Tiffany extracted another oath that the nymphs would not harm the fae before she could set up a meeting with the weres and Duke Millanthropas.

The baby landed a solid kick on Tiffany's bladder. She must have winced because Bebe was immediately by her side. "What's wrong?"

"Nothing that enrolling the kid in soccer classes won't fix." She rubbed her belly.

"I don't think you should go tonight," Miko added.

"I agree," Saif Al-Issa added. The vampire enforcer's eyes glowed golden despite the bright kitchen fluorescents.

"We can't afford to lose another authority figure before Caesar and Duncan get back. You two need to be here." Tiffany pointed at Miko and Saif. She didn't need to add the "just in case." It was clearly stamped on the senior enforcers' expressions.

"Thank you so much for including me in your expendables list." Leona's dry voice didn't help Tiffany's mood.

"You're welcome," she shot back. "Look, we need to know for sure if that fairy told us the truth. We need to know if the pack *has* switched sides. And I don't know about the rest of you, but I'm not leaving an innocent person as the fae's prisoner. There's no way we could survive long enough in Otherwhere to find Phil's contractor. This may be our only way to rescue him."

Miko opened her mouth to argue some more, but Tiffany's cell phone started playing, "Who Let the Dogs Out."

She thumbed the answer icon. "What have you got for me, Siobhan?" She listened as the were relayed Millanthropas's conditions for meeting. "Fine. See you tonight."

The other three enforcers looked at her expectantly, though the vampires could hear every word of the conversation. "La Brea Tar Pits. Tonight at ten."

"I hope you're right about this," Miko grumbled.

"If I'm not, you can always say I told you so." Tiffany grinned.

"That's a little hard to do when you're dead."

Chapter 32

Phillippa recognized the muffled groan of suppressed pain. She just never thought she'd hear it from Ares, much less several times in less than a day. "What's wrong?"

"She tightens the chains when it's feeding time."

Interesting. Despite the security of the bespelled metal, Lizard Girl was afraid of him.

A metallic screech vibrated through their little prison. Phillippa stopped tapping her demon-made boot. The door to their box opened, and she ducked her head because the faint sunlight blinded her after the total darkness.

And she got her first glimpse of her father. His black hair and beard were tangled and matted. His pale skin showed how long it had been since he'd been in the sun. Nothing was left of his tunic except tatters around his waist.

"Well, well, well. You're still alive, my dear. And here I heard Olympians eat their young." Lizard Girl's mockery lashed against Phillippa's shame at being caught and chained.

Ignore it, she commanded herself. *Pay attention to details.* The box sat in a truck from the lowering sun glinting off the second set of doors. No rebel demons were in sight. No vampires either, but she didn't expect to see any with the sun still above the horizon. The thicker air said they had descended from the Andes.

Lizard Girl's ugly mug still bore the marks from her encounter with the Hitching Post. But like a shark, new teeth were emerging from the sockets where the previous ones had melted.

Ares laughed. The angry malicious sound wrapped around Phillippa's heart and dragged her own emotions out. "I'm sure you're tasty roasted over a fire with a decent barbeque sauce," he said.

Phillippa struggled to control the fury bouncing between Lizard Girl and her father. It triggered her own rage, and she fought to think past the miasma. The door was open. Lizard Girl's magick that hid them would be weaker.

Alex! No answer.

Lizard Girl's tail whipped out and caught her across the face. Not hard enough to break anything, but her head rung and her eyesight blurred.

"Your boyfriend's not coming. He's a patch of slime on a mountain." The glee in Lizard Girl's voice taunted Phillippa. Things were thrown into the box, and the door slammed shut.

Jane's imposter was lying about Alex. She had to be. A smile curved Phillippa's lips as she realized how she could find out for sure.

"Bitch," Ares muttered. "Are you all right?"

"Father, I need you to calm down."

"Calm down? Are you mad?"

"She's fucking with us, but to find out something for sure, I need you to be as serene as you can. Please?"

He made a sound low in his throat, but the pressure in her heart eased. If Alex was dead and she succeeded in her plan, at least Lizard Girl could no longer hold her as a hostage against her father.

Phillippa raised her nails to her neck and dug into the spot where the jugular ran. Instantly, fire blossomed in her gut, and never had such pain been so welcome. With a strangled cry, she dropped her hand and fell to her side.

"Phillippa!" It was the first time she'd ever heard her father truly afraid.

"I'm okay," she wheezed. She pushed herself upright again and wiped her fingers on her jeans.

"I smell blood."

"I had to put something to the test."

"What? By harming yourself?"

She felt for the objects Lizard Girl had tossed in, picked them up and sniffed them. The meat was questionable at best and the bread burnt. Still, it was food and the water in the canteen tasted fresh. "Not exactly."

A soft rattle said Ares' chains had been loosened again.

"Here." She held the water out for him. His calloused fingers brushed her skin as he felt for the canteen, and he took it without a word. The faint scent of sour cream penetrated his body odor. So, she wasn't the only one embarrassed by their circumstances.

Phillippa shoved the emotion aside and ripped the meat into bite-sized chunks as he drank. Interesting that Lizard Girl hadn't tightened her chains. If their enemy didn't consider her a threat, she needed to figure out a way to use it to their advantage.

Even if Alex and Francisco reached them in time, they would be hard-pressed to take the Old Ones' servant out of the picture, assuming they still had some of Supay's bullets. The three of them had been royally creamed in the plaza of Machu Picchu.

She chewed and forced down a chunk of the questionable, unknown meat. No sense starving, and frankly, there'd been times when she had worse to eat. Or nothing. "You can't sacrifice yourself. You know what she's planning to do. And she'll kill me as soon as you're dead and the portal's open."

Ares crunched on a piece of the burnt bread. "With these chains on, my abilities are severely hampered. The servant won't release them before she's sure I've capitulated and she's about to slit my throat."

"She's stolen Supay's tumi." Crap. She'd forgotten to signal after the door closed. Her toe tapped its steady SOS. "Alex was able to hurt her with it."

"Is this Alex the paramour she mentioned?"

Was Ares actually teasing her? "He's not my boyfriend or paramour or anything like that. He's a vampire, and he happened to be the supernatural on duty when Lizard Girl or one of her cronies broke into my store and stole Supay's tumi."

"But you've known him a long time?"

She sighed. "Father, the important thing is he's not dead despite Lizard Girl's boasting."

More crunching, then he said, "You sound very glad of that."

"If it gets us out of—" The sequence of events over the last few days replayed in her mind. "Oh, shit."

"What?" Ares said around a mouthful of something.

"If Kiki's presence hid the tumi all this time, then Melissa's touch is what signaled its reappearance to both Lizard Girl and Supay. Dammit! If only I'd handled Beatrice's consignment, she and Jane would both still be alive."

"And you might be the one dead, little filly," Ares said softly. His palm rested on her arm. "Don't lash yourself over the circumstances. If this Alex is alive, will he come after you?"

"Yes." At Ares' amused snort, she added, "Because Lizard Girl murdered several people. Not because there's anything between us."

"Of course, Phillippa." Humor tickled her father's words.

But could Alex reach them before Lizard Girl tried to sacrifice Ares at the seal?

Chapter 33

The Nazca Plain was so still that Alex could have heard a leaf drop from miles away. If there were any leaves. The air was cold and dry and sucked the moisture from his very skin. "How close are we?"

Francisco cocked his head, listening to something Alex couldn't hear. "We're about ten klicks from the seal." His rotting lips spread into a cocky grin. "From Phillippa's signal, they are still an hour away."

Alex scanned the area. With the goddess's blood coursing through him, the stars might as well have been klieg lights. "Not much out here for ambush cover."

"Trust me. We'll be fine." The demon bounded off into the desert. "We'll beat her to her goal."

"Right. That's what you said when I got in your damn plane." Alex ran after Francisco as the demon's chitter-cough laughter rang through the night.

Tiffany parked the Suburban in the visitor's lot of the La Brea Tar Pits and struggled to climb down from the armored SUV. It was getting harder and harder to get in and out of vehicles as her pregnancy progressed. Leona rushed around to the driver's side and hovered.

"You need to stop. You're totally destroying my hard-ass image," Tiffany snapped.

"You look like a Weeble," the vampire shot back. "And you walk like one, too."

"Then why did you come with me?"

"I drew the short straw."

It wasn't true, and they both knew it. This meeting with the fae was a calculated risk. With Kensai, Jamal, Selene and Ptolemy all dead, Uncle

Duncan had become Caesar's second-in-command in name as well as fact. Millanthropas wouldn't want to piss him off any more than he already had this year by harming the vampire's only Normal family.

Assuming the Seelie duke truly wanted a truce. If Ptolemy were here, he'd be creatively cursing her for coming to this rendezvous without more backup.

Ptolemy. A wave of old grief passed through her. She missed arguing with him. Between Max and the baby, she thought of him less and less over the past five months. For some strange reason, she felt guilty, as if she'd betrayed him. The vampire had been nothing more than a teenage crush. Even at fifteen, she knew nothing would ever come of her feelings.

"Tiffany?" Leona's eyes gleamed gold in the darkness. "Is it the baby?"

This coddling shit was getting totally out of hand. "Just trying to control myself." She felt in her pocket for the steel throwing stars. "This is the bastard who ordered his bitches to torture Duncan. I blame him and his games for ruining my wedding."

"You're not the only one." Vampire fangs gleamed under the rising moon.

"Let's get this over with. Anything we need to worry about?"

Leona inhaled deeply and her eyes appeared to watch something invisible in the distance. "Only the two fae and Lannigan's pack." She returned to the here-and-now. "Siobhan's coming."

A wolf trotted from behind the visitor's center, her reddish-brown fur rippling under the security lights. Her tongue hung out of the side of her open mouth in a doggie grin. Tiffany breathed a sigh of relief at the familiar muzzle, but as Siobhan approached, she slowed, cocked her head and sniffed. A low growl sounded deep in her throat.

Tiffany crossed her arms over her belly. "I know it's bad form to bring silver, but until I'm sure your father's not stabbing the coven in the back, it stays with me. You're lucky I'm honoring Alex's promise to share information." She graced the pack beta with her own evil smile. "I've also got iron and C4 in the bag if it makes you feel better."

The were shook her head in a very human gesture before she turned and stalked into the park. Siobhan wasn't stupid. She had to have guessed something was up when Tiffany asked for this meeting. She adjusted her messenger bag and set off after the wolf.

A snicker came from the vampire. Tiffany glared over her shoulder at Leona. "What's so fucking funny?"

"The fact that you have no problem threatening everyone at a diplomatic meeting."

"Keep laughing and you'll find out just how much wood I can shove through your heart."

Stars whirled in their graceful waltz overhead. Alex hadn't seen this magnificent of a display in decades, but the discordance of the magnetic lines gave him a slight headache. The subsonic thrum felt as if Lucifer were playing his fiddle in Hell. Was the sensation because of Mamapacha's blood, or would the vibration been intolerable without it?

"This still doesn't make sense," he whispered to Francisco. It didn't seem right to talk normally. The still desert air carried sounds for miles, that was true. But it felt as if making too much noise would attract the wrong kind of attention. Things far worse than Supay or Lizard Girl. "Sacrificing Phil isn't enough to break the seal."

The demon reached over and smacked the back of Alex's head.

"Ow! What was that for?" He rubbed the spot.

"Remember what your Amazon said at the banquet in my lord's palace about who Lizard Girl would select as her sacrifice?"

"Yeah. Snatch a god from another pantheon and . . ." He finally caught up with Francisco's train of thought. "Oh, shit. Lizard Girl has Phil's dad."

Francisco nodded. "It is the only logical reason to want her. And he faces the same choice that was given me by a vampire centuries ago. Submit and save my daughters, or watch them die."

There were no words for the pain and determination Alex saw in the demon's fierce orange eyes. "I'm sorry. I didn't know."

"No matter now. My job will be to get the tumi away from Lizard Girl. Yours will be to free your lady love and her father."

"You're making this sound like a piece of cake."

"Surprise is on our side." Francisco smiled his rotten-teeth grin. "Lizard Girl will be expecting a representative of Supay. She will not expect a vampire she believes is dead."

"You don't have a weapon." Alex reached into his waistband for the Glock. "Your lord's bullets are all we have to hurt her."

"No, my friend." Francisco held up his wicked talons. "I'm very much looking forward to testing these on her."

Tiffany kept an eye on the three figures she approached and a hand on a throwing star in her pocket. Both John Lannigan, alpha of the Los Angeles werewolf pack, and Millanthropas, duke of the Seelie Court, scowled at the exact same moment, meaning they scented the silver and steel she carried.

"You brought weapons to this meeting." Lannigan didn't so much as twitch at his statement. He was experienced enough not to telegraph any move.

"And witch magick," the fae growled.

Tiffany left her right hand in her pocket. The charms Bebe placed on her wedding ring and Leona's cross would make the fae think twice about slinging spells. Fae and witch magick reacted like matter and anti-matter. But that wouldn't stop the duke and his bodyguard from a conventional attack. "If you're dumb enough to start a fight, we all go poof. Now, talk. Why is this truce so important?"

Leona stepped to the side, giving herself room if a battle broke out. Millanthropas' bodyguard mirrored the vampire's move.

"The little Normal thinks she's brave," the fae lord mocked.

Not this crap again. Tiffany managed to swallow those words. "Augustine Coven has been attacked three times in the last twenty years. Most recently by a necromancer you've been in bed with." Tiffany smiled. "And I mean that both literally and figuratively."

The change in his expression was so subtle she would have missed it if she hadn't been watching carefully. "My people paid for that mistake in blood."

"Am I supposed to cry over that?" She hardened her tone. "That doesn't repay me for the money I lost when you ruined my wedding. It doesn't take away the scars you gave my uncle when you tortured him. And it sure as hell doesn't bring back the eleven guests who died in your buddy's zombie attack."

Millanthropas gave what he probably thought was a charming smile. "I'm not responsible for your host duties and protections."

Tiffany examined her nails on her left hand. "And I'm not responsible if your queen discovers what you've been up to either." She looked up at him. "Your Grace."

His female bodyguard started to draw her sword. Tiffany wasn't sure if the fae paused because of Millanthropas' signal or Leona's threatening step forward.

"I came in person with an honest desire for peace." The duke's eyes narrowed. "If Augustine hides behind a child—"

Tiffany snorted. "Yeah, I figured this alleged truce was for show. Or an attempt to assassinate our master." She gestured to Leona. "Let's get out of here."

"Shall I tell my queen your *master* will retaliate with that creature of his?"

We have him. It took everything Tiffany had to suppress her grin as she faced the fae once more. "First of all, my sister-in-law is not a creature. Second, she hasn't been the one picking fights. Third, I heard how she wiped the floor with your zombified troops. Which, by the way, I suspect you deliberately volunteered for their *alteration* as it were."

She held up her fingers and blew a piercing whistle. It was gratifying to watch John and Siobhan jump when the nymphs drifted out of the trees with their prisoner. Melissa slammed the male fae down on his knees.

Millanthropas' bodyguard reached for her sword again, but didn't draw. Siobhan shifted to human form.

Tiffany crossed her arms once again and tapped the toe of her boot. "Now, we know you didn't trash my foster mom's store, but you want to tell me why you felt the need to kidnap her contractor?"

A little part of her was gratified to see shock on the werewolves' faces. They didn't know. Caesar would be pissed as hell if his compact with the pack collapsed.

Either Millanthropas was one hell of an actor, or he was truly caught off guard as well. Tiffany wagered on the former. Deniable plausibility after all.

The bodyguard hissed something in the fae language, her disgust evident. "He belongs to the Summer Queen."

Tiffany stilled her foot. "And why should I believe you?"

"Because if you don't kill him, we'll have to." No more mocking, sly looks or insults from the duke. "He's heard too much."

"No one touches him until my lover is returned," Melissa spat. Fingers turned to needle-sharp branches and dug into the fae's neck. Her sisters formed a protective circle around the furious nymph and her prisoner.

Tiffany had to give the kneeling asshole credit. He didn't so much as whimper.

Millanthropas whispered with his bodyguard for a moment before he said. "Our retrieval of the mortal will prove our intentions."

"I have no proof you weren't the one to nab him in the first place," Tiffany said sourly.

Siobhan stepped forward. "I'll go with him. Assuming you still trust me."

Before Tiffany could say anything, John's graying hair stood on end and his hands turned furry. "No, I'll go. One of your vampires can come with us and observe." The alpha smiled, showing some very pointy canines. "If Millanthropas is lying, his heart is mine."

I'd volunteer, but I can't leave you unguarded, Leona's voice whispered through Tiffany's mind.

She shook her head. "Go. I won't let that Normal stay in a Seelie barrow longer than necessary. I can make it home alone."

"No." Siobhan's expression showed downright embarrassment. Tiffany wondered if the she-wolf had ever been caught off-guard like this. "I will escort you home."

"Not naked you're not."

The were sighed. "I left my clothes at the visitor's center."

Leona touched the spot where her cross hung inside her shirt. "I'll let Bebe know if something goes wrong."

Tiffany nodded. The vampire disappeared into the vegetation with John and the fae. The nymphs literally faded back into the surrounding trees with their prisoner.

She rubbed her belly. All this stupid intrigue exhausted her in a way the pregnancy didn't. She pivoted and headed back for the parking lot, Siobhan padding silently beside her. Still naked.

Tiffany stifled a couple of yawns as she waited, leaning against the visitors' center. Thankfully, it took the were less than a minute to retrieve and don her t-shirt, sweatpants and slip-on Keds. Tiffany took a step toward the parking lot when Siobhan yanked her backwards and down.

Thunk!

Brilliant scarlet feathers bloomed on the visitor center's wall where Tiffany had been standing. A trank dart? "What the fuck!"

Siobhan slapped a hand over Tiffany's mouth. "Don't say a word," the were hissed.

Chapter 34

The magick woven into the titanium made the detection of outside sounds and movements almost impossible to distinguish, but Phillippa roused when the subtle vibration of the truck's engine died. "We've stopped again."

"Here. Put on your boot," Ares murmured. He'd taken over tapping a signal while she slept. "Think it's another landslide?"

"Maybe."

The journey south should have only taken a day. But every hour or so, Lizard Girl's convoy stopped. Once when Marcus had been the one to feed them, Ares overheard the rebel demons muttering something in their own language about their brothers still loyal to Supay being behind the troubles. Demon John's sister had swiftly and fiercely ended the gossip before the door slammed shut again.

Phillippa wanted to pray to Gaea it wasn't a coincidence, but she didn't dare. She couldn't be sure what the magickal prison would do to her father. She sought and gripped his hand tightly. "Listen to me. You cannot give in to her demands. No matter what happens."

"Don't ask this of me. As you pointed out millennia ago, your sisters' deaths were my fault."

"Then I ask for my daughter's unborn child," she whispered. "Please."

His fingers tightened around hers. "Truly?"

"I've already lost one girl I considered mine to this Chaos Lord's bitch. Don't make me lose another. Father, please." She'd never begged him for anything before, but for Tiffany . . .

"Do you trust me, little filly?"

Did she? All the old anger lay under the surface of her emotions, but here, now? What choice did she have? Alex may be alive, but would he reach the seal in time?

She squeezed Ares' hand in return. "I will this time. Don't make me regret it, old man," she growled.

He chuckled. "Oh, yes, you are definitely my daughter."

Shouts and gunfire erupted around the La Brea Tar Pits visitors' center. Instinctively, Tiffany curled around her protruding belly. The hot skin and heavy muscle of Siobhan covered her. Around them were the sounds of struggle, sirens and the screech of tires.

Tiffany shook, cried, and cursed the were and her own PTSD. Dammit, she was finally getting over the fucking nightmares of the wedding zombie attack.

"Baby, we got 'em!" Jorge Sifuentes' shout rang through the trees surrounding the parking lot. Floodlights pierced the gloom outside of the range of the center's little security lights. Ozone filled the air though there wasn't a cloud in the sky.

It's clear, Tiffany. Bebe's mental whisper flitted through her head.

In a flash, fear turned to rage. Tiffany shoved at Siobhan. "Get the fuck off me!"

Siobhan rolled smoothly to her feet and held out her hand. Tiffany ignored the offer and climbed laboriously to her feet. *I do not need this shit. I'm supposed to be on fucking maternity leave.*

She stomped in the direction of Sifuentes' voice. "What the fuck is going on?"

People in black were lying on their faces while LASO deputies secured them with handcuffs and zip strips. She glimpsed an all-too-familiar gold pin on the turtleneck of one of the prone prisoners. An eight-legged reptile superimposed over a star.

Tiffany reached into her messenger bag and pulled out her semi-automatic. It was all too easy to aim it at the bastard's head. "What are these assholes doing here?"

"Put it down, Stephens." From the other side of the line of people, Sifuentes stared at her, his hand on the grip of his own piece.

"They shot at me." Her voice didn't sound natural.

"Yes, but do you really want to deliver your baby in jail? Because he's a Normal and if you do something stupid, I will arrest you."

Her attention flicked from the Sunshine Believer to the detective. "They've been targeting my family. First, Jessie. Then, Phil." Duncan hadn't wanted to tell her what really happened, but her cousin Jessie had. How the cult was going to sacrifice Jessie and her unborn baby. The beautiful boy Jessie had delivered three weeks ago.

Tiffany gagged. They planned to do the same to her.

"We know. Put the gun down, Stephens. Now." The familiar *click* of a safety released. "Besides, stupid stunts are your sister-in-law's department, not yours."

Being compared to Sam sunk through Tiffany's cold rage. She slowly raised her hands and thumbed her own gun's safety back on. "Now, you're just being a dick, Detective." Someone slid the firearm from her fingers. Siobhan.

"Get her out of here," Sifuentes snapped.

Tiffany turned and stomped toward her SUV. At least, the were was smart enough not to touch her, but she rounded the vehicle and climbed into the passenger seat.

Siobhan handed the semi-automatic to Tiffany. She shoved the weapon into its slot in her bag and slid the leather pouch behind the seat.

The wolf broke the silence by saying, "Dad's not going to underestimate you after this." She chuckled. "I don't think the fae will either." She buckled her seatbelt before regarding Tiffany. "You'll need to watch your back with them."

Tiffany slung the SUV into reverse, narrowly missing a parked sheriff's cruiser. "I've been doing that all my life. Selene tried to have me assassinated in my crib. You gonna to tell me why your husband and half the sheriff's department were at the park tonight?"

"Head down to the main station. We're meeting Miko there."

"Why?" Tiffany snapped. She was in no mood for more bullshit.

"Do you want your answers or not?" Siobhan shot back.

There really was nothing to say to that question other than the obvious one, except Tiffany didn't feel like a detour to the ER after the damn she-wolf bit off her middle finger. Siobhan wisely kept her trap shut on the drive to the headquarters of the Los Angeles County Sheriff's Office.

The moon rose over the eastern Andes, spilling silvery light across the plateau. Alex peered over the lip of the depression he hid in with Francisco. "She's going to know we're here," he breathed.

"No," the demon whispered. "Same reason it's difficult to speak telepathically here. Too much psychic and electromagnetic scarring of the very fabric of the universe. That doesn't discount the possibility of scouts."

Three delivery trucks, similar to the one used to snatch Alex from the Lima airport, and several smaller cars and pickups had parked a quarter mile away. Lizard Girl had a handful of Normals with her, but they were sorely outnumbered by the rebel demons and rogue vamps that had poured from all the vehicles except the middle truck.

Alex snorted. "How does a decrepit piece of shit like that hold a god?" Much less Phil, and so far there hadn't been any sign of her.

"Can't you smell it?" Francisco said as a couple of vampires swung open the rear doors of the truck in question.

"The only thing I smell is your godawful stink—" Ozone hit Alex like a two-by-four between the eyes. For the odor to be that powerful, Lizard Girl had to have cast one hell of a spell.

Shouts and growls rolled over the desert, reminding him just how easily sound carried out here. A mix of Latin and Italian was punctuated by the chitter of Uku Pacha and the sibilant consonants of Lizard Girl. Over everything came the eye-splitting screech of metal-on-metal as a team of vamps and demons pulled a huge box out of the bed of the truck.

Unease flickered through Alex's gut. The unit was far too similar to the sensory deprivation chamber that Mallory's so-called scientists used.

Lizard Girl snapped another command. Chains were quickly attached to the container, and her minions dragged the box across the red pebbles that littered the desert floor. From the amount of ozone, Lizard Girl must be using all her strength to keep Ares and Phil contained.

"I guess I should be happy," Alex whispered.

"Why?" Francisco said.

"You and I wouldn't be having this conversation if Ares wasn't occupying most of Lizard Girl's attention."

Francisco nudged him. "Your friend has it."

Sure enough, Marcus stood apart from the mass of creatures hauling the container across the desiccated gravel. A soft white glow surrounded the tumi hanging from his belt. The traitor was too near the box for an effective divide and conquer tactic.

"If I create a distraction, do you think you can blend in with the other demons?"

"What did you have in mind?"

Alex pulled out his Glock and grinned. "I'm a mite curious to see what your lord's present will do to a gas tank."

Chapter 35

When their cage doors swung open this time, moonlight blinded Phillippa. Two of the monkey demons dragged her from the box by the chains on her wrists. Fresh blood oozed from the deep slice to her shoulder. The scent sparked blood lust in the closest vampires. Within seconds, the surrounding area was lit up with neon yellows, blues and greens.

Sharp talons dug into her cheeks, and an iron grip forced her head up to meet Lizard Girl's flat onyx stare. "Aren't they pretty when they get excited?"

"He won't do it. He won't submit to you."

"Oh, boss, you don't understand. He'll do anything to save his precious baby." Lizard Girl ran a talon from Phil's ear to the base of her throat, but not deep enough to slice the jugular or carotid. Fresh blood welled and dripped on her collar. The other side of her face and shirt were stiff with dried blood from the fight in the old city.

Fangs and the fresh-bread odor of hunger surrounded her. She was immune to the V-virus, but that didn't mean a vampire couldn't rip open an artery and drain her. *All I need is one little distraction.*

"I said I'd cooperate as long as you didn't harm her." Ares stood tall and proud despite his captors best efforts to hold him in check. The pole and chains must not be as strong as the box itself. Or else the efforts of holding both her and her father had drained Lizard Girl's strength.

"Harm? A little scratch like that?" the over-sized gecko sneered. How she didn't cut herself on her own teeth was beyond Phillippa's understanding.

All I need is a distraction. The tumi hung on Marcus's belt. Interesting. Why was he holding it? She couldn't imagine Lizard Girl letting anyone touch her prize since it would be the only way to kill Ares. And she would have to release Ares in order for the sacrifice to be willing. Maybe it was time to resort to a method that worked so well for Tiffany at age four.

Phillippa flung herself on the ground and started wailing. "Don't kill him! Please don't kill him! I'll do anything you want!" A peek said that everyone, including Lizard Girl, stared at her as if she'd lost her mind.

Ping.

Maybe Aunt Athena was listening to her. The first truck exploded into a ball of flames.

"I cannot believe your bastard of a husband used me as bait." Tiffany's toe tapped a furious rhythm as she, Siobhan, Bebe and Miko watched Sifuentes and another detective interrogate the guy they had determined to be the leader of the Sunshine Believers.

Or at least this particular merry little band of assholes.

"If it makes you feel better, my dad's going to be more pissed off than you," Siobhan said.

"You lied to your father?" Tiffany stared at the were.

"Had to in order for it to be convincing in front of Millanthropas. And I trusted his pride to kick in when you sprung that nice little nymph surprise on us." She continued to watch the three men through the two-way mirror.

"I'm not apologizing for that."

"Don't expect you to." Her attention flicked to Miko. "You're not the senior enforcer. I figured you were under orders."

Miko crossed her arms. "I'm not apologizing either. We had sufficient reason to suspect the pack may side with the sidhe instead of the coven."

"Which is why I contacted Jorge directly before one of you idiots got a bunch of people killed," Bebe snapped.

"Bitch," Tiffany muttered.

"I'm smart enough to use a condom when my partner's fertile," the witch shot back.

Tiffany threw up her hands. "How many times do I have to tell you people—we did! It's not our fault it broke!"

"For two Normals, that takes some serious gymnastics. Those things are tough to break." Siobhan said with a smirk.

This time all restraint broke, and Tiffany flipped off the were.

Siobhan laughed. "Well, I wouldn't get you pregnant."

"Shush, you two," Miko said. "I'm trying to hear this."

". . . a pregnant Family member of Augustine Coven." The Sunshine Believer stared at the mirror as if he could see right through it. "The prophet said if we controlled the child, we could control the war."

"What war?" Sifuentes said.

The cultist's gaze shifted to the detective. "The one you and your little harem behind the glass are trying so desperately to prevent, Lieutenant."

"When you say control, you mean kill, right?" the other detective said.

"Matthew Kline was overenthusiastic and prone to disregarding direct orders from the prophet. That's the reason she left him and his toxic little group behind bars." A creepy smile spread across the Sunshine Believer's face.

Siobhan shivered, and Tiffany stared at her. She couldn't remember any pack member showing that much discomfort. "You okay?"

"Kline's the one we interviewed at the nut house," the were said softly.

Sifuentes slid a piece of paper across the table. "Recognize any of these names?"

The cultist flicked his attention toward the paper, but didn't pick it up. "Should I?"

"They were all pregnant women who were murdered,"

Another slimy smile. "Maybe you should be questioning Matthew."

Sifuentes leaned forward. "Is there only one prophet?"

Tiffany jumped when the door to the observation room opened. A uniformed deputy entered and arrowed straight for Bebe. They whispered, but Tiffany couldn't catch what they were saying.

A horrible laugh crackled through the speakers, jerking her attention back to the interrogation. ". . . can't stop them, Lieutenant. They aren't of this universe. Not you, your wolves, the two witches in the observation room, the vampires or their minions. No one."

In the interrogation room, Sifuentes rose. "Eddie, take him down to the psych section."

"With pleasure," the other detective muttered.

Three seconds later, Sifuentes entered the observation room and flipped on the lights. He closed the door and rubbed the back of his neck. "Well, honey, it's nice to know we only got in the Sunshine Believers' way with our investigation. They have a serious hard-on for the Augustine Coven though."

"I ran down the research on the earlier murders you wanted, Lieutenant." The uniformed officer handed over the sheaf of papers he carried. "You were right."

"You were right about what?" Tiffany glared at the detective.

"One of my first cases. Anita Warren. Eight months pregnant. You don't want to know the details." Sifuentes flipped through the pages. "Good job, Wolowitz."

The deputy flushed at the compliment.

"What does this Anita Warren have to do with the Sunshine Believers?"

Sifuentes leaned against the desk in the corner between the door and the observation window. He exhaled wearily. "She would be yours and Osaka's sixth cousin by marriage. The Sunshine Believers don't quite understand Family relationships, so they haven't been taking any chances. Apparently, they've been grabbing any pregnant woman remotely related to Augustine Coven over the last ten years. You heard what he said about that prophecy of theirs."

Tiffany rubbed her belly. Her cousin Jessie's kidnapping last December hadn't been some random event by crazed fans or everyday psychos.

"Look at it this way, Tiffany. You were right about your coven getting picked on," Siobhan ribbed.

"This isn't funny." She stopped rubbing when her daughter kicked at her hands.

"What worries me more is that there's two more of those lizard creatures running around," Miko said.

Tiffany met her cousin's eyes and saw her own fear reflected. "Two more?"

"If you and Siobhan hadn't been so busy sniping at each other you would have heard that asshole," Miko snapped.

Sifuentes shook his head. "Wolowitz, can you—"

"Paperwork's prepared, sir." The deputy pointed at the bottom of the pile the detective held. "I just need your signature to start the DNA processing on our suspected Sunshine Believer vics."

Tiffany stepped closer to Sifuentes. "While I appreciate being tonight's bait—not—how'd the Sunshine Believers find out where I would be?"

He handed the paperwork to the deputy who headed out of the room. "We've never been able to get an undercover into the cult. Since Alex and Phil are chasing their so-called prophet through Peru, I took a chance. Planted the info." He shrugged. "It worked. Sue me."

"You ever dangle me like that again—"

"Then don't put my family in the middle of your pissing contest with the fairies." He narrowed his eyes.

Sad part was that she understood his position. Amazing how a husband and a baby changes priorities. As hard as it was, she swallowed her pride and held out her hand. "Deal on one condition."

Sifuentes cocked an eyebrow.

"Don't ever mention tonight to Max. I'm supposed to be on maternity leave, and he'll kill us both."

Shrieks filled the night as the expanding fireball caught a couple of vamps who weren't fast enough to avoid the flames. Alex lined up the next shot and squeezed the trigger. The gas tank of a pickup blew, but its incendiary display wasn't as big as the delivery truck's.

"Muzzle flash," Marcus shouted. "Behind that ridge!"

Alex had to give the rogues credit. They jumped to obey that yellow-bellied bastard. Didn't the idiots notice Giovanni didn't join them?

By the time the first vampire took one step, Alex had already moved to a dip in the landscape three hundred yards away. Another bullet ripped through the third delivery truck's gas tank.

A third explosion lit up the desert night. He scrambled to his next position. The speed he was now capable of exhilarated him, but he clamped down on his emotions. Otherwise, the glow of his eyes would provide the same target the other vampires gave him. A decent sniper's rifle would have worked much better as far as accuracy went, but he worked with what he had.

Taking aim at any eyeballs glowing yellow, green or blue, he squeezed off successive shots. Even with Mamapacha's supercharged blood heightening every sense, he didn't want to chance hitting Francisco by aiming for the orange eyeballs. The rogues didn't explode with the force Lizard Girl's partner had. Instead of craters, it was like sticking a firecracker in a canister of baby powder.

He snapped in the second clip, but had to take his time selecting targets. The dust from the rogue vampires' deaths was rapidly obscuring the area. More shouts penetrated the gray cloud of vampire dust. Human-sounding screams of pain followed by the fingernail-on-chalkboard wail of demons.

Time to grab Phil and her dad and hightail it away from the plateau. He hoped Francisco had succeeded in nabbing the tumi. Otherwise, they would still be in trouble with Supay, not just Lizard Girl.

Alex started to rise, but the slightest change in air pressure warned him. He ducked and rolled to his left.

Stones screamed as talons tore gouges into them. The same stones that had been right under his neck a moment ago. Lizard Girl crouched, her rows of teeth gleaming in the moonlight. "I'm going to flay you and eat your heart. Just like I did the Amazon's bitch."

Chapter 36

Phillippa yanked the right chain out of the grip of the rogue vampire as the idiot stared open-mouthed at his dying compatriots. Momentum wrapped the links around the neck of the one on her left. A quick jerk snapped his spine. It wouldn't kill him, but it would keep him incapacitated, hopefully long enough for her to eliminate the ones holding Ares.

The first rogue gathered his wits and rushed her. She pivoted and swung the left chain. It caught the vampire across the throat and smashed his windpipe. The motion and jolt drove screaming pain through her arm and shoulder. She gritted her teeth and searched for her father.

He had taken advantage of the confusion. Demon and vampire bodies were scattered at his feet. More tried to hold him, but his chains twirled as fast and as lethally as blades. The only vulnerability was the pole dangling from his titanium collar. Even as she analyzed the situation, she spotted Marcus Giovanni leaping, the tumi in his hand.

"Father!"

Too late. The vampire yanked Ares off his feet through sheer momentum. Supay's weapon gleamed next to his throat.

"Stand down, Phillippa," Marcus growled in Ancient Greek. "Or he dies."

Alex jumped back to avoid another blow of Lizard Girl's tail. Taking her head-on had not been part of the original plan because she would be too close to Phil and Ares. Now, he couldn't pause long enough to draw bead on the bitch.

"You should be dead!" she screeched.

"Your buddy Marcus always did suck at following orders."

She responded with an incomprehensible scream. Talons flashed so fast he'd be dead without the goddess' blood. He dodged and wove, always in the direction of the fires and chaos.

"Where's the other one?" Lizard Girl finally calmed enough she was understandable.

"Dead. Just like you wanted."

"Liar!"

Technically, no, but she wasn't about to stop long enough to debate the issue. He couldn't waste any more time. His job was to retrieve Phil and Ares. So he took a page from Marcus Giovanni's book.

He turned tail and raced for the fires.

Dammit! Francisco ground his teeth in frustration. The tumi had almost been in his grasp when the rogue vampire started to give him orders. Lizard Girl was nowhere in sight. And now, the rogue held the Lord's tumi at the throat of the lovely Phillippa's father. This simply would not do.

He bound forward. If he could grab one of the loose chains . . .

"You!"

He froze.

Bright orange eyes examined him. The lady llama trotted closer. "You're not one of mine."

Francisco grinned. "You're right."

She reared, and he ducked under her hooves. His brand-new claws gutted Demon John's sister from stem to stern. Pleased, he rolled away and scrambled for the vampire holding the tumi.

Something walloped him in the back of the head, and he flew through the air. His landing didn't hurt as he expected. It did send up a small cloud of desiccated skin and hair.

He sneezed, shook his head and looked up. Phillippa stared at him. He'd literally fallen at her feet. "I know you don't need rescuing Senorita Mann, but may I be of assistance?"

"Francisco?" From her incredulous expression, she must not be caught off guard much.

"Kill the spy! Eviscerate him!" Demon John's sister paid no attention to her path. Her eyes were locked on him. She bowled over Marcus as she raced for Francisco, trailing rotten entrails behind her.

Chapter 37

Phillippa blinked again. The question of how the Lima vampire ended up as an Uku Pacha demon could wait. "I'll take the llama. Help my father."

She stepped in front of the charging demon. Not surprising, the rest of the Uku Pacha rebels held back. Those that were still standing anyway. The rogue vampires alive drove off in any vehicle still mobile.

What she wouldn't give for her Glock or the tumi right now. She whirled the right chain and launched it at the llama as she dodged. The links tore through the demon's shoulder, shredding gray hide and muscle. No blood though.

The llama skidded to a stop on the gravel, slung herself in a U-turn and charged again.

Phillippa jumped aside, but the last few days of injuries and lack of decent food took its toll. She panted as she ran through strategies. Titanium wasn't much of a conductor, so lassoing and electrocuting Demon John's sister was out of the question.

The truck that had been her prison the last couple of days was still intact. The rogues hadn't taken it due to the heat from its burning fellows. A grin tugged painfully at the cut on her jaw as she considered the corrugated steel.

She ducked the llama's third charge and sidled closer to the vehicle. This was going to take perfect coordination. This time that damn llama wouldn't stop until her hooves were buried in Phillippa's brains.

A body slammed into the side of the truck and tumbled to the ground. A body with familiar shaggy blond hair. Glowing blue eyes stared up at her before Alex's mouth split into a ferocious grin. "Hey, gorgeous."

But the disconcerting thing wasn't his eyes. It was the fact that his entire body radiated with godlight.

Relief didn't begin to describe Alex's joy. Phil was bloodied and bruised but relatively intact.

Her lips quirked into a wry smile. Or the right side did. Her left jaw was swollen with a nasty cut that barely missed taking her ear off. "Move it, cowboy, unless you want to become llama chow."

They both scrambled out of the way as Demon John's sister crashed into the truck's side just below the dent from his body. She screamed something that sounded stranger than usual in the demon's language. Electricity crackled, ozone filled the air, and smoke wisped from her ears.

Confusion reigned until the picture made sense. Phil had lashed the demon to the delivery truck with the chains still manacled to her wrists and fed a lightning bolt through the truck's steel panel. Dry hide and hair caught fire. The demon screamed again, a wordless thread of panic and agony. She went up like flash paper. A few stray bits floated in the air currents created by the fires.

Green and yellow streaked past his vision. Before he could shout a warning, Lizard Girl jumped Phil, and the Amazon, trapped by her own chains, couldn't do a damn thing to protect herself.

And he had no idea where his Glock with the bullets from hell had landed.

Francisco had to give the Augustine traitor credit. The vampire *tried* to put up a fight. He even was smart enough to use the tumi instead of any of the other weapons upon his person. Not that it mattered.

The vampire. *At the start of this mess, I was one of them.* Funny how one's perspective changed upon death.

A wild swing by this Giovanni was all the opening Francisco needed. He sliced down, severing the vampire's hand, and caught the tumi as it fell.

Giovanni stared at the appendage twitching in the gravel, made even redder by the puddle of blood, before he turned and raced into the desert.

Francisco chuckled to himself. The rogue wasn't his problem anymore. Since Alex and his plans had gone to Uku Pacha in a hand basket, he turned to the next order of business. He shuffled closer to the disheveled man standing in a pile of corpses and bowed his head. "May I be of assistance, Lord Ares?"

The fires were reflected in the Greek god's eyes, or the orbs became flame themselves. Either way, they narrowed with suspicion. "You are one of Supay's."

Marvelous. Now he'll destroy me thanks to the rebels. "Yes. Please let me free you from the chains."

"Why should I trust you?"

"Until I died two days ago, I assisted your daughter in tracking down her friends' murderer. I have my lord's leave to complete my pledge." Francisco shrugged. "Besides, I'm speaking English. How many of my rebel brethren have you heard use the tongue of the land where your daughter currently resides?"

The titanium chains twitched, and for a moment, Francisco feared he'd pushed the god too far. Instead, Ares burst out laughing before he said, "Do it, little demon."

All Francisco had to do was strike each of the four manacles with the tumi. The metal peeled like rotten fruit. He spotted Alex and Phillippa next to the remaining truck.

"Thank you." Ares grinned and ruffled the hair on Francisco's head.

He swallowed his grimace. "Sir, it's best if we collect your daughter and—"

"Phil!"

At Alex's shout, Francisco could only watch in horror as Lizard Girl jumped on the Amazon. Blood and bits splattered the heat-warped panels of the truck.

He was too far away, but the American wasn't. He glanced at the object in his hand. "Alex!" He threw the tumi.

Chapter 38

Alex leapt and snagged the weapon in mid-air. Instantly, the inlays glowed white-hot but the tumi felt icy to the touch. He landed within reach of Lizard Girl and swiped the business end of the tumi across her back.

An unearthly shriek issued from Lizard Girl. Her hide parted and noxious smoke issued from her thick, black blood. She twisted and lashed out. Her backhand knocked him ten yards, but it got her away from Phil.

He climbed to his feet. Now that he had Lizard Girl's attention, what the hell did he do? The tumi may damage her, but that meant getting up close and personal. Not even Mamapacha's blood would keep his guts inside his body if Lizard Girl eviscerated him.

"I should have killed you in Los Angeles," she hissed.

He shrugged and backed away, keeping the glowing tumi between them. "They say hindsight's twenty-twenty."

"Whose blood did you drink?"

Now why was that important to know? He kept a close eye on her swishing tail. "Well, I know it wasn't yours."

The green and yellow tail darted. So damn predictable. He swung the tumi. The partially re-grown tip flew into the air. Black blood arched across the gravel. Pebbles and rocks shivered and screamed. His swing continued, slicing across her face.

But the tail was a feint. Talons raked his chest. Cotton shredded and fire exploded in his sliced skin. He fell backward and planted his feet in her gut.

Another unholy shriek split the night as she tumbled over his head. He completed the somersault and swung the tumi behind him. A full pivot landed a roundhouse kick to the nasty cut across what would have been the bridge of a human's nose.

Ugly boot-shaped burns marred the scales on her abdomen and face. Alex grinned. He'd forgotten Phil wasn't the only one with demon-made boots. He jabbed at Lizard Girl, driving her further away from the helpless Amazon.

"Give it to me, and I'll make your death merciful."

"As merciful as you made Jane and Beatrice's." Damn, the cuts she had landed felt like she'd poured whiskey on his chest. Were her talons poisoned like her blood?

She laughed, a high-pitched grating that could ruin eardrums. "Petty little insects killed the bitch who betrayed me, but her heart was so delicious while it still pumped."

His anger burned as cold as the tumi. She evaded another slice, dancing just out of reach. What was her game?

With a bull roar, Ares slammed into her from the side. The two tumbled to the ground. Gravel flew in all directions as they scrabbled for purchase. Talons dug furrows in the god's arms and torso, but the blows he landed left scorch marks on her hide. Alex circled, searching for an opening, but he was as likely to get himself killed as to take her out.

A crack of bone was followed by Ares' bellow of agony. Lizard Girl lifted him over her head and threw him at Alex.

So much for Mamapacha's gift. He couldn't evade the missile. And the god was a lot heavier than he looked. The dead weight plowed into Alex and knocked the tumi from his grasp.

Everything turned to slow motion. A few yards away, Francisco had untangled Phil from the truck. He bolted for the tumi as it lazily spun in the air.

Alex shoved at Ares. The god realized their danger and rolled off. They both scrambled to their feet and raced for the weapon, but Alex had a slight head start.

Green, yellow and black flashed under him as he dove for the tumi. His hand closed around air. Talons dug into his neck as Lizard girl wrenched him to his knees.

She said something in a language never meant for this universe. The sounds ripped into his soul. The air behind them cracked his flesh. But he got the gist. She was tired of his interference, and the last few seconds of his life were going to be excruciating.

"Get your paws off my boyfriend, bitch." Phil stood by the truck. Her left arm dangled uselessly, but her right was rock steady with the Glock he had dropped. Her smile was a crimson rictus.

"Blood. Already," he wheezed.

Phil gave the slightest of nods. She understood his message. The bullets were already primed. Death would be all right. She called him her boyfriend. For her, that was an undying declaration of love.

There was a soft click, a pop. As gravity changed her mind and the world tumbled into pure chaos, he felt a hand close around his and pull him into a tight embrace.

Chapter 39

The first thing Alex noticed was the odor of gunpowder, steel and C4. He didn't remember those smells in Uku Pacha, and he couldn't imagine them in Heaven. Someone shook him.

He blinked grit out of his eyes. A wild man with crazy hair and dressed in gray dust crouched over him. The man's lips moved, but no sound came out. Alex couldn't hear the crackle and pop of the dying fires either.

The explosion. Phil had shot Lizard Girl with one of the bullets Supay had supplied.

He sat up. Too fast apparently, because the wild man split into two, then four wild men. All four wild men laid their hands on his shoulder, their mouths moving in unison but with no words.

"I beg your pardon, but I can't hear you."

This better? The cannon ball ripped through his skull.

Father, tone it down. That voice was much gentler. Alex blinked again.

I was making sure I got through the interference caused by the seal. The four wild men pouted together.

A wavering vision of Phil knelt next to him. Ash drifted from her matted curls, little gray snowflakes landing on the bloody mess of her shoulders.

How many fingers am I holding up, cowboy?

His vision wavered. "More than a human should have."

I'm not human, remember? She smiled.

"You're still gorgeous." It didn't matter if she killed him now. She called him her boyfriend. If only the desert floor would stop rocking, he might actually make it to his feet.

Well, Miss Phillippa, you managed to take care of our last ride. Francisco stood behind the wild man, the tumi in his paw. The weapon no longer glowed.

Wild man. Phil's dad. Ares.

I can manage teleporting. His telepathic voice was quieter this time, and his smile was rueful through his tangled, filthy beard. *As long as it is not far, but I can't teleport this close to the seal.*

"Then I guess we're hoofing it," Alex said. It took him three tries and the assistance of a god and a demon to stay upright.

They followed the road north. None of them were in any shape for a cross-country trek. Francisco found some nylon rope that hadn't melted lying near one of the overturned trucks. He used it to hang the tumi across his shoulders.

Phillippa swallowed her pride and allowed Francisco to carry her. Honestly, she wasn't sure if she'd make more than a couple of miles before she toppled from the blood loss. They filled each other in on happenings after the battle at Machu Picchu.

Father didn't insult Alex by carrying him, but the cowboy definitely had a concussion. He'd walked in a straighter line after they'd split a bottle of tequila when he was still a Normal.

A faint shimmer appeared above the eastern mountains. Panic pounded her heart. How the hell could she forget about sunrise?

"We need to find shelter," she blurted.

"Why?" Ares asked.

"Francisco and Alex—"

The two in question exchanged looks and started laughing.

"In case you hadn't noticed by the smell, I'm dead, my lovely woman," Francisco said.

"And I've still got twenty-four hours of immunity thanks to Mamapacha's blood," Alex added. "We're fine, Phil." He wobbled when he turned to look at her, and her father almost lost his grip on the vampire.

Alex frowned. "There's going to be issues with Master Huamán over Isabella and Francisco's deaths. Didn't mean to cause this much trouble between the covens."

"Once I return my lord's property, I will speak with my former master." Francisco smiled. "I doubt he will be stupid enough to say no to Death."

"You hope," Alex said.

"He is a believer." The demon chuckled. "You worry far too much, my friend."

"Let it go, Alex," Phil said. Her voice sounded so damn tired to her own ears. And she was cold. And still bleeding from the dark spotted trail behind them.

"Anything for you, darlin.'" The dirt and cuts on his face couldn't hide the shitass grin he'd been wearing since she'd blown up Lizard Girl.

He kept glancing at the sun as it climbed above the mountain peaks. Her heart ached. The last time he'd seen a sunrise would have been the day after he'd rode out of San Antonio with the rest of the Ranger escort. If he and Francisco were correct in their estimate, this would be the last one he'd ever see.

When the sun was fully above the horizon, Ares said, "This is far enough."

Francisco lowered Phillippa to her feet as if she were a porcelain doll. She couldn't berate him. Her leg bones felt as if they might shatter if she were jarred too hard.

Ares cleared his throat. "I'm sorry, but I cannot take you home, Francisco."

"No worries." The demon smiled his rotten, jagged smile. "There's an entry way not far from here."

"Thank you, Francisco. Tell S—" She stopped herself in time. "Tell your lord thank you for his help, and that I'm sorry about his uncle." She kissed his flaking cheek.

Alex held out his hand, but Francisco pulled him into a bear hug and kissed both of the cowboy's cheeks in proper European fashion, much to Alex's consternation from the expression on his face.

The social dance was repeated with her father. Francisco stepped back. "Until we meet again, Alexander Socrates Stanton." With a flourished wave, the demon bounded off into the bright sunshine.

"Now, what the hell did he mean by that?" Alex stared in the direction Francisco had disappeared.

Ares huffed. "Let it go, Alex."

Phillippa giggled. She couldn't help it. Both men looked at her with perturbed expressions.

"We should leave," her father muttered.

Alex raised a dark, dirty eyebrow. "What do we have to do to teleport? Click our heels three times and say, 'There's no place like home'?"

"While I'm sure you would look adorable in glittery red pumps, I just need the name of a destination," Ares said dryly. "Preferably the best place for rest, provisions and medical attention for the two of you."

Phillippa looked at Alex. "Bebe?"

He nodded. "Yeah, Bebe and Caesar's house."

Her father shifted to wrap an arm around her waist while keeping his hold on Alex. Then the ground fell from beneath her feet.

The world popped into existence again. If there had been anything in Alex's stomach, he would have spewed it all over Caesar and Bebe's front yard. The blaring alarms and brilliant spotlights didn't help his headache one whit either.

"Alex? Phil?" Miko lowered her pistol. "What the fuck is going on?"

"Turn off the security system!"

The enforcer nodded, and the lights and sirens abruptly ceased. The neighborhood dogs picked up the cacophony. And it was still dark here in California. He'd forgotten about the two-hour time difference.

"What's going on?" Miko holstered her gun. She gave Phil's dad a suspicious look.

Alex took pity on her. "Ares of Olympus, Miko Osaka. Miko, Ares. Where's Bebe? Phil needs to get stitched up."

In a flurry of activity, enforcers appeared. So did the doctor, who only pursed her lips and shook her head.

Less than an hour later, Alex had showered. Bebe had chased him out of the infirmary while she set up an IV for Phil and dealt with the worst of the cuts. The Amazon had protested, but her dad threatened to hold her down if she didn't obey the doctor.

Alex leaned back on one of the chaises by the pool and watched the eastern sky lighten. He smelled the tart Granny Smith of Tiffany and the richer elements of Jamaican Blue Mountain coffee before Tiffany stepped around the outside patio kitchen.

"Shouldn't you be going inside now?" She handed one of the mugs she carried to him before setting hers on the little glass table. He ignored her struggle to settle herself in the second chaise.

"I've got twenty-four more hours. I plan to use every single daylight one of them." He took a drink. "That's not decaf."

"Nope." She silently sipped her coffee as orange light twinkled through the tree branches.

Once the sun was completely above the tree line, Miko joined them. Together, they laid out the events in Los Angeles while he and Phil had been gone.

He drained the last of his cup. "So, things are even crazier, and what Caesar's trying to accomplish with IC is for naught."

"He'll be back tomorrow," Miko said. "Mandatory meeting."

Alex stared into his empty cup. "Phil needs to be there, too. Caesar's not going to like one thing we have to say." Unease settled in his bones. Even if the vampire master didn't believe the younger members of the coven, he would listen to Phil. "Has anyone heard from Sam and Anne?"

"They called Bebe a few nights ago," Tiffany volunteered. "Something about treating an injured werecoyote. But nothing since then."

Alex rose and stretched. Between the V-virus and Mamapacha's blood, he felt almost normal again. He tamped down the disturbed feeling over facing Caesar. "The girls can take care of themselves. They'd yell if they need anything."

"Where are you going?" Tiffany peered up at him, shading her eyes from the sun.

He grinned. "Surfing."

"Without me?" The kid actually looked hurt.

"I've never been daytime surfing, and I can't wait until you pop." He bent and kissed Tiffany on the forehead. "We'll go together once Bebe gives you the all clear."

"Can you do me a favor first?" Miko asked.

"Sure."

"You need to talk to Phil's dad."

Was this what the feeling in his gut was about? "What did he do?"

"Doesn't take no for an answer."

This was going to take some delicacy. "I'll see what I can do."

He went up to the room Caesar kept for him in emergencies. Okay, so he was avoiding Ares. He donned swim trunks and a t-shirt. The wetsuit would be unnecessary with his supercharged metabolism, but he grabbed it anyway.

When he entered the infirmary, loud snores greeted him. Ares was out cold on one of the two beds. At least, he was clean.

"Wow," Alex said softly. "Lizard Girl must have put him through the wringer."

"No," Bebe said with a sour look. "He pinched my ass one too many times."

Phil giggled as the doctor removed the IV needle from her arm. "I told you so."

"Did Bebe give you a dose of what she gave your dad?"

The Amazon quickly sobered. "No." She eyed his bag. "Where are you going?"

"The beach." He grinned. "I've never seen the Pacific in the daytime."

She swung her legs around and hopped off the bed "Mind some company?"

"Oh, no, you don't." Bebe waggled a finger. "I just finished putting you back together. Don't make me trap you in a circle."

Phil glared down at the diminutive doctor. "I'm going to lie on the sand while Alex makes an immature fool of himself in the ocean. How much trouble can I get into?"

Bebe glared. "If you rip one of those stitches, I'll make you sleep for a month."

Phil ignored the other woman. "Can we stop and pick up something to eat on the way?"

"Sure." It was the only word he could manage. It'd been so long since Phil wanted to voluntarily be in his company when death and mayhem weren't involved that it threw off his equilibrium.

As they headed down the hallway, Bebe shouted, "You better not getting those stitches wet."

Phillippa sat on a blanket and ate her subs while Alex cavorted in the waves with some teens. As she finished her second bottle of water, Melissa walked up and dropped to the blanket beside her. The nymph was silent for a long time before she said, "I screwed up."

"Yes." Phillippa kept her eyes on Alex as she spoke. "But if you hadn't been sleeping with Roberto, you might not have noticed the substitution as quickly." She sighed. "How's he doing?"

"He fought the fae when they captured him. A few broken bones, but the healing spells are working. He should be back at the store next week."

"How's he dealing mentally?"

Melissa released a breath that wasn't quite a sob. "He says he wants some time alone to figure out how he really feels."

Phillippa felt for her. How would she have handled things if Alex had returned to San Antonio all those years ago? Would the human Alex have accepted the fact that she wasn't human?

"Give Roberto that time, Melissa. For both your sakes."

The nymph sniffed, but said nothing.

There was another hurting woman Phillippa needed to deal with as well. "Can I borrow your phone? Mine took a drink in a lake, and I haven't had a chance to replace it yet. I need to call Jane's mother."

Melissa handed the device to Phillippa. She thumbed in the memorized number. On the third ring, Kate Chevrette answered. "Yes?"

"It's done."

There was a gasp at the other end. Then a long pause before Kate said, "Thank you."

Phillippa ended the call and handed back the phone. She watched the ocean silently with Melissa for a very long time.

<h1 style="text-align:center">Chapter 40</h1>

Close to sunset, Alex dropped to the blanket next to Phil. Her olive skin was sun-kissed after an entire day at the beach. It was the healthiest she'd looked since this ordeal began.

Her curls were pulled back into a loose ponytail, but a few escaped. As much as he wanted to touch them, he wasn't quite sure where he stood with her. Sure, she called him her boyfriend when Lizard Girl was about to kill him, but she hadn't given any indication since then.

Well, other wanting to get out of the mansion.

If his own estranged father were there, he could understand wanting a little distance after the events of the last few days.

They sat in companionable silence as the brilliant orange disk plunged beneath the waves.

"Do you want me to take you home now?" he said softly. "Or do you want to head back to the mansion and check on your dad?"

"Dad's fine." She held up a smartphone. "I just checked a while ago. I left my key with Bebe. The part-time enforcer you hired—"

"Jake?"

"Yeah, what were you thinking? Hiring Sam's ex-fiancé? Duncan wouldn't just have a cow. He'd have the whole herd."

"As I pointed out to my boss, Jake was part of the team that saved his ass from the necromancer. And that if he didn't like it, I quit."

Phil laughed and shook her head. "Anyway, Jake took Father to my condo to get some rest. And just to warn you, Tiffany is dropping off Kiki at your place. The dog chewed up Max's favorite pair of slippers so Tiffany wants them replaced. She e-mailed you the L.L. Bean link."

"Great," he muttered. "Anything else?"

She smiled. Sea grass surrounded him. Her irises turned deep purple.

"Let's go take care of the dog." She paused for the barest of instances. "And go to bed."

His heart stuttered behind his ribcage. For once, common sense won, and he said nothing. They gathered their things. He returned the rented surfboard. And they climbed into Bebe's BMW and drove home.

Kiki greeted them, dancing on her hind legs. They played with the dog for a while, but Alex kept watching Phil. She seemed as unsure about her suggestion as he did. After racing around the living room as if it were the Indy Speedway, Kiki collapsed on the floor next to him, curled into a ball and started snoring.

"Phil, it's okay if you changed your mind," he said.

"No, it's not that." Her fingers brushed the bruises and stitches along the side of her face. "For once in my life, I'm a little self-conscious about how I look."

Alex climbed to his feet and held his hand out for her. Surprisingly, she took it and let him draw her up and close. "I'm afraid of hurting you. We don't have to do anything right this minute."

"You wouldn't hurt me," she whispered. "If you've changed your mind . . ."

"Did you mean what you told Lizard Girl?"

She nodded.

It was the closest he would get to her undying declaration of love, but it was enough for him. "Then you've got nothing to worry about."

Hand in hand, they walked to his bedroom. He helped her undress, not in the way he wanted to though. It was the first real look he'd gotten of the physical damage she had suffered.

He lightly traced gouge marks on her neck. It made him sad and pissed and a bunch of other things he wasn't sure of. "She actually tried to rip out your throat."

Phil chuckled. "The rest are hers. I did that one myself. She said you were dead."

There had been a couple of times he'd thought about eating the barrel of a gun, back before Duncan Turned him. He couldn't imagine Phil being that desperate, in that much pain. "You didn't try to—"

"Not exactly." Pink flushed her face. "Lizard Girl didn't know about my oath. It was a way—" She swallowed hard, the muscles in her neck bobbing under his touch. "Your last command was to—if the oath stopped me then I knew you were alive."

"Dammit, Phil." He wanted to crush her against him and kiss away the pain. This was the first time she ever looked . . . fragile. "Maybe we shouldn't—"

The corner of her mouth quirked. "Get naked and we'll see what we can manage."

After much grimacing, a little awkwardness and a lot of laughter, he settled between her thighs. She tasted sweeter than he recalled. Her fingers threaded through his hair. Her little moans and sighs were exactly how he remembered. He sucked and licked until she stiffened and bucked and screamed.

He tried to cuddle with her, but she would have none of that. "Phil . . ."

"My right hand works just fine," she growled, but there was a twinkle in her eyes as she said it.

"It's okay—"

"Lay down and shut up, cowboy."

"Yes, ma'am." He tried to hide his smile as he did so.

And she showed him exactly what she could do with only one hand.

Chapter 41

Whining and something scratching on the blankets woke Alex. Phil was still asleep. For once, her hair was spread in a glorious array on his own pillow. The sight sent warmth through him, along with heat in parts south. Once Bebe took all those stitches out, he'd see about loving Phil properly.

Kiki gave another insistent whine.

"Okay, okay," he whispered.

The little fluff mop raced ahead and he padded behind. The microwave clock shone at three a.m. No one around at this time of the morning so he didn't bother grabbing sweats or shorts.

Kiki jumped around at the patio door and yipped once.

"I swear you have a bladder the size of a teaspoon." He slid the door open and she raced for the newspaper.

While the Maltese did her business, he stepped into the warm night air. City lights twinkled and blinked. The traffic rumbled. It had been a while since he'd been camping. *Maybe head to Montana. See if Phil would be interested.* The thought didn't excite him so much as comfort him.

The fine hairs on the back of his neck rose to attention, interrupting his planning. He pivoted. Something hovered inside the shadow of the planter. Sable and ebony swirled and coalesced into a man-sized figure.

Alex groaned. "Not again."

Supay materialized. His visage stern, proud and etched with awful sadness.

"You understand the situation." The multitude of the god's voices echoed inside Alex's head. "I cannot release you yet, Alexander Socrates Stanton."

"Talk to Sam. She can be reasonable if you feed her enough cheesecake."

"I cannot interfere directly." Supay smiled, an evil thing that sent a shiver up Alex's spine.

"Why not?" Alex asked, very aware that the god was dressed and he was naked as a jaybird.

"It is against the . . . rules." Supay shrugged. "That does not mean we cannot bend them."

"Why me?"

"You offered."

Alex swallowed his frustration. This was getting him nowhere. "We stopped Lizard Girl. I fulfilled my promise to you. You have your tumi back."

"There will be two more tries to break a seal. There always are."

"But we destroyed two of the Old Ones' servants."

"Not the third."

"How is Sam supposed to fight? What happens if she's the goddess of love? Or puppies?" He thought about it. "Or the goddess of sarcasm."

Supay didn't look amused. "Because death always comes first. Ask your Amazon if you do not believe me."

"I believe. I don't understand though."

Supay looked away for a moment before that awful black gaze returned to Alex. "Understand this, Alexander Socrates Stanton. A god of death is never born. We are created. And we don't fight the Old Ones. We consume them. Or they us." He darkened until his form was nothing more than a shadow. It melded into the other shadows along the balcony.

A shiver crawled under Alex's skin. *Never born. Created.*

His analysis of Supay's words and Sam's situation had been correct. The implications scared the shit out of him, but what would Duncan and Sam do when they learned the truth?

Chapter 42

The key members of Augustine Vampire Coven and Phil gathered in the office at the Brentwood mansion.

Alex watched Caesar as the other members of the coven related the events of the last two weeks. The vampire master said nothing. His fingers steepled under his chin as he leaned back in the expensive leather executive chair.

"John Lannigan is waiting to hear from you about setting up a meeting with Duke Millanthropas," Tiffany finished.

Alex suppressed his own wince as Caesar straightened and his eyes narrowed. The master's silent fury was far worse than Duncan's scowl.

"And what makes you think you have the right to speak on my behalf?" Caesar's voice was quiet and calm on the surface, but instead of their brilliant gold during heightened emotion, his eyes had turned scarlet.

The color change happened in older vamps. It wasn't something Alex looked forward to. Any more than he wanted the master's attention on him while he was this pissed off. But truths had to be told.

Alex slid his hands into his back pockets, appearing as non-threatening as possible. "Tiffany did the smart thing, sir."

Duncan's jaw dropped. *Are you mad?*

"Are you challenging my authority?" Caesar said.

Alex glared at Duncan. "No, I'm not insane." He turned to Caesar. "And you couldn't pay me enough to be in charge of this coven right now. But we will need the fae's help before this is over."

He laid out Demon John's story of Supay's origins and how close they matched Sam's. The weakening of the seals. The Old Ones. The only thing Alex couldn't speak about was his private conversations with Supay, or that he was still in the god's service.

By the time Alex was done, everyone but Phil, and surprisingly Bebe, were staring at him slack-jawed. As the implications sank in, the red faded from Caesar's eyes until they became their normal gold-flecked brown.

The witch nodded thoughtfully. "It explains the complicated DNA pattern that the nanites are constructing in Sam. I didn't have any pure god DNA to compare with hers in order to understand what was happening."

"My father's staying at my place for now. I'll see if he might be willing to volunteer a sample to check against Sam's." Phillippa held up her hands. "I'm not guaranteeing anything."

"The question becomes do we tell Sam of Alex's suspicions," Caesar said.

"They're not just Alex's," Mai murmured. Miko's older sister wrapped her arms around herself. "You all saw what she did to the zombies at Tiffany and Max's wedding. It was the same thing I saw her do to them behind Anthony's restaurant at the rehearsal dinner."

"The nymphs who helped me with the wedding and bridesmaid dresses—" Phillippa halted. Alex could feel her trying to find the right words. "We saw *something* under her essence. As if the form she currently wears is nothing more than a favorite coat she clings to."

Tiffany chimed in. "It wasn't just Phil and her girls. I saw something, too, the morning of the first wedding." She sought Max's hand and wound her fingers through his.

Good. Relief spread through Alex. Some of the people in the room were taking him seriously. "Sam needs to know."

"We should not tell her," Duncan said quietly.

Alex pulled his hands out of his pockets and took a step before he quelled the desire to smack his sire silly. "Now, who's insane? Did you learn nothing from planning to move her to Las Vegas without asking her?"

"That was different." From Duncan's stiff posture, he *hadn't* learned a damn thing.

"Alex is right," Max interjected. "She needs to know."

Duncan's scowl was back. "She may not be able to handle the truth."

Max rose and crossed the room. Alex had to give the man credit. Duncan towered over his nephew-in-law by a good six inches.

"She's not just your fiancée. She's my baby sister," Max began. "I want to protect her, too. But if she doesn't know what's going on, she can't prepare. Can't learn to deal with the changes. And God help us, if Alex is right, she's the only thing standing between us and the Apocalypse."

"Miko," Caesar said. "You're the only enforcer in the room who hasn't given an opinion."

She bowed her head and stared at the carpet before she looked at the vampire master. "The Sunshine Believers are doing their damnedest to end the world. We're going to need everyone, including Sam, to stop them. Therefore, she needs to know what's going on." She faced Duncan. "With all due respect, sir, she's far stronger than you give her credit for."

The vibration in his pocket made Alex jump. It was followed by the jingle of the phone's ringtone.

"Really, Alex?" A perturbed expression twisted Caesar's mouth.

Alex yanked the device out to decline the call. But when he saw the incoming number, he muttered, "Speak of the devil."

Duncan glowered. "Why is my fiancée calling *you*?"

"Because she doesn't know you're back in the States," Alex shot back. He flicked the answer icon. "What's up, Sam?"

But it wasn't the zombie. Anne's hysterical crying blasted through the receiver.

"Anne, calm down. What's wrong?"

More sobbing, but he caught two words, "Normal" and "bit." Every supernatural in the room heard them. Alarm spiced the air.

Holy shit, what was happening in Ohio? "Anne, darlin', can you put Sam on the phone?"

The crying faded. Then Sam's voice saying, "Alex, give me a second." In the background, Sam said, "Leslie, can you watch her for a minute? Don't let her pull out that line." All sound abruptly cut out. "Okay, I'm outside, and I can think."

Alex glanced around. Everyone else was waiting, even though they were worried. Duncan, on the other hand, was getting way too close and personal trying to hear his fiancée. "Caesar and Duncan are back in town. I'm putting you on speaker." He clicked the icon.

"Hey, guys." The zombie/goddess sounded exhausted.

"What the bloody hell is happening there?" Duncan shouted.

"I love you, too, sweetheart." Sam's voice didn't just drip with sarcasm. It was an out of control fire hose.

Alex's gaze met Phil's. She hid a smile behind her hand. At least, it was a full smile now that the swelling along her jaw had subsided. *He's going to pay for that when she gets home.*

He grinned back at the Amazon before he turned his attention to the problem at hand. "Sam, what's wrong with Anne?"

She sighed. "Short version. An Unseelie assassin tried to kill me tonight. Anne dueled him and got stabbed with a silver knife. Her brother's attorney killed the fairy. Anne was bleeding out, and the stupid lawyer used himself as a donor. The witch who was with him says he was careful, but Anne insists she remembers sinking her fangs into his wrist. Said lawyer is out cold from blood loss. I've got transfusions running into both him and Anne. And from what all of you explained to me, it's too early to know for sure if he's infected since all this happened less than two hours ago."

Stunned silence filled the office.

"I keep telling you people. Murphy is the one, true god," Tiffany muttered.

"Sam sucked in a deep breath. "Caesar, I followed protocol. The Dare Coven's chief enforcer is on his way here."

"Thank you, Sam." The vampire master pinched the bridge of his nose.

In a tentative voice, she said, "We may have another problem."

"What?" Caesar sounded nearly as weary as the zombie.

"If he decides to arrest Anne, I've got the Normal sheriff's department, the local witches and werecoyotes, and the entire Amish community standing between them. She found out who committed five local murders, including her brother Thomas. They feel they owe her their lives. I'm trying to keep everybody calm, but I don't know if I can keep it up."

Alex glared at Duncan. *You need to reassure her, shit for brains.*

"Samantha, you're doing fine." Duncan glared right back though he kept his voice soothing. "Master Augustine will contact Master Dare and inform her he has been apprised of the situation. I'm sure everything will be all right."

"Thanks. Can you send the plane out to pick Anne up once the chief enforcer gets statements?" Sam's voice grew softer. "She's pretty upset, and I'm afraid she may try to hurt herself."

"I'll be there—" Duncan started.

"No." Alex shook his head. "I'll go. I have a better rapport with Anne, and you need to be here with Caesar when he meets with the Seelie. Mai?"

Their pilot rose. "We need to go now. It'll be close to sunrise when we reach Columbus as it is."

"Excuse me? I thought I was in charge of this coven." But Caesar's expression was bemused, not pissed.

"With your leave, Master Augustine." Alex bowed for good measure.

Caesar shooed them toward the door. "Go. Just go."

"Sam, we'll be there in—" Alex glanced at Mai.

"Approximately five hours," she said.

"Great." Sam sounded relieved as she clicked off the call.

As he and Mai left the office, Phil followed them out. He slowed and said, "Mai, I'll meet you in the garage in a minute." She nodded and continued down the hallway.

He turned to Phil. "You didn't say much in there."

She sighed. "What is there to say?"

He pulled her into his arms, and she surprised him by not resisting. "You're bothered by something."

Her smile was wan as she placed her palms against his chest. "We finally get our shit together, and chaos erupts. Maybe Tiffany's right—Murphy is the one, true god."

He chuckled and kissed her forehead. "Everything will be fine."

"No, Alex." She cupped his cheek. "No, it won't."

As he kissed her delectable mouth, he could hear Supay whisper deep in his mind, *The Amazon's right. Things are about to get much, much worse.*

Sam refuses to accept Alex and Phil's discovery because, well, it's totally ridiculous! Besides, she's got her own problems. Between a lawsuit against one of her zombie comedians and another one wanting to rekindle his relationship with his second wife, Sam has her hands full. But others are taking the idea of her being a goddess very seriously, namely, Baron Samedi who wants a soul back that he claims she took. And he decides kidnapping her brother Max is adequate compensation! Turn the page for a preview of *Zombie Goddess*!

Zombie Goddess

Chapter 1

I stood in the back of the dark Las Vegas showroom. On stage and under a spotlight, Lily Bell ripped through her updated stand-up act.

And she had the audience eating out of the palm of her hand.

Thankfully, she wasn't eating the audience. None of my baby zombies, as I'd come to call the people I'd accidentally returned to life after a necromancer pulled them out of their coffins, showed any signs of my insatiable hunger.

Which was a good thing because I could barely afford to feed myself, much less the baby zombies.

With a totally straight face, Lily said, "So the first customer asked to see their biggest vibrator . . ."

I winced even as a chuckle bubbled out of my throat. I wasn't a prude by any stretch, but Lily was old enough to be my great-something-grandmother. The squeaky-clean reruns of her hit show, "Lily Loves Ari," had been my after-school TV staple. A scan of the audience showed everyone having a great time, so I needed to get over my discomfort.

It helped that Lily looked exactly as she did at the height of her popularity decades ago. Since the *Parade of Stars* shows consisted of celebrity impersonators, the crowd wouldn't have believed she was the real Lily Bell, even if I showed them her empty grave back in Los Angeles. Hell, I still had problems believing she was back from the dead.

". . . and then the manager asked, 'Where's my thermos?'" Raucous laughter filled the theater at Lily's punchline.

Her grin at the audience's response was brighter than the spotlight shining on her.

Another of my baby zombies stood next to me, and he clapped as hard as the rest of the crowd while Lily took her bows. "Damn, she's still got it." Bill Faith grinned at her success. Like Lily, he had started his entertainment career in the dying days of vaudeville and segued into the upstart medium of television. Like Lily, this show gave him a second chance at doing what he did best. Like Lily, Bill was less than happy about their resurrection, but he was doing his damnedest to adapt.

The third member of my zombie trio bounced onto the stage as Lily exited. "Let's give her another big round of applause!"

Mortimer Stern, "Uncle Morty" to generations of fans, looked like he was in his mid-forties, the same age he'd been when he jumped in front of a TV camera instead of a live audience. We still hadn't figured out why my blood had reverted all three of my baby zombies to look and feel as they had in their prime, not the elderly legends they had been when they'd passed away. Out of the three, Morty was the only one who enjoyed his resurrection and took full advantage of his restored vigor. A couple of the maids at the Karnak, the hotel/casino where we all lived, had testified to his . . . enthusiasm.

Of course, this testimony was outside of what the women had assumed was my hearing range.

As Morty launched into the introduction of the next act, I gestured to Bill. He followed me out of the showroom.

Flashes popped in our eyeballs when we stepped into the lobby. Fans screamed, waving both paper and electronic pads in Bill's face as they begged for autographs. In the insanity of the modern world, the *Parade of Stars* retro act had become the hottest ticket in Vegas. Bill scribbled a few signatures before following me to the side door leading to the backstage. The security guard nodded to us as he lifted the velvet rope to let us through.

We found Lily next to one of the make-up tables, literally jumping up and down, her scarlet curls flying.

"Did you hear them?" She grabbed Bill in a bear hug.

Bill may not have been the lech Morty had been in their previous lives, but he was rumored to have dabbled on the side. Something about the beautiful redhead though turned him into a blushing teen. "Yeah, doll. I heard. You kicked ass out there."

She turned and flung her arms around me. The rib-cracking embrace reminded me all-to-well that, like me, these three would never be Normal again.

"Thank you, thank you, thank you, Sam!"

I gasped for enough air to get out, "You're welcome." If someone would have told me last year that I'd be the successful agent for three dead entertainment legends, I would have asked for a hit of whatever they were smoking.

"Samantha Ridgeway?"

Lily let go of me, and we both turned to find a cute little brunette standing next to us. "Yes?" I said.

"Your company manages the Lily Bell retro act that was just on, right?"

I took a deep breath. The scent of Fiji apples confirmed this girl was a Normal human. No honey. I'd learned to be a little paranoid since my own death in January. The fairies' contract on my head encouraged that paranoia. The actual assassination attempt last summer meant it was no longer paranoia.

"Yes." I plastered a polite smile on my face. "Is there something I can help you with?"

She smiled and held out a large envelope to me in one hand and another to Lily in the other. "I represent someone who's interested in your act."

The second both Lily and I took the paperwork, the mysterious woman's smile transformed into a toothy grin. "You've been served, bitches."

"Goddamn, mother-fucking, son-of-a—" I muttered. I wanted to kick myself. I should have known better than to take those damn papers. I'd been a tabloid reporter long enough to sniff out a process server.

For a brief instant, I considered altering her memories, but my control of my mental mojo was sketchy at the best of times. I'd accidentally left the necromancer who'd resurrected my baby zombies in a coma.

I ripped open the envelope and skimmed the contents. A cease-and-desist order along with a lawsuit claiming trademark infringement by Lily and me. The worst part was the name of the plaintiff.

"How dare you!"

I looked up from the complaint. An older woman stalked toward us. Why the hell did The Vegas Grand security let all the crazies back here? This would never have happened at the Karnak. Mainly because my vampire hunk of a boyfriend Duncan ran it. But then, most of the security there weren't Normals either.

Recognition of the screaming woman clicked. Lilianne Costas had finally given up on dying her hair black. Her short 'do was now a chic silver. Her hawk-like nose had been inherited from her crooner father Aristotle, but the dimples and eyes were pure Lily.

"How dare you profane my mother's career." She literally spat the words. I could feel the fine spray cover my face. "My mother never cursed during her act."

"I—I—" Lily spluttered. I didn't have to imagine how she felt. Her shock at seeing her daughter grated along my nerves.

I stepped between the women. "Your lawsuit's been served Ms. Costas. I'm sure your attorney wouldn't be happy about you confronting us directly. I *know* my attorney won't be."

"I want that bitch to know exactly what I think. She's a fake, and a terrible fake at that. I won't stand for her desecration of my mother's memory!" Another spray of saliva hit my face. Lilianne stabbed a finger in Lily's direction.

The process server soaked in the entire scene. An icy ball of rage froze my gut. This mess would be all over the internet gossip sites five minutes after the bitch left. I knew because I was formerly one of the people reporting on this kind of crap.

"Now, wait here just a minute, young lady." Bill stood shoulder-to-shoulder with me. "Lilianne, you can't insult your mother—"

Shut up, Bill. My telepathic warning came too late.

Lilianne's anger went supernova. "How dare you!" She exploded with enough profanity in English and Greek to seed a couple of galaxies. Finally, security noticed there was a problem. Two burly men escorted her and the process server from the backstage area. Her invectives died when the huge door slammed shut.

I turned back to Lily.

She shook her head, a defeated expression on her beautiful face. "I'm ashamed to say I taught her most of those words." Then she burst into tears.

I kept my temper under control while we took Lily back to the Karnak. Once we got the weeping comedienne into her suite, Bill promised to stay with her. I knew he'd keep Lily from doing anything stupid. The budding relationship between the two old friends was the one small favor the universe had deigned to grant me lately.

Instead of taking the elevator, I jogged down the stairs to the management section of the hotel where I'd claimed an office. No one argued with the boss's fiancée about the appropriation, especially those who knew I was a zombie.

Well, sort of a zombie. I sure as hell didn't like the Augustine chief enforcer's or my witch doctor's theory of what the damn nanites were actually turning me into. They kept me alive. That's all I cared about, even if my grocery budget rivaled a small nation's.

Alex and Bebe had to be wrong. They just had to be.

The exercise blew off some of my fury. No sense in scaring the piss out of my secretary. Not that much scared any canine were.

I burst into my office. "Staci, I need you to get Colin—"

"Shhh." Staci Warner glared at me from across her desk and held an index finger over her lips. I swear since the werecoyote had gotten married and had her pup, she'd become more of a bitch than her mother-in-law.

She stood, watching the witch in front of her desk. If his ginger scent hadn't given him away, the scarlet tendrils of energy streaming from his fingertips were confirmation. He was magickally examining a white box sitting on Staci's desk. His shoulder-wide stance gave no indication that he was aware of my presence.

I stepped inside and quietly closed the door. Mai Osaka, the head of Karnak security, watched the proceedings, and I sidled over to her.

"What's going on?" I whispered.

"You received another package." Her words were as sharp as the black suit she wore. Her almond eyes remained locked on the witch.

"I'm sure it's nothing." I wished I believed my own words.

She shot me a dirty look. "When you're head of security, you may make that decision."

"Shhhh!" Staci hissed again.

The energy tendrils sank back into the witch's dark skin. His eyes blinked and he shook out the tension from his hands. "You're right. There's a spell on the contents."

Staci looked pleased with herself.

"What kind of spell?" Mai asked.

The braided silver hoop in his left ear winked at the golden eagle in the piercing above it when he shrugged. "That's just it. It's a simple motion spell. The kind you put on a toy for kids." He ran a hand over his close-cropped black curls. "There's no blood magick or ill intent I can detect."

"I owe you one, Quinn," Mai said.

"Any time, pretty lady. It's been boring over at the Scheherazade." Ah, the casino owned by the Las Vegas witch coven. He reached out, and Mai fistbumped him.

Fistbumped.

Mai.

Who was so rigid and uptight, she made my sixteenth-century-born fiancé look like Charlie Sheen on a bender.

Staci held up a box cutter. "Let's find out what it is."

I held out a hand. "Maybe you should let me."

The werecoyote shook her head fiercely. "I'm not going to explain to Mr. St. James why you got hurt."

I scowled at the stubborn bitch. "I'm damn near indestructible.

You're not." And Alex and Bebe's half-baked theory popped right back in my head, initiating a wave of nausea in my cast-iron zombie stomach. Unfortunately, other people were latching on that self-same idiotic idea, which led to the crazy gifts landing on my plate. Like the one sitting innocently on Staci's desk.

I smiled to take the sting out of my insult to Staci's abilities. "Besides, it can't be worse than the black roses or the skull jewelry." Especially considering the jewelry had been made from actual human skulls. We weren't going to talk about what the roses did to a maid.

"Maybe I should stick around," Quinn murmured.

"That would be best," Mai said. "I may need you to separate these two."

Staci and I turned to glare at the two security chiefs before returning to our stand-off. Finally, my secretary handed over the box cutter. "Fine." She practically growled the word.

"You're sounding more and more like Leslie every day." I grinned.

This time, Staci really did growl at the mention of her mother-in-law.

I held my breath and sliced across the tape. Inside the cardboard box was a Styrofoam container, a smaller version of the type vampires used to transport blood.

Very carefully, I eased the insulated package up. Staci yanked the cardboard box out of the way, and I set the Styrofoam on her desk.

My lungs reminded me I needed to breathe, and I took a huge gulp of air. Ozone leaked from the package. Steeling myself, I cut the tape holding the Styrofoam lid in place and flipped it up.

Dry ice vapor clouded my vision for an instant. Thank god, the little mass of red inside the container didn't jump out. The other three crowded closer to take a peek.

"Well, it kind of makes sense," Staci said.

"If you're a psychopath," Mai added dryly.

"Holy shit! That's a beating heart!"

Leave it to the only man in the room to state the obvious.

Zombie Goddess is available at your favorite online retailer.

Acknowledgements

This has been one of the most difficult books for me to write, and I couldn't have done it without the following people, whether it be their actual help or their inspiration:

Col. John Payne (USAF, ret.) and Mrs. Joanne "Jody" Payne for welcoming me to their ranch with open arms and letting me borrow tons of books and CDs from their time in the beautiful country of Peru. And especially to Jody for helping me re-plot this damn story when Steven Spielberg stole the original idea and used it for *Indiana Jones and the Kingdom of the Crystal Skull*. Without you, girl, I never would have finished this thing.

Fellow physics major at Ashland College, Martin Pena, for first telling me of the wonder and tragedy of his native land.

Writer/actor/director/producer Kevin Smith for stirring the idea of what happens when a god doesn't want to take responsibility for the shitstorm he/she/it creates.

The late Kevin Tod Smith, who will always be Ares to me.

The incomparable Ivy Shorts, aka "The Happy Whisk," a good friend and fellow Wonder Woman fan who understood my need to get Phillippa "right."

And last, but definitely not least, Darling Husband and Genius Kid for learning to cook when I needed writing time.

About the Author

Suzan Harden transitioned from writing information technology manuals for companies and legal articles for a law enforcement magazine to her first love, fantasy and science fiction in all their forms. She's the author of the Millersburg Magick Mysteries, the Soccer Moms of the Apocalypse series, and the Books of Apep series.

Contact Suzan Harden

Facebook: Suzan Harden
Email: suzan@suzanharden.com
Website: www.suzanharden.com

Sign up for Suzan's Mailing List

www.ingramcontent.com/pod-product-compliance
Lightning Source LLC
Chambersburg PA
CBHW070608170726
48291CB00003B/753